Marion Harvey

The Mystery of the Hidden Room

e-artnow 2022

Marion Harvey
The Mystery of the Hidden Room

Murder Mystery Novel

e-artnow, 2022
Contact: info@e-artnow.org

ISBN 978-80-273-4302-7

Contents

CHAPTER I: THE NOTE	13
CHAPTER II: THE SHOT	16
CHAPTER III: THE POLICE	19
CHAPTER IV: THE INQUEST	23
CHAPTER V: THE SECRETARY	28
CHAPTER VI: CORROBORATIVE EVIDENCE	31
CHAPTER VII: THE LAWYER	34
CHAPTER VIII: LEE DARWIN	37
CHAPTER IX: THE VERDICT	40
CHAPTER X: JENKINS' ADVICE	44
CHAPTER XI: ARTHUR TRENTON	47
CHAPTER XII: AN EXPLANATION	50
CHAPTER XIII: THE SUICIDE	53
CHAPTER XIV: GRAYDON MCKELVIE	56
CHAPTER XV: THE INTERVIEW	60
CHAPTER XVI: THE EXHIBITS	63
CHAPTER XVII: THE LAMP	66
CHAPTER XVIII: THE SECRET ENTRANCE	71
CHAPTER XIX: THE LAWYER AGAIN	74
CHAPTER XX: DEDUCTIONS	76
CHAPTER XXI: THE STEWARD	81
CHAPTER XXII: ORTON'S ALIBI	85
CHAPTER XXIII: GRAMERCY PARK	89
CHAPTER XXIV: THE SIGNET RING	95
CHAPTER XXV: THE DECEPTION	99
CHAPTER XXVI: JAMES GILMORE	103
CHAPTER XXVII: THE STRONG BOX	106
CHAPTER XXVIII: GOLD AND BLUE	109
CHAPTER XXIX: THE REWARD	112
CHAPTER XXX: THE CURIO SHOP	115
CHAPTER XXXI: THE RESCUE	118
CHAPTER XXXII: LEE'S STORY	121
CHAPTER XXXIII: THE SECOND BULLET	124
CHAPTER XXXIV: THE WOMAN IN THE CASE	128
CHAPTER XXXV: A STRANGE ACCOUNT	132
CHAPTER XXXVI: THE TRAP	136
CHAPTER XXXVII: M'KELVIE'S TRIUMPH	139
CHAPTER XXXVIII: THE MOTIVE	143

CHAPTER XXXIX: CONCLUSION

CHAPTER I

THE NOTE

I had intended spending the evening at the Club; but after my solitary meal, I found that I was too tired to care to leave my own inviting fireside. Drawing up a chair before the open grate in my library, for the October night was chill and the landlord had not sufficiently relented to order the steam-heat, I settled myself comfortably with my book and pipe. The story I had chosen was a murder mystery, extremely clever and well-written, and so engrossed did I become that I was entirely oblivious to the passage of time.

The entrance of my man, Jenkins, brought me back to my surroundings with a start to find that the clock on the mantel was chiming eleven. A little impatient at the interruption for I had not concluded the story, I grew sarcastic.

"What is it, Jenkins? Have you come to remind me that it is long past my bed-time?" I inquired.

Jenkins' face grew longer if such a thing were possible in a countenance already attenuated by nature into the semblance of perpetual gloom, and shook his head with a grieved air as though he considered my remark an aspersion upon his knowledge of his duties as a valet.

"A man who claims to be Mrs. Darwin's chauffeur, sir," he replied in a tone that indicated that he at least would not be responsible for the veracity of the statement, "has just brought this note. He says that he will await the answer below in his machine, sir."

He extended an unaddressed white envelope with a funereal air. The note was from Ruth. The message was brief and to the point.

"Will you return at once with my chauffeur? I need you."

"My hat and coat, Jenkins," I cried, flinging aside my jacket. "You need not wait up for me. I have my key," I added.

I could have descended the stairs a half dozen times before the elevator finally arrived, or so it seemed to my impatience. The moment we reached the lobby I was out of the elevator and down the steps into the waiting motor before the boy had recovered his wits sufficiently to follow me to the door.

The chauffeur evidently had his instructions, for I was hardly within before the machine was speeding toward the Drive. My bachelor apartments were situated on 72nd Street, just off the Park, and I knew we could not cover the distance to the Darwin home on the outskirts of Riverside Drive in less than twenty minutes, even at the rate at which we were traveling.

I had stuffed Ruth's note into my pocket as I left. Mechanically I drew it forth and tore it to shreds, flinging the scraps from the window. Letters are compromising things.

What had possessed Ruth to commit herself to writing after the compact we had made to have no further communication with each other! It was she who had suggested that we become as strangers, and I could only read in this sudden appeal and the haste with which I was being whirled toward her some dread calamity. Nor was my anxiety lessened by the fact that I was hopelessly in love with her. Yes, hopelessly, I speak advisedly, because she was another man's wife, and while that man lived she would be true to him although he deserved it less than anyone I knew.

To think that a few short months ago Ruth and I had been engaged! If I had had my way we should have been married at once without any fuss, and so should have avoided the trouble that befell us, but Ruth wanted a trousseau and a big wedding, so like many a better man before me I humored her to the extent of promising to wait another month.

Did I say a month? Six have passed and I am waiting yet, while Ruth has had her wish, for her wedding was a sort of nine days' wonder, Philip Darwin having long been voted by his feminine friends as "the type of man who never marries, my dear."

In letting my bitterness run away with my discretion, I have begun my story at the wrong end, giving a false impression of the facts of the case, for I never once dreamed of blaming or censuring Ruth for the misery that her decision cost me.

Two weeks before the date set for my wedding, Ruth came to me with tears in her eyes, and laying the ring I had given her upon the table begged me if I loved her never to see her again. I was decidedly taken aback, but I retained sufficient presence of mind to laugh at her and to request her not to be absurd. She was not to be diverted, however, nor would she say anything beyond a reiteration of the fact that if I loved her I would be willing to obey her without questioning her motives.

All of which was folly to my way of thinking, and being very much in love, I refused to be disposed of in any such high-handed fashion, particularly as I felt that as her affianced husband I was entitled to some say in the proceedings. Never in the course of my life before had I been called upon to plead so skillfully, and plead I did; for it was more than my life I was fighting for, it was our love, our happiness, our future home. Gradually I wore down her defenses and finally she sobbed out the whole pitiful story.

Her brother, her adored and darling Dick, whom she had mothered almost from the time that he was born, had fallen of late under the influence of Philip Darwin, director of the bank of which her father was president and Dick assistant cashier. Handsome, spoiled, the boy had been flattered by the attentions of the older man, who explained his interest on the ground that Dick reminded him strongly of what he had been ten years before. Under his tutelage, then, the boy early became a devotee of the twin gods of gambling and of drink.

Two nights before in a questionable gambling den to which Philip Darwin had taken him, Dick, his temper inflamed by the strong liquor he had been drinking, quarreled with his neighbor, accusing him of trying to cheat. The fellow, a big, powerful chap, made for Dick, who pulled out a pistol which Darwin had given him, and fired. His opponent went down like a log, and as the man fell, Darwin extinguished the light. In the confusion that ensued the older man got the boy away to his home, where Dick gathered some things together and with the connivance of his father left for the West.

Of course the affair came out in the papers, I recalled it as Ruth spoke, and the police were on the hunt for the unknown assailant of the dead man. Fortunately for Dick, both he and Darwin attended these places in disguise and a trip West for the scion of a wealthy family was no unusual event, hence his absence from social circles was easily accounted for, and Ruth and her father were merely waiting for the furore to abate before sending for the boy, when Darwin exploded a bomb in their midst.

He had always admired Ruth, he had always wanted to make her his wife. She had spurned his love and he had accepted defeat stoically. But now things were different. Her brother was wanted by the police for murder. The police, to be sure, didn't know it was her brother that they wanted but he, Philip Darwin, was quite willing to supply them with the information unless Ruth agreed to become his bride.

"What was there for me to do, Carlton, but to acquiesce?" she had ended with a sob. "Philip Darwin is an implacable man. And even if Dick eluded the police, think of the disgrace for Daddy and for me. It's terrible enough that he should have killed a man, but that he should become a hunted thing, my little brother—! No, no! I'd rather sacrifice my love than have that happen!"

I remained silent, for I could think of no argument that would suffice to meet the situation, and taking my apparent immobility for acceptance, she continued: "It's a big sacrifice, dear, I know, but you will bear it bravely for my sake, because-because there is more in life than love alone and it's the honor of my name that is at stake."

In the face of her sublime unselfishness I felt that I could do no less than prove myself as noble as she deemed me. I agreed, therefore, to give her up and when she said we had better not meet again I consented dumbly, comprehending the wisdom of her decision even while my heart rebelled against its enforcement.

When she had gone my resentment flared full and strong, but curiously enough not against the one who had been the chief cause of the ruin of my happiness. I felt only pity, a profound and sincere pity, for the misguided boy who had committed the crime. My anger blazed toward that man who by his foolish adoration of his only son had spoiled and indulged the boy to his own undoing. What right had any man to bring up a son in that fashion? How dared his father let him loose upon the world without teaching him the first principles of self-restraint?

It was not Dick but Mr. Trenton who was to blame for the boy's act. Almost from the moment that he could make his wants known the boy had been given to understand that what he wanted was his for the asking. Everyone in the home had to give way before him. He was never crossed and never denied. Small wonder that when he grew to manhood he should expect the world to give as much and more than his father had done, that when he ran across temptation he had no moral strength to resist, and that he became an easy prey to a man of Philip Darwin's type.

Here my thoughts veered abruptly to the man who would soon become Ruth's husband and for a moment I saw red. Ruth, pure, sweet Ruth, married to that vile wretch! I could not endure it.

I had actually grasped my hat and was on the point of hastening to her home to plead with her not to sacrifice herself in so dreadful a manner, even if she never married me, when I paused, for the horrible alternative flashed across my mind. With a groan I returned to my library where the remainder of the night I wrestled with what to me seemed the only solution to the problem, the instant and speedy death of Philip Darwin.

By morning I was saner. There was not much use in jumping out of the frying-pan into the fire, and besides what did I know of Philip Darwin beyond the fact that he had been the one to lead Dick astray? For ought I knew to the contrary he might make Ruth a very good and devoted husband. There were hundreds of cases on record where a man had been reformed and steadied by marriage.

Though all this philosophizing by no means alleviated the pain in my heart, still it helped to allay the fever in my tortured brain, and from that time on I resolutely put Ruth from my mind and plunged into my work in an effort to forget.

Forget! How much had I forgotten in the six months that had passed? Not one single detail had escaped my memory and it all came back with tenfold force for having been thrust out of sight so long. With a groan I buried my head in my hands.

How long I remained thus oblivious to time and space I do not know. The chauffeur's voice brought me back to a realization that we had arrived at our destination. I alighted and as he backed the car down the drive I paused a moment before ascending the steps to try to distinguish something of this home whose mistress Ruth had become.

It was very dark, a dull, cloudy night, and all I beheld was a great black bulk looming before me like some Plutonian monster, harbinger of evil, and the soughing of the wind in the branches of the nearby trees gave me such a feeling of superstitious dread that I raced up the steps and rang the bell as though in fear of my life.

CHAPTER II

THE SHOT

The door was opened for me by Ruth herself, who drew me within, and locked it behind me. Then with a finger on her lip, she led the way in silence to the drawing-room, seeming to breathe only when the door of that room was closed against further intrusion.

"What is it, Ruth?" I asked, more and more alarmed by all this secrecy coming on top of my own foolish fears.

Instead of answering she drew me down beside her on the divan and touched with her fingers my graying temples.

"Did I do that to you, Carlton?" she murmured, brokenly. "Oh, my dear, I wonder you had the courage to forgive me!"

"Ruth!" I cried sharply and at the misery in my voice she slipped to her knees and buried her face in her arms.

"Forgive me," she sobbed. "I should not have let myself go, but sometimes I feel I must go mad, alone night after night in this great silent house with only that horrible secretary of Phil's for company!"

"Hush," I returned, drawing her to me, but she pushed me from her and raised her head in a startled way.

"Listen!" she whispered, holding up her hand. "I thought I heard someone prowling around."

More to satisfy Ruth and ease her fears, for I had heard no sound, I went to the door and flung it open. But the dimly lighted hall was empty save for the wavering shadows that lost themselves in the gloom of the stairwell. The utter silence and loneliness of the great house gave me an eerie feeling, and I was glad to close the door and return to Ruth.

She had regained command of herself and was once more seated on the divan. As I approached she questioned me with her eyes. With a shake of the head and a reassuring smile, I resumed my place beside her.

"I thought I could stand it," she said, after what seemed an interminable interval, "but you don't know what I have had to put up with. No, Carlton, please!" for I had caught her to me in my desire to shield her from all harm.

"Forgive me," I returned humbly, rising and pacing the long room, "but I can't bear to hear you say such things when I love you so!"

"I know, Carlton. I won't grieve you that way again. It was for another reason that I asked you here."

She was so long, however, in telling me that reason that I had time to study her more closely, and my heart grew ever more bitter as I saw how thin she was and how the lines of suffering had gathered on her white brow and around her sweet, drooping mouth. Verily I cursed the day that Philip Darwin had crossed Ruth's path, and if he had entered the room at that moment I honestly believe I should have killed him.

She must have read my thought for she cried out sharply, "No, no, Carlton, not that!" and when I flushed she added more quietly, "Won't you come and sit beside me, please?"

When I had complied with her request, she lowered her voice until it was the merest thread, at the same time looking around her as if she feared the presence of someone else in the room.

"You know I have a feeling that Mr. Orton, Phil's secretary, is always hanging around listening and spying upon me. Ugh, he makes me shiver with his prominent, near-sighted eyes, his eternal humility and mock grin. He reminds me of Uriah Heep in *David Copperfield*. I suppose I'm foolish, but I've been alone so much of late."

"But, Ruth, I thought your father lived here with you?"

"Yes, he did, but two weeks ago the doctor told him to take a vacation and he has been visiting friends out of town. I expect him home to-morrow or the next day at the latest. Then I shall be all right again."

She clasped her hands in her lap and strove to keep back the tears.

"Ruth, dear," I said, taking her little trembling hands in both my own, "why did you send for me? Surely there is something I can do!"

She smiled faintly as she gently withdrew her hands and reclasped them in her lap. "It was for your sake I sent for you," she said, simply.

"For my sake?" I asked puzzled.

"You'd think that I had caused you enough suffering without adding needlessly to your sorrow," she continued, as if to herself. "Oh, Carlton," turning suddenly toward me, "forgive me, but I did a very foolish thing last night. I was so lonely and dispirited and nervous with hearing Mr. Orton prowling around and seeing him appear suddenly from shadowy corners that I locked myself in my room and poured out my heart to you."

"Ruth, darling!" I murmured.

"It was foolish, Carlton, nay more, it was imprudent, and realizing this last fact I tore up the letter and threw it in my waste basket. I would have done better to have kept it, for to-night about ten-thirty, when I was on the point of retiring, Mr. Orton knocked on my door and said that Phil desired my presence in his study."

"You obeyed?"

"Yes," she answered wearily. "It is only one of the many indignities I have had to endure. So I followed him to the study and there on the table the first thing I laid my eyes on was my letter-all those scraps pasted together on a larger sheet. Think of it, Carlton!"

But I couldn't think. The petty sordidness of it was beyond me. I could only stare at her and speak a name below my breath. Orton was what I said.

"Yes, he had found the letter. He examines my waste basket every day it seems," she continued, bitterly, "in hopes of finding just what he did find this morning. An unfaithful husband is always sure to be suspicious of his wife, and her moral superiority is equally sure to gall him."

"I am not going to tell you what Phil said," she went on presently. "I couldn't, for most of it passed me by. But when he spoke of revenging himself upon you, of ruining you and breaking you, then I decided it was time to act. He told me he was going out, so I sent my maid with the note and instructions to my chauffeur. I had to warn you, to put you on your guard that you might be able to fight any rumors which he may spread. But, Carlton, please promise me that you will keep out of his way. Please, for my sake!"

She clung to me as I shook my head impatiently. "It would only make it harder for me, Carlton!" she pleaded.

"Never mind me, Ruth!" I said almost angrily. "Think of yourself for a few minutes. Why don't you get a divorce or at least a separation? You have more than enough grounds."

"No, no. He would take it out on Dick. Don't you see he has me in his power?"

It was useless to try to influence her, especially as I could well appreciate the justice of her remark. I slightly cursed Philip Darwin for a blackguard, and then turned the conversation into a side channel.

"Ruth, do you think you could get that letter for me?" I asked.

"Why, Carlton?"

"Because it is a powerful weapon to hold over you if he should ever decide to cast you aside." Seeing that this had no effect upon her, I added-would that I had cut my tongue out ere it had uttered those words! "because he can use it as a weapon against me."

Instantly she was on her feet. "He put it in the drawer of the table in his study. Stay here, dear, while I see if I can get it."

She opened the door of the drawing-room and crossed the hall to the study. The drawing-room occupied about one-third of the lower floor of the main wing and lay to the right of the entrance hall, while the study was its exact counterpart on the left, so that the door of the study was directly opposite the door of the drawing-room which was now open before me.

I saw Ruth try the door of the study and as it yielded to her hand she advanced timidly into the room, leaving the door barely ajar behind her. My view being thus effectually cut off I strained forward in an endeavor to catch the slightest sound, but was only rewarded by the most profound stillness, through which there presently echoed and re-echoed the voice of the old clock in the hall proclaiming the midnight hour. Then, as if that ancient time-piece had been the signal previously agreed upon, there rang through the house from the direction of the study the sharp report of a pistol, followed by silence, absolute, profound!

A moment I remained petrified, then with a bound I gained the study door, my one thought for Ruth. But on the threshold I stood rooted to the spot by the sight that met my eyes!

In the patch of light cast by a small lamp upon the study table, lying back in his chair with a sardonic grin on his face and an ever-widening stain upon his shirt front, was Philip Darwin, while beside him as if turned to stone, stood Ruth with a pistol in her hand!

CHAPTER III

THE POLICE

"Ruth!"

My cry startled her. Dropping the pistol and flinging out her arms, she laughed hysterically and stumbled toward me. Something in my face, perhaps the horror I could not help revealing, arrested her before she reached me.

"Carlton! Surely you can't think I killed him!" she cried. "It-it would be too monstrous!" And with a fluttering sigh she sank in a heap on the floor.

Tenderly I gathered her limp form in my arms and was on the point of bearing her from the room when suddenly without any warning the study was flooded with light and Philip Darwin's secretary was standing obsequiously before me.

"Shall I telephone for a doctor, Mr. Davies? And for the police?" with a glance at his erstwhile master.

At mention of the police I frowned though I knew of course that their presence was inevitable. But there was no need to bring them buzzing about our ears any sooner than was absolutely necessary.

"A doctor, yes. The police can wait," I said abruptly.

"Just as you say, Mr. Davies," he returned with a leering smile. "I'll call Dr. Haskins."

He stepped to the table and picked up the phone and while he summoned the doctor I looked at him more attentively. He was just as Ruth had described him and instinctively distrust of this pale-faced secretary arose in my mind, distrust of him and his pussy-footing ways. I had not heard him enter the room behind me. For ought I knew to the contrary he might have been in the study when the shot was fired, sulking among the shadows in the corner while awaiting a chance to kill his employer. But then how in the name of all the gods had Ruth come by the pistol!

Which brought me back to the realization that I was still holding her unconscious form in my arms. I must carry her upstairs to her room. Yet I disliked intensely leaving the secretary alone with the dead, fearing I knew not what perversion of justice, dreading also that he might take the opportunity to summon the police before I was ready for them.

I glanced around the study and was relieved to find that the room possessed only one door, that by which I had entered, whose key was still in the lock, but on the inside. Ordering the secretary to lead the way to Ruth's apartments, I closed and locked the door of the study behind me, and pocketing the key followed him up the broad staircase.

Hardly had I laid Ruth upon her bed when a sharp ring startled me, and I glanced apprehensively at Orton. Could it be that others besides ourselves had heard the shot?

"No one could hear anything. The grounds are too extensive," he said, answering my unspoken thought. "That must be the doctor. He lives only a short distance from here."

Much as I disliked him I could have blessed him for those words, for already the plan to keep the police from questioning Ruth that night was simmering in my brain.

"Bring him here at once," I commanded, and Orton slipped noiselessly from the room.

I heard him opening the front door, heard the sound of voices apparently in consultation, and then the doctor's step upon the stair. I had expected an old family physician. The man who stepped briskly across the threshold was small and slight, almost a boy in years, yet having an air of knowing his business to perfection. Without ostentation, and also without asking needless questions, he examined Ruth quietly and attentively while I explained that she was suffering from the shock of having discovered her husband's murdered body.

"And, Doctor, could you not give her an opiate to insure a perfect night's rest," I added in a lower tone.

He gave me a swift appraising glance from his keen eyes, then as if satisfied, nodded to himself.

"Yes, I think you are right. It is far more important to save her reason than that the police should have the satisfaction of questioning her."

As he administered the dose to the now conscious girl I mentally decided that there was not very much that escaped this young doctor's observation.

"Is there no one to stay with Mrs. Darwin?" he inquired in a dissatisfied tone. "Where is her maid?"

"She sleeps in the servants' wing, Dr. Haskins," replied Orton.

"Go and get her," ordered the doctor briefly.

When the maid arrived on the scene, only half awake and very much tousled as if she had flung on her clothes without regard to appearance, the doctor bade her establish herself in the boudoir. Then satisfied that there would be someone within call in case of necessity, he asked to be conducted to the scene of the tragedy.

"You have notified the police?" questioned Dr. Haskins as we descended the stairs.

"No," I replied. "I waited to hear your verdict first."

"Better send for them at once," was his reply.

"I will do it, Dr. Haskins," put in the secretary eagerly.

As Orton moved to the hall phone I inserted the key in the lock of the study door and opened it with some trepidation, remembering what lay within. I had forgotten to turn out the lights and as we entered from the semi-obscurity of the hall, the chair and its horrible occupant seemed literally to spring out at us as we approached. To the doctor death was a familiar sight, but I could not bear to watch him as he probed the wound with skillful fingers, so I turned away and desirous of having something other than my thoughts to occupy my mind, I took cognizance for the first time of this room where the crime had been committed.

The study, as I remarked before, lay to the left of the hall and like its counterpart, the drawing-room, it was exceedingly large, a good forty feet in length at the very least. Again, like its counterpart, the side opening upon the garden was a series of French windows hung with velvet draperies of a rich brown that harmonized perfectly with the luxurious appointments of the room. Whatever one might say for his morals, one could certainly find no fault with Philip Darwin's taste in furnishing his study. It was the den of a sybarite, not the conventional study of the modern business man. The only jarring notes were supplied by the mahogany table directly in the center of the room, at whose head stood the chair in which the dead man lay, and by an immense safe let into the narrower wall, whose highly varnished surface reflected Darwin's face as clearly as any pier-glass would have done.

For a space I stood gazing at the safe, wondering what any man would want with such a gigantic contraption when I became conscious of the reflection of the doctor's occupation. With a feeling of nausea I swung away toward the windows when, struck by a sudden idea, I hastily examined them. It had occurred to me that while we were standing idle the murderer had probably made good his escape through one of them, since there was no other means of egress which he could have used with impunity. Imagine then my feelings to find that the windows were not only locked, but were also supplied with burglar alarms, which precluded beyond the shadow of a doubt their recent use by anyone intent upon escaping from the study!

With dwindling hope I tried the safe and finding that locked also, I returned to the table, where despite my aversion I could not help glancing at the man who, living, had destroyed my happiness and who, dead, was about to bereave me of all hope as well.

I had known Philip Darwin very slightly, a mere bowing acquaintance, so that it was a distinct shock to me to discover that he was so fine-looking a man. I had always accounted him handsome in a bold, dashing way, with his dark hair, his gold eyeglasses, and his neatly trimmed coal black Vandyke; but, death, that dread visitant that plays such queer tricks upon us mortals, had ennobled his countenance and rejuvenated him by wiping away all traces of the dissipation which of late had coarsened his features and left its marks beneath his eyes and around his mouth. Had it not been for that red stain which seemed to mock me as I gazed, I would have said that he was merely asleep, so gracefully did he repose in the big chair, the left hand holding a small handkerchief upon his knee, the right flung out across the arm of the chair.

Just then I noticed that the doctor was gravely regarding the pistol as it lay on the floor beside the chair, and recalling where I had last seen it, I hesitantly asked the question whose answer I knew before the words had left my lips.

"Is there any possibility of suicide?"

"None at all," replied Dr. Haskins. "He has been shot through the left lung and death occurred from internal hemorrhage. The absence of powder stains and the fact that the bullet entered at an angle preclude the idea of suicide."

"Then Mr. Darwin was not killed instantly?" I asked.

"No. I should judge that he had lived at least twenty minutes after the shot was fired."

It could not have been more than twenty minutes, or at most, a half-hour since I had heard the report that had turned my world so suddenly upside down! Had he then been alive when I carried Ruth from the room? Had I locked him in to breathe his last alone, when perhaps I might have saved his life? The thought was too horrible to contemplate!

"Doctor!" I cried. "You mean he has only just died? That something could have been done to save him?"

The doctor looked at me in some surprise. "Nothing could have been done to save him," he answered quietly. "From the condition of the body——"

But we had no time for further discussion for a great pounding had ensued at the front door and in a few moments Orton returned with the police. There were five of them, the Sergeant and his two men and a couple of detectives from the Central Office, and they made an imposing array as they entered the room.

The Sergeant, a mild-looking man, nodded to us pleasantly enough, deplored the necessity which had brought him to the house, and ordered his men to guard the premises and to permit no one to leave the place under any circumstances, while the detectives made the rounds of the room, examining everything from the carpet to the ceiling.

"I do not believe I can be of further use," said Dr. Haskins. "Let me know when the inquest is called and I shall be glad to give my testimony."

The Sergeant took down his name and address, and, when the doctor was gone, turned to me and asked me who I was. I mentioned the name of the brokerage firm with which I was connected and of which I had the honor of being the junior partner. The name of that firm was a well-known one throughout the city and its effect upon the Sergeant was instantaneous. Glancing at me with marked respect he asked me to give him an account of the affair. It was precious little that I could tell him, however. I had been in the drawing-room, had heard the shot, and on rushing in had found Darwin dead.

While the Sergeant was transcribing this information in his notebook the younger of the two detectives, who had been glancing over the objects upon the table, spoke up.

"It was an inside job, then, Sergeant. The windows are all locked and anyone leaving by the door would have encountered this gentleman coming in," and he looked at me very suspiciously indeed.

The worthy Sergeant scratched his chin and looked perplexed. Then his eye fell on Orton standing meekly in the doorway.

"Hello, where the devil did you come from?" he asked.

"I—I'm the man who sent for you, who just let you in," he stammered, whether from fright or awe I don't know. "I'm Mr. Darwin's secretary."

"I see. What do you know about this affair?"

He was opening his mouth to say I know not what when he caught my eye. I was determined that Ruth should have a night's rest if I had to go to jail as the consequence.

"I heard the shot and when I entered the room Mr. Davies was looking at the body," he said with a malicious glance in my direction.

I could have laughed aloud as the Sergeant regarded me from beneath frowning brows. I was a prominent man and he dared not risk a false arrest.

"Are you the only two people awake in this house?" he inquired, to gain time.

"Mrs. Darwin heard the shot but she was prostrated by the news and the doctor does not wish her disturbed until morning," I said, purposely giving the wrong impression by my statement.

Again the Sergeant's troubled glance rested upon me. "What are you doing here at this time of night, Mr. Davies?" he asked abruptly.

"I came here on important business," I answered.

At this juncture the older detective whispered something to the Sergeant and handed him a paper he had taken from the table drawer.

"Mr. Davies, I am under the painful necessity of keeping you under surveillance until the arrival of the coroner. You will remain in this house until that time."

I bowed. "Then you have no objections to my retiring?" I asked.

"None at all, Mr. Davies. Gregory," he called, and when the burly policeman appeared in the doorway, "You will accompany Mr. Davies to his room and see that he does not attempt to leave the house."

"Very good, sir," saluted the policeman.

"Good night, Sergeant," I said. "I am sorry to put you to so much trouble." Then I touched Orton upon the shoulder. "If you will be so kind I should like to be shown to a vacant room and might I borrow a suit of pajamas?"

I linked my arm through his and forced him to accompany me upstairs. By dint of hinting that he had no way of proving that he was not in the study at the fatal moment and that my word had far more weight than his, should I choose to cast suspicion upon him, I frightened the cowardly fellow into promising to keep his knowledge to himself for that night at least. That the police were bound to learn that Ruth was also in the study was inevitable, but at any rate I should have gained her a few more hours of freedom, for whichever way I looked at it the case was black against her.

CHAPTER IV

THE INQUEST

When I awoke the sun was pouring into the room and my watch pointed to eleven o'clock. After hours of pacing the floor in utter anguish of spirit while the specter of murder stalked hand-in-hand with innocence and love, outraged nature had asserted herself and I had found respite in oblivion. But now the weary round of thoughts must be taken up again and it was with a sigh of relief that I obeyed the summons to present myself in the study where the coroner was holding the inquest.

The body had been removed and in the chair where it had so lately rested reposed the coroner with his papers spread out on the table before him. I noticed that he had taken the chair from the head of the table and had placed it around the corner on the right side, facing the direction of the door instead of the safe.

In the corner opposite the door sat the younger of the two detectives who had accompanied the Sergeant to the house the night before. Beside him was Orton, looking pale and dispirited, while huddled in the adjacent corner like a herd of frightened cattle stood the servants, their eyes fastened upon the coroner, watching his every movement as if in terror lest they be accused of having murdered their master. Grouped around the table but slightly behind the coroner sat the jury, and I was glad to note that the coroner had had the good sense to pick a fairly respectable set of men to judge the case, from which I argued hopefully that the gray-haired, heavy-set gentleman in charge of the case might possess a modicum of intelligence and a keener brain than the average coroner.

Back of the jury stood Dr. Haskins, in conference with a rotund individual whom I assumed rightly to be the coroner's physician. Beyond the doctors sat the assistant district attorney, surrounded by the very few newspapermen who had got wind of the affair and had insisted upon being present.

Passing the jury I seated myself near one of the windows beside a man whom I recalled having seen, but whom I could not at the moment place, and looked around in vain for Ruth. Evidently Coroner Graves (I obtained this information from the man beside me) intended to spare her as much as possible, for which consideration I thanked him from the bottom of my heart.

They must have been awaiting my presence since I was no sooner seated than the coroner called on Doctor Haskins to give his testimony. The doctor repeated what he had previously told me, that Philip Darwin had been shot through the left lung, that death had resulted from internal hemorrhage, and that the victim had lived at least twenty minutes after the bullet had penetrated his body. Asked if he had examined Mr. Darwin immediately upon his arrival, the doctor replied that he had first attended Mrs. Darwin and that it must have been ten or fifteen minutes later that he had entered the study. He had found Mr. Darwin lying back in his chair with a smile on his lips, one hand closed over a handkerchief, the other hanging limply over the arm of the chair. From the condition of the body he must have been dead from twenty to thirty minutes. Also there was a small abrasion on the little finger of his left hand, as if a ring had been violently removed. Questioned as to whether he was the family's physician, he said no, that he only knew Mr. Darwin by sight and had probably been summoned because he was the nearest doctor.

This evidence was partially corroborated by the coroner's physician, who added that he had made a post-mortem examination and had extracted the bullet, which had narrowly missed entering the heart. From the nature of the wound it would have been impossible for him to have shot himself, and the absence of all powder stains pointed to murder rather than suicide.

Then he continued, with a slightly commiserating look in Dr. Haskins' direction: "You have heard Dr. Haskins' testimony, your honor, that the victim lived twenty minutes after he was shot, and that at the time that the doctor examined him he had already been dead from twenty to thirty minutes. This last statement is correct. The post-mortem examination proves conclusively that Mr. Darwin died at midnight or shortly thereafter. From questions that I have already put to Mr. Orton I have learned that the shot was fired as the clock finished striking twelve, therefore since that was the only shot fired Mr. Darwin must have died immediately, or at the best, must have lived only five minutes, for Dr. Haskins was in the study by twelve-thirty."

"But," interrupted Dr. Haskins, "the nature of the wound is such that instantaneous death could not have possibly occurred."

"Please do not volunteer information unless you are being questioned," returned the coroner with some asperity. He turned to his physician, "You were saying, Doctor?"

Dr. Haskins shrugged his shoulders at the coroner's words, while his boyish face flushed angrily at the rebuke, and he walked away from the table, but turned to listen as the physician took up the cudgels again by answering the query he had propounded.

"Dr. Haskins is young in his profession and this is his first criminal case, hence his natural inference that because in his medical books such a wound should produce such results, therefore it must be so in practice," said the coroner's physician, with pompous superiority. "Now as a matter of fact where one man will live an hour another will survive only a few minutes, depending on the life each has led. Now Mr. Darwin, I have been told, led a very fast life, which probably accounts for his quick demise. After all, you see, it's a question of fitting your facts to the circumstances of your case and in this instance no other conclusion is possible."

I could see that Dr. Haskins was not at all convinced, and I set it down to professional jealousy and his desire not to be outdone by the coroner's physician. I can imagine that that "is young in his profession" rather stuck in his gorge.

When the physician had seated himself the coroner took up the bullet and called the detective, to whom he handed it along with another object that had been lying upon the table. Whereupon the detective took a step forward and held up the object for our inspection. It was a long-barreled thirty-eight caliber revolver, just the sort of weapon a man would keep in his house for use against burglars, since it insured a fair chance of more accurate marksmanship.

"This revolver, gentlemen," said the detective, speaking to the jury, "was found on the floor beside the chair in which the victim lay. As you can see for yourselves," here he broke the pistol, "it is fully loaded with the exception of one chamber, which has recently been discharged. The bullet extracted from Mr. Darwin's body corresponds in every respect with the bullets remaining in this pistol. Therefore I have no hesitation in stating that the deceased was killed with this weapon in my hand."

He passed the revolver and the bullet to the jury, adding that Mr. Darwin had been standing when he was shot, and that as he had been engaged in writing the moment before, the inference was plain that he had risen to meet the person who killed him.

"What makes you certain he was standing when he was shot?" inquired the coroner.

"The carpet, if you'll notice," replied the detective, whose name, by the way, was Jones, "has a very heavy pile. The marks made by that arm-chair as it was pushed back from the table were apparent to me when I examined the carpet around it. Now Mr. Darwin had been writing, for we found a half-finished word on the paper before him, and must therefore have been seated in the chair. Hence the only person who could have produced those marks in the carpet was the victim himself, and they could only have been made if, as I said, he had risen suddenly to meet his murderer, who was evidently known to him, since Mr. Darwin was smiling when he was killed."

There was a murmur of admiration for the clever way in which he had deduced his statement, and the man beside me softly clapped his hands as he whispered to himself, "admirable, marvelous. Upon my soul I could not have builded better had I tried."

The thought came to me that my companion might be a detective also, and that he was delighted with the intelligence displayed by his professional brother, but I had no time to nurse idle speculations, for Jones had resumed his seat, and I expected the coroner to make an attempt to discover the ownership of the pistol. To my surprise he ignored that point and turned his attention to the servants.

The butler, who was the first servant called upon and who was a vigorous old man about sixty years of age, gave his name as George Mason and stated that he had been in his position for thirty years. I saw the coroner's face clear at this statement, for surely a man who had been the family retainer for so long a time could be relied on not to pervert any knowledge he might possess of the events of the previous night. The coroner should have recalled that though not given to perverting justice old family servants have a faculty for forgetting what they would rather not explain.

"I understand that it is your duty to secure the house at night," began the coroner.

"Yes, sir."

"What time do you usually lock up?"

"When Mr. Darwin left the house for the evening, sir. Or if he was away, as he sometimes is, for days together, it would remain locked while he was gone. That is, it was that way before his marriage, sir. Now I lock up when Mrs. Darwin goes upstairs."

"What time did you close the house last night?"

"At nine-thirty, sir."

"You are sure you locked all the doors and windows securely?"

"Oh, yes, sir, everything except the study, for to my surprise Mr. Orton was in there and said he'd lock the windows himself, sir."

"Why did Mr. Orton's presence in the study surprise you?"

"Because Mr. Darwin always keeps the study locked, sir. I have a duplicate key to let the maid in to clean, sir, and it was my custom in my rounds at night to knock on the door. If I got no answer I went in to see that everything was all right, sir."

"How long has Mr. Darwin been in the habit of locking his study?"

"A good many years, sir, ten or more."

"For what reason?"

"I do not know, sir."

"Did Mr. Orton explain how he came to be in the study?"

"No, sir. When I found him there I withdrew at once."

"After that, what did you do?"

"I saw to it that all the servants had left the main wing and closed the door into the servants' wing. When that door is closed it is impossible to hear what goes on in the main part of the house, sir. We went to bed and did not know the master was dead until Mr. Orton informed us this morning, sir."

"I see. This applies to all the servants, you can swear to that?"

"Yes, sir, to all except the valet and Mrs. Darwin's maid. They do not leave the main wing until dismissed for the night."

"Who opened up the house this morning?"

"The police, sir."

The coroner looked inquiringly at the detective, who answered promptly: "Nothing had been tampered with. The burglar alarms on the windows were all intact and the front door was double-locked when the doctor arrived."

The coroner turned once more to the butler. "When did you last see Mr. Darwin alive?"

"Yesterday about six o'clock, sir. He was just going out."

"Then he was not home for dinner?"

"No, sir. Mr. Orton and Mrs. Darwin dined alone, sir, for even Mr. Lee was away."

"Who is Mr. Lee?"

"Mr. Darwin's nephew, sir. He has lived here ever since he was a lad, sir."

Coroner Graves pondered a moment, then asked abruptly, "Have you ever noticed any signs of ill-feeling between your master and mistress?"

The answer came without a moment's hesitation, "No, sir, and even if I did it was not my place, begging your pardon, sir, to pry into the affairs of my betters."

The jury smiled, but the coroner frowned as he told Mason that he was through questioning him, for he was evidently a stickler in regard to upholding the dignity of the law as embodied in his own proper person, of course.

The examination of the other servants was a mere formality. None of them knew anything of the tragedy and they were disposed of in a group with the exception of the valet and Ruth's maid.

The former, being questioned, stated that his master had given him the evening, that he had left the house at six and had not returned until eight this morning. Where had he been at midnight, why at the Highfling, on Fourteenth Street, dancing with his girl.

The coroner summoned a policeman and sent him out to verify this statement, then called Ruth's maid, who supplied him with the first bit of tangible evidence against her mistress.

"How long have you been in your present position, Annie?" he asked, glancing at the sheet he held in his hand.

"Five months, sir," answered Annie, with a grin and curtsey. She was quite a pretty girl and it was evident that she was bursting to tell all she knew, so the coroner asked her to relate everything that had happened the night before, admonishing her to be careful not to forget a single detail.

She tossed her head. "As if I'm like to forget, sir, with it all ending in murder, sir." She spoke the word in a thrilling whisper, enjoying to the full her connection with so sensational an affair.

"Last night, sir, about ten-thirty, as I was getting my mistress ready for bed, came a knock at the door and who should it be but Mr. Orton, saying that the master wished to see my mistress in the study. Quick as a wink she was after him down the stairs, and I hadn't hardly had time to fix the bed before she was back again——"

"Be more definite," interrupted the coroner. "Was she gone five minutes?"

"Nearer ten, sir," came the ready answer.

"Were you making the bed that it took you ten minutes to fix it?" inquired the coroner, sharply.

The girl hung her head. "No, sir. I went out in the hall to see if I could hear anything, but there was no sound and when I saw my mistress coming up the stairs I ran back in the room and noticed the clock said about twenty to eleven, sir."

"Be careful how you give false impressions, my girl. Remember that we always learn the truth," said the coroner, severely.

The girl was quite abashed and just a little frightened. "It wasn't any harm, sir," she murmured, "and I didn't hear anything, so I thought it didn't have to be told."

"Go on with your story," shortly.

"Yes, sir. My mistress came back looking very excited and sat down at her desk. She wrote something on a paper and put it in a white envelope, then she told me to give it to her chauffeur and to tell him to go for Mr. Davies and bring him back as fast as possible. She said I needn't come back to her, so I did what she told me and then went to bed. I don't know how long I'd been asleep when Mr. Orton woke me and told me my mistress was ill. I flung on some clothes and followed him to her room, where the doctor told me to stay the rest of the night. I didn't know the master was dead until I went to get my breakfast. The butler told me, and that is all I know, sir."

"You have no idea what was in the note?"

"No, sir. It was sealed."

The chauffeur was called next and testified that what the maid had related with regard to him was correct. He had taken the note to my house and delivered it to my man. When I had entered the machine he had driven me to the Darwin home and left me at the front steps.

"Did the maid give you Mr. Davies' address?" asked an inquisitive juror.

"No, sir. I was Mrs. Darwin's chauffeur before her marriage and had often driven Mr. Davies home, sir."

"Then Mr. Davies was acquainted with Mrs. Darwin before her marriage?" This from another juror.

"Yes, sir."

"Did you not think it odd that your mistress should send for Mr. Davies at that time of night?" inquired the coroner.

"I didn't think about it one way or 'tother. I'm paid to obey orders, sir."

There was nothing more to be obtained from him and as by this time it had grown late a short recess was called for luncheon. I had hoped to see Ruth, but I was disappointed for she kept her room and so, not caring to join the others in the dining-room, I had Mason bring me a bite in the room adjoining the study.

When the inquest was reopened I once more took a chair near a window but above the table instead of below it, where I could watch more closely the witnesses as they were called. To my surprise my companion of the morning again chose a seat beside me.

Then the coroner rapped for order and inquired if Gregory had returned.

"Yes, sir," answered the policeman promptly, coming forward and saluting. "The valet's alibi is O. K., sir. The music hall attendant remembers speaking to him at midnight, and his girl corroborated his testimony."

"Very well. That effectually disposes of the servants," remarked the coroner. "Now for the more important witnesses."

I was hoping that he would call me first, but the name that fell from his lips was that of Claude Orton, private secretary and creature of the murdered man.

CHAPTER V

THE SECRETARY

What was Orton going to say? How many of last night's events had come under his notice? I had no recollection of having seen him until he had turned on the study lights, yet Ruth had been manifestly uneasy and had thought that she had heard his step in the hall. Where had he been when Ruth left the drawing-room and how close was he to the scene of the tragedy when the shot was fired? But all this was idle conjecture. I would know soon enough what I had to fear from this man, and as I caught the ugly gleam in his prominent eyes when he turned them for an instant my way I realized that he would do his very best to hurt me. My peremptory manner last night would be paid back in full, measure for measure, and he was cunning enough to guess that he could wound me most through Ruth.

"You are Mr. Darwin's secretary?" the coroner was saying when I was once more cognizant of my surroundings.

"I am his private secretary. I have charge of his business affairs," with a trace of condescension beneath his apparent humility.

"Where do you discharge your duties?"

"At his office in Broad Street. I attend to his correspondence."

"Is it not odd that a man of Mr. Darwin's—er-wealth-should introduce his secretary on an equal footing with his family?"

The secretary squirmed and the man beside me grinned delightedly through his forest of red whiskers.

"I am a distant connection of the family," answered Orton. "I—er-he asked me to make my home with him a month ago."

"And how long have you been in his employ?"

"About two months."

"You are then acquainted with his private affairs also?"

"Not at all, only those relating to his business."

"And what is this business you are always talking about?" inquired the coroner ironically. In his opinion rich men evidently had no need of occupation.

"He was director of the Darwin Bank," answered Orton, discomfited. "He also played on the market."

"A speculator, eh? Did he also play fast and loose in his domestic affairs?" continued the coroner with a shrewdness I should not have given him credit for.

For a moment Orton was puzzled, then a great light dawned upon him and he laughed feebly. "Yes, he was not on good terms with his wife, if that is what you mean. He was not what you would call a model husband."

"What an infernal idiot that fellow is," said the man beside me with a sneer, but I was too much concerned with what Orton would reveal to take any interest in side comments.

"You testified last night that you had heard the shot?" remarked the coroner, changing the subject abruptly. "Where were you at that particular time?"

"On the stairs. I had been doing some work in the little room beyond the study and on my way to my room had paused on the lower step to count the strokes of the hall clock. Just as I finished counting twelve the shot rang out," answered Orton very humbly, as if anxious to efface his personality from the minds of his listeners.

"What did you do then?"

"My first impulse was to flee up the stairs. I am a timid man and dislike the sight of bloodshed. But sometime previously I had heard a step in the hall and looking out had seen Mrs. Darwin enter the study. Fearing that it was she who was hurt I followed Mr. Davies into the study."

He wiped his brow with a trembling hand and I mentally decided that he had had a bad minute concocting that piece of testimony-for one part of it at least was a decided fabrication. Ruth had been in the study only a minute and had not gone in some time before, as he tried to imply.

"Mr. Davies entered ahead of you? Where did he come from?" queried the coroner.

"He was in the drawing-room, which is nearer the study than the stairs, and so he reached the room first, but he paused at the door for a minute and I was right behind him when he spoke to Mrs. Darwin."

"What did he say to Mrs. Darwin?"

"He cried out, 'Ruth!' and she dropped something shiny from her hand and fainted. While Mr. Davies picked her up I turned on the light and noticed for the first time that Mr. Darwin was dead."

Another prevarication! He could no more have helped knowing who had been shot than I if he was right behind me as he said!

"The study was in darkness then?"

"No. There was a small lamp lighted on the table but it did not give sufficient light to distinguish clearly the rest of the room."

"And when you turned on the light how many persons were in the room?"

"Just Mr. Davies, Mrs. Darwin, and I."

"Might there not have been someone else who left by the windows before you lighted the room?"

"No, for I locked the windows at Mr. Darwin's request a half-hour before, and they were still locked when the police arrived."

"Could anyone have escaped by the door then?"

"Impossible, for I should have seen that person. Besides, Mr. Davies was at the door almost immediately after the shot was fired."

"You said Mrs. Darwin had something shiny in her hand. Were you able to tell what it was?"

"Yes, it was a pistol," he said, with a triumphant look in my direction.

"That's a lie!" cried a man's voice, and Ruth's chauffeur detached himself from the group of servants to shake a finger beneath Orton's nose. "It's a lie, you miserable little worm! Take it back or I'll wring your neck!"

I think he would have done it, too, had not a policeman thrust him out into the hall, where he remained to curse Orton roundly before he moved away. A servant's loyalty to a sweet and gentle mistress, and I determined it should not go unrewarded, for nowadays such loyalty is rare.

The murmur of approval that followed this act showing in what odium the secretary was held by the servants, made the coroner a little doubtful of his man and more than ever anxious that his statement be properly substantiated.

"Have you any reason to suspect Mrs. Darwin other than the fact that she held the pistol in her hand?" he asked after due deliberation.

"She knew that Mr. Darwin kept a pistol in the drawer of this table and she had quarreled with him an hour and a half before," replied Orton with a triumphant expression on his pale face.

"She quarreled with him, you say? Tell me all you know about it."

"Mr. Darwin was away for dinner and I believe he returned about ten-thirty, but of this I cannot be absolutely sure, since he has a key of his own and I was in the study with the door closed."

"What were you doing in the study?" interrupted the coroner.

"I was answering some letters which Mr. Darwin had left for me," replied Orton.

"Mason testified that the study was usually kept locked," continued the coroner. "Have you also a duplicate key?"

"No, I have no key. He told me he would leave the door open for me and he unlocked it before he left the house," returned Orton, quietly.

"Go on with your story."

29

"At ten-thirty Mr. Darwin entered the study and told me to call Mrs. Darwin," resumed Orton. "She, as you know, answered the summons. At first they talked in low tones, but presently from their raised voices I knew that they were quarreling and quarreling bitterly, for I heard Mr. Darwin threaten to do something or other to Mr. Davies. Then Mrs. Darwin opened the door and rushed upstairs and Mr. Darwin called me to him. He said that he was expecting a visitor but wished me to watch Mrs. Darwin's movements and, when he summoned me, to report them to him. After which he closed and locked the door. It was then that I heard Mrs. Darwin telling her maid to make haste. I hurried to the back stairs and followed Annie to the garage where I heard her instructions to the chauffeur. Coming back to the house I hung around the darkened hall and while I waited I heard voices in the study, but I was unable to distinguish whose they were. Then Mrs. Darwin came downstairs and I drew back into the little room next the study to await developments. She lighted the drawing-room and about eleven-twenty-five she opened the front door, admitted Mr. Davies, locked the door, and led him into the drawing-room. It must have been about five minutes later that Mr. Darwin called me to the study and asked for my report. He was seated in that chair leaning back with his pen in his hand and in just the same position as we found him when he had been shot. I told him what I had seen and he laughed and clapped his hands softly as if something tickled his fancy."

"'So we've a broker in the house, eh?' he said. 'He should know how to play fast and loose, eh? I'll make him useful, this broker lover of our stainless Ruth!'"

Orton got no further. It was more than flesh and blood could endure to sit and hear him repeat that odious man's remarks in that softly insinuating voice. "Stop!" I cried, springing to my feet. "Your honor, I protest against such things being dragged into this court of inquiry!"

"That will do, Mr. Davies," said the coroner stiffly. But I believe he feared to antagonize me too far, for he said to Orton, "You need not repeat Mr. Darwin's conversation."

Orton bowed obsequiously in deference to his superior. Ugh, how I despised him!

"It was then that he told me to lock the windows and he was laughing when I left the room," finished Orton.

"Do you know what occasioned the quarrel between the husband and wife?" suddenly inquired the inquisitive juror.

"It was a love-letter that Mrs. Darwin had written to Mr. Davies," said Orton.

I think the coroner was afraid he was going to divulge its contents, for he interposed hurriedly, "Did anyone else know that the pistol was kept in this table drawer?"

"No, only Mrs. Darwin and myself."

"Is this the pistol in question?" pointing to the revolver.

"Yes. It belongs to Mr. Darwin and has his initials engraved on the handle."

The coroner nodded in confirmation. "Do you recognize this handkerchief?" holding up a dainty lace-covered bit of cambric partly stained with blood.

"I have seen Mrs. Darwin carry one like it."

"Are you and Mrs. Darwin the only members of the household?"

"We were last night. Mrs. Darwin's father has been away for two weeks on a vacation, and Lee Darwin, Mr. Darwin's nephew, left the house yesterday morning."

"What do you mean?"

"He had a dispute with his uncle and I overheard Mr. Darwin tell Lee to get out and stay out, which he promptly did. He went to the Yale Club and has not been back since."

"That is all, Mr. Orton. Gregory," called the coroner.

"Yes, sir," answered that worthy.

"Go to the Yale Club and inquire for Mr. Lee Darwin. If possible bring him here."

"Very good, sir."

When the policeman had gone the coroner turned to me. "Now, Mr. Davies, we will hear what you have to say."

CHAPTER VI

CORROBORATIVE EVIDENCE

How I wished that I had been born blind, or failing that, that I had been a thousand miles away when that fatal shot was fired! A coward's attitude? Perhaps, but for the life of me at that moment I could not see how my testimony could be anything but damaging to the girl I loved.

"Mr. Davies, will you tell the jury what happened last night," said the coroner.

Very calmly I told them all that had happened, saying that I was a life-long friend of Ruth, that she had asked me to come to the house, and that in the course of conversation I had urged her to get me a paper which was of value to me. She entered the study and almost immediately the shot rang out. I ran to the door and found her standing beside her husband. The shock of his death caused her to faint and I carried her from the room.

When I was through, the coroner stroked his chin reflectively. I was hoping he would dismiss me without further parley, but instead he began his cross-examination.

"Mr. Davies, did you not think it strange that she should send for you so late at night?" he commenced, after a slight pause.

"Under the circumstances, no," I replied.

"Under what circumstances?"

"In the interview between Mr. and Mrs. Darwin, of which you have heard, Mr. Darwin threatened to ruin me. Mrs. Darwin sent for me because she desired to warn me against her husband."

I saw several of the jurymen nudging each other and even the coroner's brows shot up a trifle, but I decided that it was far better to strengthen the case against her than to have them construing all manner of scandal from my refusal to answer.

"Could she not have written to warn you, just as well?" pursued the coroner.

"She believed that I would take no notice of such a warning unless it were given in person," I replied.

"Would not the next morning have been ample time?" caustically.

"I can't presume to say," I shrugged.

"You were acquainted with Mrs. Darwin before her marriage. Was it merely in the capacity of her friend?" He spoke diffidently, as if anxious not to offend my sensibilities.

I debated the point and finally came to the conclusion that there was no object in airing the family skeleton, more particularly as it might get Dick into trouble with the authorities and thus set at naught Ruth's dearly bought sacrifice.

I bowed therefore and replied quietly, "Yes, your honor, I was merely her friend."

The coroner gave me a swift glance from beneath half-closed lids as he fingered a sheet of paper thoughtfully.

"You said that Mrs. Darwin entered the study to reclaim a paper which was of value to you, did you not?" he inquired.

"Yes," I answered, briefly.

"Is this the paper?" he continued in a peculiar tone, holding up the letter that Ruth had described to me.

"I have no idea," I retorted.

"What do you mean by that?" he continued sharply.

"Mrs. Darwin simply told me that in the study-table drawer was a letter which her husband could use against me. I urged her to retrieve it. Never having seen it I cannot possibly say whether the paper in your hand is the one or not," I returned, quietly.

For a moment he was nonplussed, and then he asked: "You heard Mr. Orton say it was a love-letter written to you by Mrs. Darwin?"

"Oh, yes, but I didn't hear you ask him how he knew this. No, nor did I hear him tell you that he fished the torn scraps of Mrs. Darwin's private correspondence from her basket and pieced it together for her husband's delectation," I replied, scornfully, glad of the chance to let the jury know the truth concerning that letter.

I saw the look of disgust with which various of the members of the jury favored Orton, and even the coroner was impressed to the point of laying the letter aside and resuming his attack upon a different line.

"When you sent Mrs. Darwin into the study you were both aware, of course, of Mr. Darwin's presence in that room?"

"No. Mr. Darwin had told his wife he was going out and we had no idea there was anyone in the study."

"But finding him there unexpectedly might she not have shot him to secure the letter?" pursued the relentless voice.

I shook my head and replied abruptly (I have learned since that he had no right to ask that question, but I had no knowledge of legal technicalities): "Impossible. She was in the study only a minute before the shot was fired. This I am positive of, Mr. Orton's evidence to the contrary. She had left the door slightly ajar and I remember listening for sounds from the study just before the clock struck twelve. I heard no voices. Besides, the study was in total darkness——"

"You are sure the study was in darkness?" he interrupted with an odd look.

"Yes, I think I can safely say it was."

"It has been proven that Mr. Darwin was writing just before he was shot. Do you think he was in the habit of writing in the dark?" he inquired sarcastically.

I reddened. The detective's statement had slipped my mind, but I refused to be ridiculed into changing my opinion. I could have staked my life upon it that the study was dark.

"Of course I was not in the room itself," I returned stiffly, "but by the hesitating way in which Mrs. Darwin entered and from the fact that no glow came through the doorway as she opened the door, I judged that the study was in darkness."

"The lamp on this table could never give sufficient light to be seen from that doorway, Mr. Davies," remarked the coroner.

I shook my head impatiently. "Nevertheless, I am convinced the study was in darkness," I reiterated stubbornly.

Seeing that he was getting nowhere he dropped the point, and asked: "Did you also see the pistol in Mrs. Darwin's hand?"

There was no use in quibbling since the fact was known, and I had no idea of what Ruth herself would say on this point, so I replied in the affirmative, adding: "As I stood in the doorway I could see that Mr. Darwin had been shot as plainly as I could see that Mrs. Darwin was standing beside his chair."

"I thought you said the study was in darkness?"

"It was, but the lamp was lighted as I sprang for the door."

"Then you think there may have been someone else in the room?"

"Yes."

"Could you see the door of the study from your position in the drawing-room?"

"Yes." What was he getting at, anyway?

"So that you could see whether anyone came out of the study, or entered it after Mrs. Darwin?"

"Yes."

"Did anyone come out or go in?"

"No."

"You heard the evidence concerning the windows?"

"Yes."

"Do you still persist in saying there was someone else in the study?"

So that was it. He was trying to trap me into making a contradictory statement to pay up for my stubbornness concerning the study. But I had no intention of being trapped by him.

"I cannot be absolutely positive, your honor," I said, "but of this I am certain. I had no knowledge of Mr. Orton's presence until he lighted the study. Whether he was already in the room when Mrs. Darwin went in, or whether he entered behind me, I am not prepared to say."

"That's not so!" cried Orton, his face more pallid than ever. "I was out in the hall, your honor, I was out in the hall!"

The detective said something to him in an undertone, whereupon he subsided tremblingly, but it was very plain to be seen that the coroner, who had not been previously impressed with the man and who had since come to regard him in the light of a sycophant, began to be suspicious of the secretary, eyeing him with great disfavor, wondering, no doubt, whether he were as innocent as he gave out. I began to breathe more freely for Ruth, but at the coroner's next words my hopes were dashed once more.

"Knowing that Mrs. Darwin was in the study, why did you give the police the impression last night that she had heard the shot from upstairs?"

"She was ill. I didn't want her disturbed," I explained.

"In other words, you feared to tell the truth," he commented.

I made no answer. Protestations would only have made a bad matter worse.

"Mr. Davies, you know, of course, that if a man dies intestate, his wife inherits his property?"

I nodded, but was decidedly puzzled.

"Mr. Darwin died intestate," he continued quietly, watching to note the effect upon me.

"I don't understand you," I said, and I spoke the truth. I was out of my depth, for he surely couldn't suppose that I was intimately acquainted with Philip Darwin's personal affairs! Either that, or else he possessed information of which I had no knowledge. It proved to be the latter case.

"In the waste basket we found partially burned scraps of what was presumably a will, Mr. Davies, and here," holding up a heavy paper, "is what Mr. Darwin was at work upon when he was shot. It is a will, Mr. Davies, or rather the beginning of one, and it is not in Mrs. Darwin's favor."

I made no comment, but I could see what he was driving at. This was another powerful factor to be added to Ruth's motive in taking her husband's life.

"This will is in favor of Cora Manning. Did you ever hear of her, Mr. Davies?" continued the coroner.

"I can't say that I have."

"Do you also identify this handkerchief?"

"No, I have never seen it before to my knowledge."

"It might be Mrs. Darwin's?"

"I don't know."

"That is all at present. Mr. Cunningham, please."

CHAPTER VII

THE LAWYER

At the coroner's words the man beside me arose and walked to the front of the room. He was about Philip Darwin's build and height, but his face was fleshier, and he wore a full, square beard of a peculiar mottled red, the same shade as his hair, as though both had been liberally sprinkled with gray. He was very fastidiously dressed, I might say almost foppishly so, even to the point of wearing spats and an eyeglass, which he was continually screwing into his eye as he spoke.

"You are Mr. Darwin's lawyer?" asked the coroner.

"Yes. You will pardon me if I reply rather briefly. I have a bad throat to-day and find it trying to speak at length," he apologized in a husky voice.

"Certainly, certainly. This is a mere formality," responded the coroner affably, whereat the lawyer smiled, rather sardonically, I thought.

"Mr. Cunningham, do you know whether the will that was destroyed was in Mrs. Darwin's favor?"

"It was."

"Are you absolutely certain?"

"Yes. I made it out when Mr. Darwin was married."

"Do you know whether Mr. Darwin keeps any of his valuable papers in that safe?"

"I am sure he keeps nothing of value in it. His papers are in his vault at the bank."

"Have you none, then?"

The lawyer shook his head and replaced his eyeglass with great deliberation. "Two nights ago Mr. Darwin removed the last of his securities from my office," he said with evident difficulty.

"The last of his securities? Do you mean that he had been gradually removing them from your care?"

This time the lawyer nodded.

"For what purpose?" asked the coroner.

"I do not know," was the candid answer. "He was rather secretive. I surmised he needed them in his dealings in Wall Street."

"He did not actually say so?"

"No. He told me nothing."

"Since he was so secretive, might he not have put some of his securities in that safe?"

"No, I don't think so. However, you might have it opened-to satisfy yourself," with a slight, rather mocking accent on the last word.

"I think it just as well," responded the coroner, briskly. "Mr. Cunningham, you don't by any chance happen to know the combination?"

"No, I do not."

"Jones, can you open that safe?" inquired the coroner.

"I think so." The detective rose and advanced down the long room to the safe, where he knelt down, the better to hear the fall of the tumblers. While he twirled the knob of the dial now this way and now that, Mr. Cunningham, as if in no way interested, moved to the window, where he stood looking out with his back to the room. Now it happened that I was sitting so that I could see his reflection in the window-pane, and I was surprised to note the look of diabolical joy that overspread his countenance as he rubbed his hands together in unholy glee, for it seemed to me that such levity was decidedly out of place at this particular time.

But now my attention was diverted, for the detective straightened to his full height and opened the safe door, which swung back on noiseless hinges. As the detective darted within the cavernous depths, the lawyer turned toward the room once more with a remnant of his smile on his lips as he stroked his beard with a well-kept white hand. And then it flashed across me where I had seen him before. It was on the Knickerbocker Roof, late one evening in September, where I was supping with my partner after the show. Cunningham had come in with a couple of chorus girls and my partner had mentioned that he was a gay old boy, to which I had agreed after watching him as he stroked his beard and made love to the girls. I had not seen him since that night, roof gardens not being much in my line, and so, of course, I had failed to remember him until that gesture which seemed habitual with him recalled him to my mind.

"Nothing, your honor," reported the detective, emerging with a crestfallen face. "Nothing but a few receipted tailor's bills, an empty cash box and a stoneless ring."

"A what?" The coroner screwed himself around in his chair and the jury strained backward as Jones spoke.

Mr. Cunningham involuntarily put out his hand for the bauble as the detective passed him, but Jones shook his head with a smile, as he returned to the front of the room and placed the objects on the table before the coroner.

Coroner Graves examined with meticulous care the sheaf of bills, the empty box. Then he put them aside and turned his attention to the stoneless ring.

"Odd, very odd," he said. "Why should a man like Mr. Darwin preserve a stoneless ring?"

"I think I can explain that," said the lawyer, coming forward very leisurely. "May I look at it?" He held out his hand and the coroner placed the ring within it. "Ah, yes, it is the same." He handed it back with a courteous air, but I could not help feeling that somehow he was merely amused by the attempts of the coroner to solve the problem. But it must have been my own overwrought fancy, for his voice was sinister enough through its throatiness, as he said:

"My client, as perhaps you know, was very fond of the ladies. Before his marriage he met a very beautiful young lady-her name does not matter, it was not her own, for she was an actress, I believe-of whom he became very fond. In fact, he told me he was going to engage himself to her, and showed me that ring which he had bought her. It held within that now broken setting a magnificent blue-white diamond. If you will look within you will see the inscription which Mr. Darwin had engraved upon it."

He paused, as much to rest his voice as to give the coroner the opportunity of reading aloud for the benefit of the jury the sentiment which graced the ring: "To my one love —D."

"I remonstrated with him, told him she would take the ring and leave him high and dry, but he would not listen and bestowed it upon her," resumed the lawyer. "A week later he received a letter from her enclosing that." He waved his hand toward the golden circlet contemptuously. "She had kept the diamond and returned him his ring. She left the country and he never heard from her again. Why he kept that empty shell I don't know. Perhaps he put it in the safe and forgot it was there."

"Where did you find it, Jones?" asked the coroner.

"In one corner of the top shelf. I only discovered it because as I passed my hand over the shelf the broken prong scratched me," replied Jones.

The coroner nodded. "A thin bit of gold not worth considering," he said, adding as the lawyer was about to return to his seat: "Mr. Cunningham, do you know Mr. Darwin's nephew?"

"Yes, I have met him several times," responded the lawyer.

"Was there not a will in his favor before the wedding?"

"Yes, but it was destroyed when the new will was made."

"Did Mr. Darwin mention to you recently that he intended changing his will?"

"No."

"Have you ever heard of Cora Manning?"

"No."

"Yet Mr. Darwin had written her name on the will he was making at the time he was shot, Mr. Cunningham."

"Indeed? This is all news to me, sir. My client, as perhaps you have heard, was exceedingly peculiar. He did not confide all his affairs to me. In fact, he often employed more than one lawyer."

The coroner raised his brows. "Well, he certainly was peculiar if he did that. One lawyer ought to be enough for any sane man."

"Quite right," responded Mr. Cunningham with an odd smile. "But perhaps my client wasn't quite sane."

CHAPTER VIII

LEE DARWIN

The coroner's retort, if he made one, was lost to me, for at this moment loud voices were heard in the hall and a burly policeman came hurriedly into the room.

"What is it, Riley?" asked the coroner in an annoyed tone.

"Beggin' yer pardon, sorr, but there's a young man out here and a divil of a strong young man he is, yer honor," said the policeman.

"What does he want?"

"Shure an' he says he's Lee Darwin, but Oi'm on to their little tricks. An' shure by the looks of him I'd say he was one of thim fresh cub reporters that worries the life out of us huntin' for noos."

"Reporter be hanged!" exclaimed a wrathful voice, as a young man strode into the room.

Here the details of the scene before him, the frowning coroner, the amazed jury, the dignified lawyer, sank into his consciousness and he stopped abruptly a few feet from the table.

"What is the meaning of all this?" he inquired, but in a more subdued tone. "Mr. Cunningham, what are all these people doing here?"

Before the lawyer could answer him, he cried out suddenly, "My uncle! What has happened to him!"

"Mr. Darwin was shot last night," answered the coroner.

"Shot? You-you mean murdered?" in a horrified whisper.

The coroner nodded, then said briskly: "I am glad you are here. There are several questions I should like to ask you."

"I am at your service."

The defiant lift of the head as he spoke, and the fiery look he cast around the room as if challenging us to contradict him, were so like the actions of a creature at bay that I examined him more attentively. He was a tall, broad-shouldered, dark, young man, with a pair of snapping black eyes that roamed restlessly about the room during his entire examination. It was evident that he was laboring under some strong emotion, for much as he controlled his voice and strove to appear calm the muscles of his face betrayed him by their involuntary twitching, and his hands were clenched convulsively at his sides.

"You had a misunderstanding with your uncle yesterday morning. Is my information correct?"

No answer, only a savage look in Orton's direction, as though he divined the source of the coroner's knowledge of his affairs.

"I should like an answer, if you please," with some asperity.

The young man laughed harshly. "I'd call it a quarrel," he said.

"A quarrel, eh? What was the subject of this quarrel?"

A slight pause while he mentally debated the wisdom of replying, then with a sudden abandonment of his former brief manner, he said quickly: "I objected to the way my uncle treated his wife. He took umbrage at what he called my impertinence and told me to clear out. I did. It was none too congenial here."

"What do you mean by that last statement?"

"My uncle was always at dagger's points with his father-in-law."

"For what reason?"

"I do not know. I fancy, though, that it was something pretty strong that my uncle held over Mr. Trenton. I have heard him say things that had I been Mr. Trenton, instead of listening meekly, I'd have jumped up and knocked him down."

"What was Mr. Trenton's attitude toward your uncle?"

"He was always very pleasant to him, and never seemed to take offense at what my uncle said."

37

The coroner made a note on one of his many papers and then resumed his questions. "What brought you back this morning if you had left the house for good?"

"I came to get the rest of my belongings. I left rather suddenly yesterday."

"When did you last see your uncle?"

"In this study when I quarreled with him yesterday morning."

"Did you notice whether he was wearing a ring on the little finger of his left hand?"

Was it my fancy, or did he pale?

"My uncle never wore any rings," Lee Darwin answered.

"Yet the physician testified that a ring had been pulled off his finger."

"He wore none when I saw him last." How proudly, and it seemed to me how sadly, that was said.

"Mr. Darwin, did you ever see that handkerchief before?"

As the coroner held up the dainty trifle the young man started and with a quick indrawn breath he leaned closer to examine it. Then with a look of relief he straightened to his full height.

"No, I do not recognize it," he said.

"Whose did you think it was when I first held it up?" Again Coroner Graves surprised me by his astuteness.

"Why-why, Ruth's—Mrs. Darwin's," stammered the young man, somewhat taken aback.

"And it isn't hers?" persisted the coroner.

"No, I'm positive it isn't."

Certainly he was a young man after my own heart.

"Would you swear to that fact?" went on the coroner inexorably.

"Look here, do you think I'm lying to you?" demanded Lee Darwin, angrily.

"Would you swear to that fact?" repeated the coroner monotonously, taking no notice of the outbreak.

A dull red suffused the young man's dark face and his eyes smoldered as he glanced at the coroner. "I refuse to answer," he said, sullenly.

The coroner shrugged, having won the battle by creating just the impression that he desired, namely that the handkerchief was Ruth's and that for some reason Lee was trying to protect her. I swore softly below my breath at the blunder young Darwin had committed in becoming angered, for though I knew he could possibly have no motive for shielding Ruth, having heard none of the previous evidence, he had yet managed to strengthen the case against her by his strange attitude.

"Mr. Darwin, did you ever hear of Cora Manning?" suddenly inquired the coroner.

Lee Darwin had himself better in hand this time, for his face did not change from its sullen aspect, but he could not help clenching his closed hand tighter until the knuckles showed white through the flesh. That action alone told me that he knew the woman whose name was on Philip Darwin's unfinished will. It also told me that he would deny it. So I was not surprised when he said, a little stiffly, as though he found it hard to speak at all:

"No, I do not know her."

"When you first recognized my official capacity what made you think something had happened to your uncle?"

For a moment he seemed nonplussed, then he answered readily enough, "I suppose it was because I was entering his house and the thought of its master and our last meeting was uppermost in my mind."

"You are sure that it wasn't because you knew beforehand that he was dead?"

I thought he was going to faint, so pale did he become, but he rallied instantly and said, haughtily, "Do you presume to intimate that I killed my uncle?"

"Not at all, since you could not possibly have been in the room at the time," responded the coroner. "I merely wished to learn, whether when you were standing outside the house late last night, you saw what occurred in the study."

This statement created an immense sensation. Everyone looked at everyone else and then at Lee Darwin, who stood before the coroner with blazing eyes and head flung high.

"I came here to get my belongings and not to be questioned about an affair of which I know nothing!" he exclaimed angrily. "I refuse to answer further."

The coroner shrugged. "Of course it is not really important. You can tell your story in court when you have been arrested as an accessory after the fact."

"I know nothing about it, I tell you!" cried Darwin in exasperation.

"Your footprints were found in the flower-bed, outside the study window. What were you doing there at that time of night?"

Lee Darwin laughed outright, whether with relief or hysteria I don't know, though I incline to the former.

"Your honor, your minions are not as clever as they seem to think. I made those footprints yesterday morning when I left the house through the study window. I turned around and stood there a moment to shake my fist at my uncle," he said, sarcastically.

"Just a moment, Mr. Darwin. Mason," called the coroner.

The old butler came forward timidly. "Did you see Mr. Lee Darwin leave the house yesterday morning?" inquired the coroner.

"No, sir. I knew he was in the study after breakfast but I did not notice whether he came out," he answered, peering anxiously at the young man.

"That will do. Mr. Orton, please."

The secretary rose and took the butler's place, and as though he had anticipated the question he said eagerly, "Mr. Lee Darwin left the house by the window yesterday morning."

It struck me he was trying to curry favor with young Darwin by the way he spoke and fawned upon him.

"You are positive of this?" said the coroner.

"Yes, Mr. Lee was just leaving the house when his uncle said something to him and he followed him into the study. I was waiting for Mr. Darwin in the hall, and after the quarrel, I entered the study at Mr. Darwin's summons in time to see Mr. Lee leave by the window and then turn back again, as he said."

"Now that the word of a gentleman has been vouched for by that of a miserable spy, I trust you will permit me to go to my apartments." The sneer that accompanied the words made Orton wince, but the coroner remained imperturbed. He granted the permission with a wave of the hand.

"Would it be asking too much to allow me to see my uncle's body?" inquired the young man, pausing in the doorway.

"Unfortunately your uncle has been removed to the undertaker's," responded the coroner affably. "If you care to call on them ——"

With a gesture of disgust the young man left the room and the coroner was human enough to enjoy his advantage after his own discomfiture at young Darwin's hands.

And now only Ruth remained to be questioned. Would he tell me or Orton to summon her? To my surprise he called Cunningham to him and after a whispered consultation the lawyer left the room and I heard him ascending the stairs.

This unexpected move the coroner explained in a few curt words. "Under the circumstances Mrs. Darwin is entitled to counsel," he said. "Mr. Cunningham has kindly consented to act in that capacity this afternoon."

Had the case against her progressed to the point where she needed legal advice? Then, indeed I had nothing to hope for from the interview which was now about to take place.

CHAPTER IX

THE VERDICT

A few moments later Cunningham returned alone, and presently I heard Ruth's step upon the stair. I arose and as she entered the room I hastened to her and led her to a chair, giving her a reassuring smile as I did so. She looked so little, and so tired, so in need of comfort that it seemed a sacrilege to question her. As for believing her guilty of murder, that was too preposterous!

But then the coroner was not in love with her, and he had his duty to perform. I will give him credit for this, that as he looked into her sweet, gentle face his duty became none too pleasant for him and he conversed with a stranger who had entered the room before he again took up his burden of office. When he did it was to say:

"Mr. Ames, the finger-print expert, has a word to say before we can pass verdict on this case."

Before Ames could speak, Cunningham held up his hand.

"I would like you to hear what Mrs. Darwin has to say first before you attempt to actually incriminate her," he said.

At his words Ruth turned and glanced at him sharply, with a puzzled expression on her face which I could not account for, as she stared at him uncomprehendingly, but as the full meaning of his words dawned upon her, she turned her terrified eyes in my direction.

"Carlton," she said, and she raised her right hand solemnly, as though I were the judge before whom she was taking an oath, "I am innocent of any crime. In God's name, tell me you do not believe me guilty!"

She caught my hand and drew me down so that she could see my face.

"Ruth," I replied-it cost me an effort but for her sake I strove to speak quietly—"when I found you in the study I was startled, but never once have I believed you guilty, and now I know that you are innocent."

She released my hand and settled back in her chair with a sigh of relief. As long as I knew her innocent what mattered what anyone thought, was her attitude. But, alas, it was not I but the jury she would have to convince.

"Mrs. Darwin, I should like very much to have your version of the events of last night," said the coroner, and his voice was very gentle as he addressed her.

"Ruth," I interposed quickly, "be careful what you say." I was in mortal dread lest she incriminate herself beyond redemption, and yet I knew her to be innocent! Explain the paradox as best you may. I could not.

"Well meant, but ill-advised," said Mr. Cunningham. "Your best plan, Mrs. Darwin, is complete frankness."

Again that strange puzzled look on Ruth's face as she turned toward him, then as if his words found an echo in her own heart, she looked once more toward me and said simply, "Yes, Carlton, why shouldn't I tell him all since I am innocent?"

I groaned and mentally anathematized the coroner for his choice of counsel. I was powerless to help her in the face of her guileless attitude and evident inability to realize the danger of her position.

Very quietly and very candidly she told the coroner all that had occurred that fateful night, most of which was already known to those present in the room, the only new evidence being her account of what took place after she entered the study.

"The study was dark and as I left the door only barely ajar and the hall was dim, it was impossible to see any objects in the room. I knew however about where the table was located and I groped my way to it, and found the drawer. It was closed and I had to pull quite hard to open it. As I did so I thought I heard someone breathe quite close to me. I was paralyzed with fright, but as moment after moment passed and I heard no further sound, I decided I was mistaken and slowly put my hand in the drawer and felt around for the letter that I had come to get. Just as my hand closed around it I heard again that sound. Oh, it was horrible! Like someone trying to breathe who couldn't!"

She broke off and hid her face in her trembling little hands, and at my suggestion Mason brought her a glass of water. When she had sipped it she thanked him with a sweet smile and I saw the old man hastily wipe away a tear as he departed. I am not sure but that I did the same myself, as Ruth resumed her narrative in a voice not quite so steady as before.

"I snatched my hand from the drawer and had taken but two swift steps away from the table, as I thought, when there was a sudden deafening roar. I stood stock-still, unable to move, and when I did finally take a step I trod on something hard. Mechanically, I stooped and picked it up. It was then that the lamp lighted and I saw Phil lying there-dead-almost beside me. I was stunned and stood like one stricken until I heard Carlton's voice. I had no idea what I had picked up until that moment, but when I saw what it was and what Carlton was thinking, I cried out in horror-and fainted. That's all I know," she ended, faintly.

I don't think they really believed her. The skeptical smile on the coroner's face was reflected on the countenances of the jury. It was an ingenious account but there was entirely too much that was still obscure.

"Why did you not light the study instead of groping in the dark?" asked the coroner.

"Because I knew that Mr. Orton was spying upon me, because I saw him in the hall as I entered, and did not wish him to follow and see what I was doing," she answered quietly, thereby drawing the noose tighter about her own neck by providing with a perfectly good alibi the only other person who could possibly have been in the room at the time!

But she was ignorant of their suspicions and failed to see the look of relief that crossed the secretary's pallid face.

"Mrs. Darwin, do you recognize this pistol?"

"Yes. It is Phil's. It's the one I picked up."

The coroner scratched his head in perplexity. Either she was innocent or she was a magnificent actress, for only in those two instances could she answer these questions with so much directness and sincerity. I could see that he inclined toward the latter assumption for his tone grew harsher as he said abruptly: "You were not on good terms with your husband. Did you know that he was making a new will when he was shot?"

Ruth opened her eyes wide in astonishment. "Why, how could I know what he was doing when I did not know he was at home?" she asked naïvely.

"Do you know anyone by the name of Cora Manning?" pursued the coroner.

"Cora-Manning? No." Her voice trembled slightly as she pronounced the name.

"You are sure?"

"I do not know her," repeated Ruth firmly.

"She is the lady whose name is on the unfinished will. Evidently your husband must have thought a good deal of her for he had torn up his old will and was apparently going to leave everything to her."

Ruth drew herself up proudly. "Excuse me, sir, but my husband's affairs were his own. I take no interest in them whatsoever."

"Not even to the extent of losing several millions?" spoke up the juror who seemed always to have so much to say.

But Ruth did not deign to answer him. Instead she addressed the coroner. "By a legal agreement entered into at the time of our marriage my husband was free to dispose of his wealth as he saw fit."

If her voice held a tinge of bitterness who can blame her?

"As you saw fit, since his murder gives it all to you," continued the irrepressible juror.

"Your honor, I protest against such insinuations," I cried, for Cunningham seemed to have fallen asleep.

41

"I don't understand you," faltered Ruth, her eyes growing dark as they traveled over the stern, set faces of the jury. Then her hand fluttered involuntarily to her throat. "I don't understand you," she said again.

As the juror opened his mouth to reply, the coroner silenced him with a gesture. "Kindly permit me to conduct this investigation," he said curtly, then to Ruth, "Mrs. Darwin, was your husband in the habit of wearing rings?"

"I never saw him wear any," she answered. It was plain she was puzzled by his question.

"Yet he might have done so last night?"

"I suppose so."

"You didn't happen to remove it, did you?"

"Most certainly not," she said, highly insulted by the implication.

"Your honor, may I make a suggestion?" Cunningham awoke suddenly to the exigencies of the situation.

"Certainly, Mr. Cunningham," responded the coroner graciously.

"It has occurred to me that perhaps Mr. Darwin had in a moment of sentiment slipped that stoneless ring on his finger, and then had trouble in removing it. Of course it is only a suggestion," apologetically.

"No doubt it was just as you say," answered the coroner. "After all, the ring has nothing to do with the actual murder. Thank you, Mr. Cunningham."

As the lawyer resumed his seat with that sardonic smile upon his lips, the coroner picked up the handkerchief. "Is this yours, Mrs. Darwin?"

"No."

"Are you sure?"

"Yes."

"May I see that handkerchief that you are holding so tightly in your hand?"

Without a word she passed the bit of cambric to him and he held it up beside the blood-stained handkerchief. They were exactly the same, texture, pattern, and design!

"Well?" The coroner laid the two articles upon the table and bent a flashing look upon her.

"I don't understand how it can be just like mine when it doesn't belong to me," she said in a frightened voice. "Phil bought it for me at the church bazaar-just after we were married. He-he only bought me one."

"Wasn't it strange-his buying only one?"

"No-no. I wouldn't let him get me any more. I—I didn't want him to buy me anything at all."

"Then since it is quite evident that you did not love Philip Darwin, will you explain why you married him at all?"

"Ruth," I said, warningly, and this time she heeded my advice.

"I can't discuss my private affairs, sir. They have nothing to do with-with Phil's death, and they are my own," she said with troubled dignity.

"Do you realize that your silence will militate against you?"

"I can't help it, sir," she answered with tears in her eyes.

"Just one thing more. What is your father's present address?"

"Daddy's address? Surely you can't think-but he wasn't here last night!" she cried in terror.

"I know. It is merely a formality," replied the coroner, in a soothing voice.

"Shall I tell him, Carlton?" she asked me, ignoring her counsel.

"Yes, I suppose you had better," I returned.

"He is staying with Mrs. Bailey at Tarrytown."

"Thank you, Mrs. Darwin. If you will remain where you are, please, we will now hear from Mr. Ames," said the coroner.

The finger-print expert stepped forward. "My evidence is of the briefest," he said. "I have examined the pistol and have taken an impression of the finger-prints upon the handle. I have the enlargements with me and I should like to compare them with a set made by Mrs. Darwin. If you please."

He extended an inked pad toward Ruth and showed her how to make the impressions that he desired. Then followed silence while he compared them with the enlargements. Then with a brisk nod he passed the plates to the jury.

"Well, Mr. Ames?" asked the coroner.

"Finger-prints, as you know, are infallible evidence," said the expert. "The finger-prints on the handle of the pistol are the same as those made by Mrs. Darwin here in your presence and there are no other prints of any kind upon the pistol. Therefore I do not hesitate to say that the only person who handled that revolver last night was Mrs. Darwin."

The expert sat down, and satisfied that the chain of evidence was complete the coroner ordered the jury to leave the room and arrive at a decision. We had not long to wait. No sooner had they filed out than they were back again, nor do I think that anyone was surprised when they found that the deceased had come to his death by a pistol shot fired at the hands of his wife, Ruth Darwin.

"Carlton, do you still believe in me?" she asked dully.

"With all my heart and soul, Ruth, dear. I shall always believe in you even against all the world," I answered simply.

She gave me a look of love unutterable, then for the second time in twenty-four hours crumpled in a heap on the floor beside me.

CHAPTER X

JENKINS' ADVICE

Philip Darwin was a man of so great wealth and social prominence that the news of his murder and the subsequent arrest of his wife aroused the public to such a pitch of sensational excitement and furor that the district attorney, an exceedingly clever man by the name of Grenville, was forced to set the trial for the end of November, within two months from the date of the murder.

Whereupon I hastened to lay the case before my lawyers, who were also the Trenton solicitors, since I took no great stock in Cunningham for the reason that he had been Darwin's attorney. Therefore, as I remarked before, I went to the firm of Vaughn and Chase, where I found the senior partner in his office. I would rather have spoken to Chase, who was younger and more enthusiastic, but he was out of town, so I had to content myself with Richard Vaughn.

The senior partner was the old-fashioned type of lawyer, cautious and unimaginative, and he listened to my rather disconnected statements with patient tolerance. When I had finished he shook his head and eyed me rather pityingly.

"You know of course that we do not make it a practice to take up criminal cases?" he said with indulgent kindliness.

"I didn't know," I said, rising and walking toward the door. "I came to you because you have handled her father's business for years, but I certainly won't trouble you to defend her since it might break a rule of your firm," and I flung open the door.

"Tut, my dear boy, don't fly off the handle at my first remark. Close the door and sit down, please. Of course we'll take the case," he continued as I resumed my seat, "or rather we shall see to it that she has proper counsel at the time. But you must realize for yourself that we haven't much evidence to go on."

"You have a good knowledge of her character, you know she is incapable of murder, and you have her account of what happened in the study," I returned.

Again he bent upon me that tolerant, pitying look. "My dear boy," he said, laying a hand on my knee, "you are young and in love and as is only natural you are letting your heart run away with your head. Besides you know nothing of courts and their proceedings. Mrs. Darwin's account of that minute or two in the study is, to say the least, extremely fanciful."

"But true," I interrupted with conviction.

"Yes, yes, of course," he replied soothingly. "But remember that a jury of twelve honest, but more or less stolid, citizens is convinced by facts and not by fancies."

"What do you advise then?" I asked dully.

"I shall call on the little lady myself and have a talk with her and arrange for her defense. I shall also try to make her more comfortable. My advice to you is, get more evidence, good, substantial, unshakable evidence."

It was all very well for Mr. Vaughn to talk of getting further evidence, I muttered savagely to myself as I dined that night. But where in Kingdom Come was I going to find it? Over and over I reviewed the coroner's inquest and the more I studied the facts the blacker things grew for Ruth.

In utter weariness of mind I finally flung myself into my chair, from which I had been called so abruptly two nights before, and waived aside the newspapers that Jenkins was offering me. I had caught a glimpse of the headlines. Philip Darwin's life history, his penchant for chorus girls, his wealth, and his prominence, were blazoned forth for all to read. Even his wedding was raked from the files, and old pictures of the wedding party were on display. I had no desire to go over the sickening business again.

And then as Jenkins laid the papers on the table, the name, Cora Manning, caught my eye and I picked up the discarded sheet and avidly devoured the column devoted to this woman whose name had appeared on Philip Darwin's will. An enterprising reporter had discovered where Cora Manning lodged and had forthwith set out to interview her. But the only person he saw was the girl's good-natured landlady who declared that Cora Manning had left the house at eleven the night of the murder, carrying her suitcase and that she had told her landlady that she was going on a journey of great importance and not to worry in the least about her. When the reporter asked where the girl had gone the landlady returned that she had no idea, but that since she had taken artists, writers, and actors as lodgers, she had ceased to worry herself about their comings and goings so long as they paid their board, for according to her they were all erratic and far from responsible.

All of which, contended the reporter who had made the scoop, only corroborated the statement which he had made the previous evening as to what actually took place in the study between the husband and wife. Mrs. Darwin had entered the study and had quarreled with her husband about the letter. Mr. Darwin in anger had torn up his will and had defiantly begun a new one, writing down the first name that occurred to him to annoy his wife, whereupon she snatched the pistol from the drawer and killed him.

"Fool!" I muttered, flinging the paper into the fire in my indignation. "Of all the idiotic trash that has been printed that's about the worst. Does the young idiot think all that could happen in two minutes? Ye gods, has the whole world gone mad that they can believe her guilty!"

"It's a dreadful thing, sir," said Jenkins respectfully, as he replenished the fire that I had so signally extinguished.

"It's a miserable business and blacker than Egypt," I answered dismally. Then recalling Mr. Vaughn's words I said abruptly, "Jenkins, if you were the jury, knowing what you have read in the papers, would you say that Mrs. Darwin was guilty?"

"If I were twelve easy-going men not given to much reasoning, I'd say she was, sir," he replied deferentially, adding before I could speak, "But knowing Mrs. Darwin-as it were-personally-sir, I'd say she was innocent."

I buried my face in my hands with a groan of utter despair. If Jenkins, a servant, albeit an ultra-intelligent one, was as persuaded as Mr. Vaughn that the jury would find Ruth guilty, I might as well give up at once.

"If I were you, sir, if you will pardon the liberty of my giving advice, I'd ask Mr. McKelvie to help me, sir."

I raised my head. "Who is Mr. McKelvie, Jenkins?"

"He is a gentleman, sir, who is interested in solving problems of crime. It's a sort of hobby with him, sir," said Jenkins, his usually somber eyes beginning to sparkle as he spoke.

"You mean that he is a private detective?" I asked, not overly pleased, for Jones of Headquarters had struck me as being up to snuff and yet every clue that he found had only drawn the net more tightly about Ruth. It was no wonder therefore that I was chary of detectives, for except in books, I deemed them all cut out of the same mold and after the same pattern.

"Oh, no, sir," returned Jenkins, horrified. "He's not a detective in the ordinary sense of the word. He is what you call an investigator of crime and he only takes cases that he thinks are worth-while solving. He does it mostly to amuse himself, sir."

"Oh, I see. A second Sherlock Holmes, eh?" I said ironically.

Jenkins looked hurt. "He says, sir, that there is no one who can equal Sherlock Holmes. He says, sir, that beside Holmes he's only an amateur burglar, though begging his pardon, I don't agree with him, sir."

"How does it happen that you know so much about him, Jenkins?" I asked suspiciously.

"He once saved my life in the Great War, and in return I help him with his cases when he needs me, sir."

"Humph. I thought I employed you, Jenkins."

"Well, yes, sir. But I have my free hours, sir." The poor fellow's face grew so very mournful at my insinuation that I could not help smiling even in the midst of my despondency.

"I'm not blaming you, Jenkins. I was merely wondering why he didn't hire you altogether," I said.

"He's rather eccentric, sir. He does not want to be bothered with servants."

"And do you think this very strange gentleman will condescend to help me, Jenkins?" I inquired dubiously.

"Oh, yes, indeed, sir, if I ask him."

"Do you really believe that he can find a ray of light amidst the Stygian darkness of this horrible business?" I asked, interested in spite of myself.

"I'm sure of it, sir."

"Very well, then. Get me my hat and give me his address. Anything is better than this deadening inaction."

When he returned with my overcoat and hat, Jenkins handed me a folded note. "If you don't mind, sir," he said apologetically. "Mr. McKelvie doesn't always receive strangers, sir."

Queer customer, I reflected as I departed on my errand and I had my doubts of his ability to aid me, grave doubts which were only increased by the faded gentility of the old house on Stuyvesant Square, and far from quieted by the sight of the darky who popped her head out of the front window at my ring. It was a head calculated to frighten away any but the boldest intruder, a head bristling with wooly gray spikes set like a picket fence around a face the whites of whose eyes gleamed brighter and whose thick lips flamed redder against the shiny blackness of her skin.

"Courageous man to employ such an apparition," was my thought as I proferred my request.

"Mistuh McKelvie?" she repeated after me, parrot-like. "No, suh, he ain't home, no, suh."

"Are you sure?" I persisted, holding out the note; for I recalled Jenkins' remarks.

"Ah ain't 'customed to tellin' no lies, young man," she responded with a haughty toss of the head.

"Will you please tell me then when I can find him at home?" I continued, too weary to be amused by the incongruity of unkemptness trying to look haughty and dignified.

"About a week, suh. He's away, yessuh," and she pulled in her head and slammed the window in my face.

CHAPTER XI

ARTHUR TRENTON

Discouraged I returned to my car and as I drove across the Square it suddenly occurred to me that it was somewhere in this vicinity that the evening paper had stated that Cora Manning lodged. Her name carried me back to the inquest and the coroner's attempts to learn the girl's identity. It seemed strange now that I thought of it dispassionately, that of all the persons present in the study not one had any idea who she was. I did not for a moment credit the statement of the reporter who claimed that Darwin had put down the first name that had occurred to him merely to annoy Ruth. Men as a rule do not leave their fortunes on impulse to the first person they happen to think of, and I was pretty certain that Philip Darwin was no exception to this rule. If therefore the uncle deemed her worthy to become his chief legatee, was it not more than likely that the nephew was also acquainted with the girl? I recalled the fact that Lee himself, in view of Ruth's statement, was Darwin's real heir, yet he had not seemed to take it amiss that his uncle intended to disinherit him, and I also recollected his peculiar actions as he denied all knowledge of Cora Manning, and my own belief at the time that he knew the girl well.

Now I was convinced of the fact and acting on the impulse I headed the car in the direction of the Yale Club, determined to see Lee Darwin and learn the truth from him. When I arrived at my destination, I eagerly ascended the steps and entered the club; for though not a member myself I foresaw no difficulty in the way of securing an interview. To my chagrin the steward to whom I confided my errand told me that Lee Darwin had gone South the afternoon of the eighth, ostensibly on business, nor as far as I could discover had he left any address behind.

That he should leave the city the day after the murder without waiting to attend his uncle's funeral, which was scheduled for the morrow, seemed to me the height of disrespect. I began to wonder if Lee Darwin had had a very urgent reason for leaving town as soon as possible. He had sensed that his uncle was dead when he saw the coroner. Was it because he was the murderer? If so, why had he been foolhardy enough to return to the house, and how in the name of goodness had he vanished from the study after killing his man in the dark!

Whereupon I gave it up in disgust and went home. Jenkins had waited up for me and had evidently been listening for my return, for hardly had I inserted the key in the lock when he opened the door.

"There's a gentleman waiting to see you, sir. He is in the library," he said in a low tone, as he helped me off with my overcoat. "He refused to give his name, sir."

"Very well, Jenkins." I started down the hall when I heard him again at my elbow.

"Pardon my curiosity, sir," he whispered eagerly, "but did you see Mr. McKelvie, sir?"

"No. He is unfortunately away and won't be home for a week," I said bitterly, realizing for the first time how much I had unconsciously counted upon this man's aid.

"Never mind, sir. The trial is two months away and in seven weeks Mr. McKelvie can solve anything, sir."

"Thank you for your encouragement at any rate," I answered, touched by his desire to console me.

"It's the truth, sir," he replied simply.

"I wish I could think so," was my comment, but I did not speak it aloud. Not for anything would I have hurt his feelings by displaying the doubts which had descended upon me again as to the ability of this man he so evidently worshipped. Instead I nodded agreement and stepped into the library.

"Mr. Trenton!"

Ruth's father was the last person I had expected to see, for I still held him responsible for all my misfortunes and I believe he was aware of the state of my feelings in the matter, since

47

he had refused to give Jenkins his name, fearing that I might beg to be excused from seeing him. But he had taken me unawares and there was no retreat after my first exclamation.

"Carlton, have they really dared to commit Ruth to jail?" he asked in a voice that trembled with anger and emotion.

I nodded dumbly, and abruptly he sat down and hid his face in his hands, then as abruptly he rose and fell to pacing the room in an agitated manner. Apathetically I watched him. I too had had my siege of walking the floor. It was only fair that he should have his turn.

That he was suffering as I had suffered I divined, but it had no effect upon me beyond rousing a dull wonder and perhaps anger, that he should look no older than when I saw him last, six months ago. But, no, I was wrong. He was still the same spare man with a magnificent head of snow-white hair above a massive brow and a pair of gray eyes, deep-set and penetrating, but sorrow and pain had left their trace, for so I read the meaning of the deep lines that had graven themselves around his mobile mouth and sensitive nostrils.

"Has counsel been appointed to defend her?" Mr. Trenton spoke so low and his voice was so charged with emotion as he sank wearily into my big chair, that his words made no impression on my brain and he was forced to repeat them before I could comprehend sufficiently to answer in the affirmative.

"Mr. Vaughn will arrange for her defense," I added.

"You will be permitted to testify in her behalf?" he inquired.

"No, I'm the chief witness against her," I answered sadly.

"What!" He was absolutely dumbfounded.

"Haven't you read the papers?" I asked him.

He shook his head. "I have been ill for days. To-day the doctor told me I could go out. I overheard my hostess asking her husband if he thought it would hurt me to tell me about Ruth. I at once demanded an explanation and when I had been told that Ruth was in jail charged with the murder of her husband, I waited to hear no more but took the train and came straight to you. I naturally supposed—that is, of course-knowing your love for her I assumed you would do your best to free her by-by taking her side," he said brokenly.

I sighed. Once more the miserable details had to be recounted and then I laughed harshly. Mr. Trenton looked at me as though he thought that I must have taken leave of my senses. For the moment I verily think I had, for the thought came all unbidden that I was another Ancient Mariner relating my tale to all who crossed my path, only I could not remember what crime I had committed that I should be punished in so terrible a manner.

"Do you suppose it could have been in a former reincarnation?" I asked him in all seriousness.

"For heaven's sake, man, brace up!" cried Mr. Trenton alarmed. "You can't afford to go to pieces now!"

I passed my hand wearily across my brow. "I—I guess I'm pretty nearly all in," I mumbled, sinking into a chair.

Ruth's father looked across at me compassionately. "Poor boy," he said gently. "I won't worry you for your story to-night."

"Have you any objections to my remaining here with you?" he continued presently, as I preserved an unbroken silence. "I—I can't bear to return-to that crime-haunted house," he added with a shudder.

"Certainly. Glad to have you. I'll ring for Jenkins," I murmured vaguely, trying to rise. But my legs refused to support me and my head fell back heavily against the cushions.

When next I opened my eyes I was in my bed and Jenkins was moving softly about the room.

"What time is it, Jenkins?" I asked, sitting up.

"Twelve-thirty, sir," responded Jenkins, pulling aside the curtains to let in the light of day.

"Have I been asleep all that time?" I inquired aghast.

"You were very tired, sir. You hardly slept the night before," he apologized for me.

"Mr. Trenton is waiting luncheon for you, sir. He wants to know how you are feeling, sir," he continued presently.

The events of the previous evening flocked into my mind, and I felt the blood surge into my cheeks. What a chicken-hearted fellow her father must have thought me!

"Tell Mr. Trenton I'll join him in the library in half an hour," I said decisively.

"Very well, sir."

It was more than thirty minutes before I made my appearance, but I had myself well in hand now and after luncheon, at which we spoke only of common-places, I told him that I was ready to give him the details of the case. Immovably he sat with his head bowed upon his hands while I related the facts, nor did he interrupt by word or gesture at any time during the recital.

When I had finished he raised his head, and I was startled by the old and haggard look upon his face. He had aged ten years in as many minutes.

"The sins of the father," he said, hoarsely. "Carlton, it's all my fault that Ruth has killed that wretch!"

CHAPTER XII

AN EXPLANATION

When a human being has run the gamut of horror and suffering in a short space of time his mind ceases to be affected by further sensations. At any other time I should have been appalled that Mr. Trenton could even for a moment believe his daughter guilty. As it was, I merely accepted his words as one more link in the chain of evidence against her.

"My boy," he said humbly, "I know that you have held me responsible for your misfortunes. And you are perfectly right to feel so. I, and I alone, am to blame for all that has happened."

He paused to wipe the moisture that had gathered on his forehead, showing what an effort he was making to control his emotion.

"But if I am to blame in spoiling the boy, I have been punished beyond my due. You do not know, I hope you may never know the anguish, the torture, the awful horror, of learning that the being you have worshipped and adored is worthless clay, a —a common murderer! I was frantic, crazy, and to save my boy I sacrificed my girl. And now, and now —" He broke off with a sob and buried his head in his hands.

"Mr. Trenton, don't. I'll stake my life that Ruth is innocent." I held out my hand, touched as I had thought I no longer possessed the power to be touched by his sorrow. Certainly if I had suffered, he had been in hell.

"My boy, you give me new life," he said, raising his head and taking my hand. "I do not deserve your forgiveness."

"It's all behind us, Mr. Trenton, and can't be undone. The task before us is to free Ruth. We will work together toward that end," I answered.

He was silent a moment, evidently pondering mentally some question, then he said with the air of one who has arrived at a decision by which he will abide whatever comes, "And the first step is to show you something that I had hoped not to reveal. The very day of the murder I received a letter from Dick stating-but you had better read it yourself."

He took from his wallet a single sheet of notepaper which he handed me. It was dated from Chicago two days before the murder and written in Dick's unmistakable flowing hand.

"Dear Dad," it began.

"Philip Darwin has persecuted the Trenton family for the last time. I have a weapon to use against him which will free Ruth and myself from the bondage we are in to that cur. I am leaving for the East to-morrow and when my task is completed, I shall call upon you at Tarrytown.

"Your repentant son,

"Dick."

When I finished reading I looked across at Mr. Trenton, wondering if to him too had occurred the thought which possessed me. Could the weapon be murder and the answer to the problem the fact that Ruth was shielding her brother again? Then I shook my head.

"If Dick was in the study how did he get away without my seeing him?" I said aloud. "He couldn't vanish into thin air."

"Carlton!" The word was a cry. "No, no, he would not dare again!"

"What did he mean by weapon then?" I inquired bluntly.

"Not-not murder! I could not bear that! No, I am sure he meant that he had learned that Philip Darwin was his uncle," he said low.

"His uncle!" I gasped, horrified.

"Yes, his uncle. But not Ruth's, Carlton! No, no, she was no relation to him," he reassured me quickly.

My head began to whirl. Affairs were growing too complicated for me. "I don't understand what you are talking about," I returned wearily.

"I'll explain. It all happened so very long ago that I never mention it, but the fact is that two years after Ruth's mother died I married Philip Darwin's sister."

"Darwin knew then that Dick was his nephew?" I asked when he paused.

"No. No one knows it except myself. Philip Darwin could not have been more than ten or so at the time, and I doubt if he remembers that he ever had a sister. You see when I met her I had no idea who she was, for she was acting under an assumed name. She had been on the stage six months and was heartily sick of it when I was introduced to her. We fell in love with each other and before the wedding she confided her story to me.

"Her father, Frank Darwin, was a stern, unyielding, puritanical man, who had no use for what he called the lure of the world. On the other hand, Leila was just eighteen, beautiful, proud, wilful. She had read of the wonders of the stage and when her father opposed her desire to become an actress she ran away from home. When he learned that she had actually joined a theatrical company, he disinherited her and refused to have anything further to do with her, forbidding his two sons, Robert, who became Lee's father, and Philip, from ever mentioning her name or seeing her again. She died when Dick was born, poor little girl, more than twenty-five years ago, and I think I had almost forgotten the relationship. A quarter century is more than ample time to erase a memory," he ended with a sigh.

I was silent for a while and then asked him why he had not told Philip Darwin that Dick was his nephew, thus avoiding all the dire consequences which had followed Darwin's threat of exposure.

"Because it would have made no difference to him at all," answered Mr. Trenton. "He wanted Ruth and if she had refused him he would have revenged himself by exposing Dick, knowing that we would suffer far more than he. Besides, he would have demanded proofs. I had none which I could give him."

"What about family resemblance?"

Mr. Trenton shook his head. "They are both dark and about the same build. That is as far as the resemblance goes, and that's no proof, for Ruth is dark, too."

"And you really think that Dick—"

"Yes, I do. I believe that in some way the boy learned that he was Darwin's nephew and hoped to use the knowledge to force Darwin to divorce Ruth," he interrupted.

This time it was I that disagreed. "But you said yourself that the knowledge would cut no ice with Darwin," I said, impatiently.

"But Dick wouldn't know that. He is young and to him it would seem only natural that an uncle should desire to shield his nephew. The husband bound to secrecy to preserve his good name would be unable to fight proceedings if Ruth brought suit for divorce against him. At any rate, that is how I read it."

I did not like to say so, and thus shatter his fool's paradise, for he was entitled to any consolation which he could draw from his deductions. To me, however, there were two flaws in his reasoning. In the first place, if Mr. Trenton was the only one who knew his wife's identity and he had almost forgotten it, how in the name of all the gods had Dick learned it? And in the second place, I was firmly convinced that Mr. Richard Trenton stood in no ignorance of Mr. Philip Darwin's true character and would be under no delusions as to the exact reception such knowledge would receive.

No, Dick had some other weapon in mind, and the only one which would free both himself and Ruth at one stroke was the death of Philip Darwin. Dick had killed a man once under less provocation. What was to prevent his repeating the act when he realized the injustice that had been done Ruth in forcing her to marry such a man? But in that event why had he not come forward to free Ruth from jail? Surely he had not sunk so low that he would permit her to pay the extreme penalty for his act. It's true that she was allowed to shield him once, but I very much doubt whether Dick knew anything of it until after the wedding when his coming forward would certainly have created a terrible scandal without in the least bettering conditions for Ruth.

Besides, the whole thing was illogical. If Dick killed Darwin to free Ruth, it was ridiculous to suppose that he would then run away and leave her to face the consequences. I was more inclined to believe that the boy had discovered some counter-knowledge which would buy his freedom from exposure. He had been in New York the day of the murder, or should have been, according to his letter. Why then did he remain in hiding, or had he returned to Chicago without making use of his "weapon" when he learned that Darwin was dead? On the other hand, that would also be a senseless proceeding, for Darwin dead, he, Dick, had nothing further to fear.

The whole affair was a muddle and growing more complicated at every turn, and I heartily wished that Dick would show up to settle all doubts on his score at least.

As if in answer to my thought, the phone in the hall rang sharply and Jenkins appeared to announce that Headquarters would like to speak with me. I sighed. What new evidence had they discovered now, I thought savagely, and my "hello" must have sounded like a roar in the Inspector's ear.

When he was through explaining I leaned limply against the wall and wiped my forehead with a trembling hand.

"Jenkins!" I said hoarsely. "Ask him if-if-it's really true!"

Jenkins took the receiver from my nerveless hand and spoke into the phone. "Yes, sir. I'll tell him, yes, sir." He rang off and turned to me, his long face graver than ever.

"He says there is no mistake, sir. And he'd be obliged if you and Mr. Trenton would receive Detective Jones and give him all necessary information, sir."

"Would you tell him-now?" I asked dully.

"It would be far kinder, sir," answered Jenkins. "I'm very sorry, sir."

I went slowly back into the library wondering how best to break the news to Mr. Trenton. My face must have told him much, for he sprang toward me with a sharp exclamation.

"Dick!" he cried. "You have news of Dick?"

I nodded, for I was unable to speak.

"Don't keep me in suspense, Carlton! What is it? Have they—" Then he turned away and sought a chair. "You need not tell me," he said very quietly. "I know that he is dead."

"Yes." I found my voice, but I hardly knew it for my own. "Yes, he-he drowned himself in the East River early this morning!"

CHAPTER XIII

THE SUICIDE

I had anticipated trouble when I gave Mr. Trenton the Inspector's message, but shock seemed to have rendered his sensibilities numb for the time being and he made no demur about receiving the emissary from Headquarters.

It was just two-thirty, the hour set for Philip Darwin's funeral, when the Inspector called me and while I awaited the arrival of Detective Jones my thoughts reverted to the funeral. I pictured to myself the solitary coffin being lowered into its grave unmourned and unattended by any save the faithful Mason, for I do not count the idle and the curious who merely come to gape and stare and be amused.

He had been rich and popular, with a host of friends, yet I was willing to wager that not one had taken the trouble to escort the body to its final resting-place, and though I had never had any use for the man while living, still my heart was strangely stirred by the spectacle of desolation which I had evoked. Death is after all dread enough without the added knowledge that no single human being will shed a tear at our passage from this earth. Even his own flesh and blood had turned from him, and for a minute I was sorry I had not attended. If I have one regret in all this terrible business it is that one omission to accompany the dead on its journey to the grave.

"Mr. Davies, how do you do, sir," said Jones, entering and breaking in abruptly on my thought, for I had not heard his ring. "And this gentleman is Mr. Trenton, I take it?"

"Yes, Mr. Jones. I have told him the sad news. You-you wish him to identify the body?" I asked, returning to earth with a decided jolt, mental if not physical.

"Unfortunately," answered Jones, with a commiserating look at Mr. Trenton, who sat staring vacantly into space, "the body has not yet been recovered. I really don't need it, but thought I might as well have an identification of his belongings."

He placed the package he had brought with him upon the table and opened it, exposing to view a gray suit of good material, a rather shabby cap, a watch, and a pocket notebook.

"These articles," he said, speaking rather loudly to attract Mr. Trenton's attention, "were found in a lodging-house on Water Street. Yesterday about noon, a dark young man, not any too well-dressed, and looking dishevelled and unkempt, applied for lodgings, and was taken in by the landlady, Mrs. Blake, herself. He spent the afternoon and early evening wandering about among the wharves and spoke to several loungers to whom he made no secret of where he was staying. This morning, before it was light, this strange lodger arose and went out. Mrs. Blake saw him go, but thought he was going to work. Fifteen minutes later someone banged on her door to tell her that her lodger had thrown himself into the river and had drowned. She was frightened and called the police. On the wharf was found the cap he had worn and in his room those other articles in a suitcase."

The detective paused in his narrative to pick up the watch. "The clothes are new and give no clue except that they evidently belonged to a gentleman. This watch is more helpful. Do you recognize it, Mr. Trenton?"

Mr. Trenton, still somewhat dazed by the rapid sequence of the other's story, received the watch with tender reverence, looked at it, nodded, and passed it to me. How well I remembered that gold time-piece of biscuit thinness, with its plain R. T. engraved upon the back, which Mr. Trenton had given Dick on his twenty-first birthday! And in further proof, if such were needed, the inside of the case held a round kodak picture of Ruth and Dick, taken on the same day!

No, there could be no mistake as to the identity of Mrs. Blake's lodger!

"The watch is really superfluous evidence," continued Jones. "In that notebook we found your name, Mr. Trenton, written along with his on the sheet reserved for identification."

He opened the book and showed us the page which had a place for name, address, parentage, age, height, etc. Dick had filled in only his own name and his father's.

"You identify the handwriting?" asked Jones.

"Yes, it's my son's," returned Mr. Trenton in that same monotonous tone in which he had first spoken of Dick's death.

"Knowing that these articles belonged to Mr. Richard Trenton, and knowing also that he was Mrs. Darwin's brother, we had these things brought to Headquarters for investigation, because we thought there might be some connection between this suicide and the murder of Philip Darwin."

"I don't believe that Dick had anything to do with the murder," I said slowly. "Surely you are not of the opinion that he killed Darwin?"

"Well, hardly, since he wasn't in the study when the crime was committed. What I meant was that he might have been the instigator; and she, the tool, as it were."

I stiffened. "What do you mean?" I asked coldly.

"This." Jones spoke sharply. "I have been delving into Richard Trenton's past history. One of the things I learned from a former servant was the fact that six months ago Richard Trenton came home hurriedly one night in company with Philip Darwin and that after a consultation with Mr. Trenton, the boy was packed out West. The next night, according to the same servant, Philip Darwin came to the house and was closeted with Mr. Trenton and his daughter for several hours. When Darwin finally left, Mr. Trenton looked ten years older and Miss Trenton was in tears. Two weeks later, to the servant's astonishment, she married not you, but Philip Darwin."

He looked at me shrewdly and I nodded in confirmation of his story. "Having satisfied myself that there was decided connection between the flight of the brother and the marriage of the sister, I proceeded to trace Richard Trenton's movements on the night of the murder. He came to New York on the seventh of October and arrived at Grand Central at 10.10 p. m. From there he took a taxi to the Corinth Hotel. He registered, went to his room, and in a few minutes came down again and went out on foot. He returned to the hotel about one o'clock. According to the night clerk he looked haggard and weary. The next morning he paid his bill and again left on foot. To-day, the tenth, he commits suicide. Mrs. Darwin declares she has not seen her brother since he left for Chicago, but admits corresponding with him and refuses to say about what. Now, the question is, What was he doing between the time he left the hotel and one o'clock on the night of the murder? Where did he go between the morning of the eighth and the afternoon of the ninth? Did he instigate the murder and then in remorse commit suicide?"

"No, I don't believe it," I said stoutly. "You have learned so much that I think the best course which I can follow is complete frankness. However, there is no need to rake dead ashes, so I will merely say that Dick was forced to leave New York and that Philip Darwin had the boy in his power because he knew the reason for Dick's flight. And basely Darwin used his knowledge to force Mrs. Darwin to marry him to save her brother from exposure."

"I see, and of course it strengthens my point. Driven to desperation young Trenton may have returned with intentions to kill Darwin," put in Jones.

"Yes," I interjected eagerly, "and very probably he went so far as the Darwin home that night. Then he may have thought better of it and tramped about as one will when fighting a mental battle. In the morning he left with intentions of returning to Chicago. Then he read of the murder in the papers and decided to lie low and see what happened. When he learned that his sister was arrested, he probably considered himself the primal cause of all the trouble and in a fit of despondency drowned himself."

I was quite proud of the theory I had evolved and doubtless it was the right one. Jones weighed it in his mind and then he said, "You're right, Mr. Davies, that's probably just what did take place."

"Besides, if he had instigated the murder, since he was putting himself beyond the power of the law, he would have left behind a written confession to that effect," I added.

"Yes, that's so. Well, I guess we can say he had nothing to do with it after all. Probably thought he was morally responsible. 'In pace requiescat.'"

"Amen to that," I answered so surprised to hear him quote Latin that for a space I could find nothing to say.

"There is no hope of finding the body?" I asked when I had recovered my mental balance.

"I'm afraid not. It has probably been carried out to sea."

"You are certain that he drowned himself," I persisted, for I recalled that Dick could swim.

"Yes, he was seen and recognized by the men to whom he had spoken the previous evening. They saw him throw himself into the river. Before they could reach him he had gone down beyond recall."

"I should like to interview Mrs. Blake and the others," I said, not with any hope of discovering a flaw in the evidence, but because I could not endure to witness the poor father's silent grief.

"Certainly, Mr. Davies. I have my car outside. I will take you there myself," answered Jones affably.

As the detective began to wrap Dick's belongings, Mr. Trenton, who I am confident had heard no word of our conversation, suddenly realized that the conference was over and leaning forward took the watch from the table.

"May I keep it?" he begged.

"Yes, we have sufficient evidence in case we should need it," answered the detective.

"I'll be with you in a moment," I said, for I wished to give Jenkins directions to keep an eye on Ruth's father. When I returned Jones had his package under his arm and though he said good-by, Mr. Trenton did not respond.

"Poor old chap," he whispered. "It must have been an awful blow to him."

"Worse than anyone can imagine," I returned, thinking of the confession he had made. So we went out, leaving him there alone with the thoughts of his dead.

We drove in silence to Water Street and pulled up before a shabby old house. Decidedly Mrs. Blake's was not the type of home I should have picked out to live in, but when one has no intention of using one's lodging, the more obscure the better, I imagine. And it certainly was obscure, and dingy and ill-smelling.

I was shown the room in which Dick had slept and where he had left his clothes, and it struck me that if he hired that room to remain unknown, he had been very negligent in leaving his belongings around. Then I decided he chose that locality because it was near the river and the river was the most convenient end he could think of. Poor Dick!

I talked with the men who had witnessed the suicide, I was even shown the place where the event occurred, and the point where the body submerged! It was all very gruesome and alas, all too true! The only thing that puzzled me was why the lad had done it.

It was one thing to convince Jones, but quite another to satisfy myself that my reasoning was correct. Dick was not despondent by nature and though he might hold himself responsible for Ruth's marriage, surely he would have the sense to see that committing suicide would only add to her sorrow without in the least aiding to free her. I gave it up unless he really killed Darwin and feared to face the consequences, but that would make him out a despicable creature indeed, and I resolutely closed my mind to such a suggestion.

When I reached home Mr. Trenton put into words the thought I had refused to harbor.

"Carlton," he said, with the calm of desperation. "I have been thinking things over and I believe you are right. We will go to Ruth and tell her that it is useless for her to shield Dick any longer."

CHAPTER XIV

GRAYDON MCKELVIE

It was easy enough for me to procure through Mr. Vaughn an interview with Ruth and the next afternoon Mr. Trenton and I visited her in the prison, or rather in that gray reception-room which is as far as outsiders may come in the Tombs. She was delighted to see her father, concerning whose silence she had been quite worried, and when he broke down and told of yesterday's happenings, she wept with him for a few minutes, then quietly dried her eyes and set herself to comfort him. What she said I do not know, for I did not like to intrude myself upon their sorrow, and I withdrew to the other end of the room and looked out the grated window.

To think that Ruth, my beloved, should have to spend her days in such a place, barred from association with her friends, and from the blessed light of day, innocent of any wrong, yet suffering for some wretch's crime! Ruth and the horrible creatures who infested the jail! The thought goaded me to desperation. Abruptly I swung back toward her and spoke hoarsely,

"Ruth, for God's sake if you are shielding Dick, tell us at once, for I can stand this suspense no longer!"

She had been seated on a chair beside her father, but at my cry she jumped up and came to me. Verily I must have been mad, I think, for I caught her to me and kissed her again and again. A moment she clung to me, then she pushed me away.

"Carlton! No, you must not!" she sobbed. "No, no," as I followed her, "not until I am cleared of the shadow of murder!"

"You have committed no crime," I replied savagely. "What do I care for the world's opinion!" And I caught her to me once more.

"Carlton! If you kiss me again I—I shall hate you!" she whispered fiercely.

Instantly I released her and walked rapidly away to the other end of the room.

"Carlton, please don't be angry," she said, brokenly, timidly touching my arm with the tips of her fingers, "but, oh, my dear, if you kill my self-respect what in all the world have I left to offer you!"

Humbly I carried her hand to my lips. "Forgive me, dear. I don't deserve to be allowed even the privilege of looking upon you."

She gave me a smile so forgiving that it brought the tears to my eyes, and seeing how I was moved she turned away to her father.

"Ruth," he said, relieving the tension, "we have come here, Carlton and I, to ask you a question."

"Yes, Daddy," she replied, softly, sitting down beside him again.

He drew out Dick's letter and handed it to her. When she had read it he explained the process of reasoning that had led him to believe that Dick had killed Darwin and had then committed suicide.

"And now, Ruth, if you saw him there in the study and helped him to escape, if you are shielding him as you did once before, I hope you realize that he is quite unworthy and that it is too much of a sacrifice for you to suffer for his crime."

He had spoken with difficulty, showing how much the words cost him, yet determined to make amends for all the wrong that had been done to Ruth, both by himself and Dick. When he finished she looked from him to me in utter bewilderment.

"I am shielding no one, Daddy. And as far as I know Dick was not in the study when I was there."

There was no mistaking her sincerity. She was telling the truth and the whole business was a worse tangle than ever before.

"Besides," she added, "I do not think Dick would do such a thing."

"He did once," returned her father, gloomily.

"But, Daddy, dear, he did not know what he was doing and it-it was Phil's fault for giving him that pistol. I have mothered him for years and I know. Whatever reason he had for committing suicide, Daddy, rest assured in the conviction that he did not kill my husband."

A ray of hope lighted Mr. Trenton's face. "You really believe that, Ruth? You are not saying it just to comfort me?"

She laid a hand upon his arm as she answered quietly, "I don't believe it, Daddy. I know he did not murder Phil."

After that we could not believe it either, and so we were back once more exactly where we started from. In other words, we were moving in circles which ended where they had begun: namely, in the police's assertion that Ruth was guilty, a beginning which we knew to be false on the face of it, but which we had no means of proving to anyone's satisfaction.

"The only thing to do is to hire a competent detective," said Mr. Trenton emphatically, that night at dinner.

This recalled McKelvie to my mind. "I have one in view," I answered, "but he is away at present."

"Hire another one then," he retorted.

But I preferred to wait, for as I said before I had not much use for detectives, private or police, and the only reason that McKelvie appealed to me at all was because he did not seem from Jenkins' account to have much in common with the usual sleuth. Then Mr. Trenton wanted to rush out and employ a man on his own initiative, but this also I negatived, since no detective was far better than a mediocre fellow without a grain of imagination. I remembered Jones, and shuddered for Ruth.

I should like to say right here that if the reader thinks that both Mr. Trenton and I got over our grief at Dick's horrible end very rapidly, he must remember that human beings cannot be kept at high tension for a great length of time or the brain would snap. Everyday occurrences and the dire need of doing something for Ruth pushed to the background more recent happenings, particularly when Jenkins brought me word late that same night that Graydon McKelvie would see me at his home.

Mr. Trenton of course desired to accompany me, but I finally dissuaded him, telling him that it was better that only one of us should apply to McKelvie, especially as I had been forewarned that he was rather eccentric. To which Mr. Trenton grudgingly agreed, and I set out to interview this solver of crimes with a fluttering heart, for upon him I based all my remaining hopes.

As I sat in the cosy little sitting-room of the old house on Stuyvesant Square to which I had been conducted by a better combed and more civil Dinah with the announcement that "Mistuh McKelvie'll be down in a secun', sah," I conjured a vision of the type of man I expected to see. I evolved a cross between an oddity and a mental Sampson, a fretful, thin man, with a head too big for his body, who would speak in a querulous high-pitched voice.

The man who entered the room at that moment and came toward me with extended hand was none of these things. He was a slender, well-dressed young man, well above the medium height, with a pleasant, but rather rugged cast of countenance, whose main features were a tenacious chin and a pair of brilliant black eyes. But when he spoke my name I forgot his appearance. Never had I heard such a melodious voice. It soothed the ear with its mellow richness and remained in the mind long after it had ceased, like the echo of some clear-toned bell. And such was its power that by merely pronouncing my name he had made me believe that he alone of all the world could possibly solve the problem which was well-nigh overwhelming me.

Later I came to know him better and I should have liked him even without the added attraction of his voice, for he was a refined and cultured man, extremely clever, if eccentric, whose main idiosyncrasies seemed to be confined to a whole-souled worship of Sherlock Holmes, a decidedly autocratic manner, and a fondness for speaking satirically, even at the expense of his friends.

"Jenkins has told me that you have a problem which you wish me to look into," he said, motioning me to be seated as he settled himself in a large arm-chair. "Will you give me briefly the details of the case?"

I am afraid my story was far from brief, for I told him everything from the moment I heard the shot, through the inquest, to Dick's suicide. He listened attentively to every word without comment and when I was through he briskly assumed command.

"I have read of the crime in the papers," he said, "but I must study the coroner's personal notes of the inquest, before I come to a decision."

He rose and walked to his desk as he spoke, where he scratched off a few lines on a sheet of notepaper, which he enclosed in an envelope.

"What was the reason for young Trenton's removal from New York six months ago?" he asked abruptly, turning toward me as he sealed the envelope.

"Is it necessary to the investigation?" I inquired, loth to reveal the family skeleton.

"I do not ask unnecessary questions," he returned coldly.

Without more ado I related the affair in all its sordid details. When I finished he held out the envelope which he still retained in his hand. "Kindly tell Jenkins to take this note to Coroner Graves," he said. "Meet me here at ten o'clock to-morrow for your answer. Good-night, Mr. Davies."

Before I could adjust my thoughts to his rapid speech I found myself in the street looking in some perplexity at the closed door of Graydon McKelvie's house.

"Well, I'll be hanged!" I exclaimed wrathfully, as I climbed into my car.

I drove away in no very pleased frame of mind at the reception I had received, for when I reviewed the conversation I realized that he had not compromised himself to help me at all. The moment I reached home, however, I forgot my annoyance at the cavalier way I had been treated. The sudden transformation of Jenkins' lugubrious countenance into an ecstatic smile as he hastened to carry out McKelvie's command, for that's just what it was, made me feel sanguine once more of that gentleman's aid. I put down his manner, therefore, to eccentricity and the natural desire to know more of the problem before he promised to bring his faculties to bear upon it.

I passed the evening in Elysium and I came down to earth with a bang when promptly at ten o'clock the next morning, in answer to my query, McKelvie tossed a sheet of paper across the table to me with the remark:

"Find the answers to those questions and you'll have the name of the person who committed the crime."

I looked at him, sitting smoking unconcernedly, to the paper in my hand, undecided which to tackle first, when my mind caught the sense of the words before me. After that I forgot my surroundings until I had absorbed every line that McKelvie had written. The document was drawn up in the form of a series of questions, with sufficient space below each one to insert the proper answer, and it read as follows:

(1) Why was the pistol fired at midnight?
(2) Did the murderer also light the lamp?
(3) How did the murderer enter and leave the study?
(4) What was the motive for the murder?
(5) Why did the doctors disagree, and which was in the right?
(6) Why did Philip Darwin put that ring on his finger and then pull it off?
(7) Whose is the blood-stained handkerchief?
(8) Where did the second bullet go?
(9) Why is there so much evidence against Mrs. Darwin, and who would most desire to injure her?
(10) Is Cora Manning the woman in the case and if so, who and what is she?
(11) What has become of Darwin's securities?
(12) What is Lee Darwin's connection with the affair?

(13) Why did Richard Trenton come to New York and then commit suicide?
(14) What is the relation between Mr. Cunningham and the murdered man?
(15) Which one of those having a sufficient motive for killing Darwin answers to the following description: clever, unprincipled, and absolutely cold-blooded?

"Find the answers to those questions!" I repeated when I had devoured the sheet with my eyes. "It would take me a lifetime! For mercy's sake, don't fail me now when I have only you to depend on to help me!" I cried.

With an odd smile he took his pipe from his mouth and tapped the bowl upon his open palm. Then he looked at me and spoke abruptly, "If I take this case it will be on one condition."

"A thousand if you wish," I exclaimed impatiently.

"No, only one, that when I give commands they shall be obeyed implicitly, even though you may not be able to perceive their wisdom at the time."

I blinked at the unexpectedness of the answer and then held out my hand. "It shall be as you say, Mr. McKelvie, only don't let them convict Ruth."

He clasped my hand. "I won't, Mr. Davies, if she is guiltless, and my first command is this: I want an interview with Mrs. Darwin this afternoon."

CHAPTER XV

THE INTERVIEW

When we entered the Tombs that afternoon I noticed that several of the wardens smiled at McKelvie, as if his presence were a familiar one in that place of horrors. The matron too was very accommodating, more so than she had been to me, when McKelvie suggested that she stand out in the corridor when Ruth arrived. I noticed, however, that though she did as he asked and moved out of earshot, she remained where she could keep an eye upon our movements.

When I presented Graydon McKelvie to Ruth and explained his mission, she gave him such a sweet, pathetic smile and wished him success in so gentle a manner that he was won over to her cause on the spot.

"Mrs. Darwin," he said, with feeling, in that wonderful voice of his, "my best is the least I can offer you."

From that moment I had no misgivings as to the outcome of the affair. Let come what would, Graydon McKelvie would prove Ruth innocent, not because he believed, but because like myself he knew her to be innocent.

"Mrs. Darwin," McKelvie was saying gently, "in order to get at the bottom of this matter it will be necessary to ask you certain pertinent questions. I trust you won't be offended by anything I may say and also that you will answer me truthfully in every case."

"I will tell you anything you desire to know," she answered quietly.

"The coroner's inquest brought out a number of facts which do not, in my estimation, agree with one another. You say the study was in darkness when you entered, yet the lamp was lighted after the shot was fired. You are sure you did not light it yourself, unconsciously, perhaps?" he inquired in a brisk manner.

"I did not touch it," she answered with conviction. "I had just picked up the pistol and was standing beside the chair some distance from the table when the lamp apparently lighted itself."

"If someone had pulled the cord of the lamp would you have been able to see that person?" he persisted.

"Yes, for I turned toward the table the minute the light went on. There was no one there—except Phil-and myself," she said low.

"Point to investigate," he muttered, making a note in a small black book. "Memo: How was the light turned on?

"Now, Mrs. Darwin, please go back in your mind to the moment when you heard the shot. What part of the room did it appear to come from?" he continued.

"I—I'm afraid I couldn't say."

"Did it sound very close to you, or far away?" he prompted.

"Quite close. It was deafening," she said.

"Did it sound in front or behind you?" he continued, patiently.

"Behind, I think."

He nodded. "You say you trod on the pistol as you moved forward. You did not hear it fall near you, for instance?"

"No, when I heard the shot I involuntarily closed my eyes. It's a habit with me when anything startles me. When I opened them again I took a step and trod on something hard. I heard no sound at all."

"I see. You did not know the object was a pistol you said?"

"I did not know it. I merely felt something hard under my foot and in a dazed way I picked it up, without actually being conscious of what it was."

"One thing more. Supposing there had been someone behind you, could you have heard that person?"

"No. The carpet is very thick and absolutely deadens any footfall. Besides I do not see how anyone could have been back of me for I heard no one breathing."

"That doesn't follow. A person might have stood far enough away so that you would not notice the breathing, particularly if that person took pains that you shouldn't. And now we come to the breathing that you did hear. Where did it seem to come from?"

"It was right beside me, very, very close."

"Was it normal, hurried breathing, or was it labored?"

"Oh, horrible! A —a gasping sort of breath!"

"What advice did Mr. Cunningham give you at the inquest?" he asked, with a sudden change of subject.

"I don't understand what you mean, Mr. McKelvie," she answered, surprised.

"The coroner appointed him your counsel pro tem. and he left the room to consult with you. Did he not tell you what you should or should not say in answer to the coroner's questions?" he explained.

"Oh, no. He merely sent word by a policeman that I was to come down and that he considered it best that I tell frankly all that had happened that night. I did not see him until I came into the study and he first spoke to me, advising me to answer," she replied.

He made one or two more notes and then held out his hand. "Thank you, Mrs. Darwin. You have helped me materially. Good-by for the present."

"Good-by, Mr. McKelvie. Good-by, Carlton. See how quickly you can solve this mystery, won't you please? It's horrible there!" and she pointed toward the corridor.

"I will do my very best, Mrs. Darwin, but don't hope too soon, for the way is long and dark," returned McKelvie with deep sympathy.

When she had disappeared from sight around the bend of the corridor, he spoke again. "She's a brave little woman," he said, greatly moved. "God grant I'm not too late!"

I was silent, for Ruth's incarceration was the one subject I dared not permit myself to dwell on if I desired to retain my sanity, and in another moment McKelvie himself had changed the subject.

"By the way, I clean forgot to ask her a rather important question," he said, and he called to the warden, who brought Ruth back as far as the door of the reception-room. Somehow I could not bear to part from Ruth again and as there was no necessity for me to show myself, I remained where I could hear him without being seen.

"I'm sorry to disturb you again, Mrs. Darwin, but I forgot to ask you this question. Why did you deny knowing Cora Manning at the inquest?"

I was surprised, but Ruth said calmly, "I don't know her, Mr. McKelvie."

"But you know who she is," he returned, smiling.

"Will it help you?"

"Very much."

"She's Lee Darwin's fiancée. I have never met her, but one day he confided in me and showed me her picture. She is a very beautiful and noble girl, so please don't drag her into this inquiry, for whatever Phil's motives in leaving his money to her, I am sure that she is innocent of any knowledge of his actions," she pleaded.

"I won't bring her into it unless it's absolutely necessary," he replied.

"Are you a mind-reader?" I inquired as we walked slowly across the courtyard to the men's building and so out into the street.

"Not that I'm aware of," he replied seriously. "What makes you ask?"

"I'd have sworn that Ruth had never even heard of Cora Manning," I said.

"That's because you hear and see without observing," he explained. "I read what you heard: namely, that Coroner Graves, dissatisfied with Mrs. Darwin's first answer, asked her again if she knew Cora Manning. The inference was plain. She knew or knew of this girl and hesitated to say no or yes. By the time the coroner repeated his question she had made up her mind."

"That's so. Now that you mention it, I recall that she seemed disturbed by the question. And so she is Lee's fiancée, yet he denied all knowledge of her," I mused aloud. "Strange that everyone should have been so intent on shrouding her identity in mystery. What was their reason, do you suppose?" I asked suddenly.

McKelvie shrugged. "I do not know-yet. 'There are more things in heaven and earth than are dreamed of in your philosophy, Horatio,'" he said lightly.

I opened my eyes wide at this apt quotation for I did not know him then as I do now and I pondered in silence upon the oddity of hearing a detective spout Shakespeare, until I remembered that Jenkins had said that McKelvie was not a detective in the ordinary sense of the word.

"Very kind of Jenkins," said McKelvie aloud. "By the way I phoned him to meet us at the Darwin house. I may need him in the course of the afternoon."

In view of his stipulation and fearing to lose him before he had begun work on the case, I murmured hastily, "That's quite all right," then I gasped and looked into his amused, slightly ironical eyes.

"Why, man, it's marvelous," I said.

"What is?" he asked coolly, although he knew exactly what I meant.

"Your reading of my thought," I replied. "Why you might almost be Sherlock Holmes himself."

"No. I lay no such flattering unction to my soul, if you will pardon the misquotation. Sherlock Holmes is in a class by himself. No one can touch him, but I have studied his methods and in this case it was not very difficult to guess what you were thinking when you eyed me so hard and murmured, 'Jenkins,' unconsciously, particularly when I know Jenkins so well."

We had been walking up Center Street as we talked, in total disregard of the fact that my car was parked in front of the Tombs, but now McKelvie paused abruptly and I saw that we were standing in front of Police Headquarters.

"I had intended going out to Riverside Drive at once, but I have changed my mind," McKelvie explained. "I want to look at the exhibits before I view the scene of the crime. The scent is decidedly cold. I must see what I can do to warm the trail."

"Do you think the police will let you see them?" I asked dubiously.

"We can do no more than ask. I have influence yonder," with a nod of the head toward the massive abode of the representatives of law and order. "Besides I would be a poor specimen indeed if I couldn't bamboozle Jones into giving me whatever I want."

"You know Jones, then?"

"We have crossed one another's paths occasionally. Why?"

"He's persuaded Ruth is guilty. He unearthed most of the evidence against her," I warned, "and he will guard it jealously."

"Not Jones. It's only natural that you should be prejudiced against him, of course. But really he's not a bad sort, and he's only doing his duty as he sees it."

"You are not small-minded at any rate," I answered smiling.

"Oh, well, I always believe in giving the devil his due," he returned with a mocking laugh as he ascended the steps.

CHAPTER XVI

THE EXHIBITS

We entered the building and at McKelvie's request Detective Jones was sent for. We awaited his arrival in silence, merely because McKelvie refused to talk, but he found his golden tongue readily enough when Jones came forward and blandly inquired what he could do for us.

The police detective was a shorter man than McKelvie, but heavier of build, with a pleasant enough face and fairly agreeable manners. He seemed to consider himself well enough acquainted with McKelvie magnanimously to overlook his eccentricities, and asked in a bantering way what he expected to get out of a case which had already been satisfactorily solved by the police.

McKelvie laughed good-humoredly, and answered in kind. "I was asked to investigate," he said, "and my aim, you know, is always to oblige."

"Whom? Yourself or your client?" inquired Jones shrewdly.

"My client, of course," McKelvie returned sententiously. "But, seriously, Jones, I did not come here to exchange witticisms, pleasant though it is to me to do so with such an opponent as yourself."

"What did you come for then, you blarneyer?" demanded Jones.

"I want a look at the exhibits. Come now, be a sport and show them to me."

"They will be of no use to you," answered Jones a trifle suspiciously. "They are all evidence against the accused."

"What's the objection then to showing them to me?" McKelvie responded. "I just want to satisfy my client that I have done everything possible to solve the case. I don't expect to learn anything from them."

Jones shrugged. "We have deduced all there is to learn and you are welcome to that," he said quietly.

"But not welcome to look at the articles themselves, is that it?" returned McKelvie, with a curl of the lip. Then he laughed outright.

"Say it. Go ahead. Don't spare me," remarked Jones with a grimace.

"I was wondering how soon it would be before you would be coming to me for advice, as you did in that last case of yours," McKelvie answered reflectively.

Jones flushed, then grinned. "You win," he said, and ushered us into his private office. From a cupboard in a corner of the room he produced the articles in question, and placed them on the flat-topped desk before us.

McKelvie picked up the pistol and examined it carefully. "Mrs. Darwin's finger-prints, I understand?"

"Yes."

"Anyone else's?"

"No."

"Dear, dear, that's too bad." McKelvie laid down the pistol and poked the bullet with his forefinger.

"Another theory gone up in smoke?" asked Jones, with a laugh.

"More or less. Sure the bullet fits the pistol?"

"As sure as human beings can be of anything in this world. We had the fellow from whom both pistol and bullets were purchased examine the weapon."

"So. You're sharper than I'd have given you credit for being."

"The police are not overlooking anything in this case," retorted Jones with some pomposity.

"Exhibit three-two handkerchiefs," muttered McKelvie. "Where did they come from?"

"The blood-stained one was in Mr. Darwin's hand. The other belongs to Mrs. Darwin. As you see, they are identical," explained Jones.

63

McKelvie sniffed at each one critically in turn, and then without any warning of his intention, passed the blood-stained handkerchief suddenly beneath my nose. Instinctively I drew back, inhaling involuntarily as I did so, and then I blinked and looked at McKelvie. But he was engrossed in reading the sheaf of bills and taking this as a sign that he did not wish his action remarked upon, I busied my brain in trying to recall the name of that delicate fragrance that for one fleeting second had assailed my nostrils when McKelvie brushed my face with the handkerchief. But try as I would I could not remember, and I decided to ask McKelvie the name of the perfume when we were once more alone. In the interest aroused by more pressing matters, however, I completely forgot the trifling episode.

By this time McKelvie had opened the cash box and was engaged in peering at the stoneless ring through his lens.

"Thank you, Jones," he said, replacing the ring beside the other objects. "But, hello, what's in this envelope?"

"Burnt scraps of the torn will. And look here, you have overlooked the will he was making," returned Jones, pushing forward a heavy sheet of paper.

"I noticed that," responded McKelvie indifferently. "May I look inside this envelope?"

"Surely. You will find that the most interesting scraps are the one with the name Darwin and the one with the partially burned letter R," explained Jones.

As in the case of the ring, McKelvie used his lens on the scraps, then he replaced them in the envelope.

"Thank you, Jones. Some day I hope to return the favor."

Jones, who had been highly amused by McKelvie's actions, waived aside the other's acknowledgment with a lordly air. "You are welcome to whatever you learned. Not much, was it?" he said.

"No, not much," replied McKelvie with a twinkle, adding as we passed out of earshot, "not much but quite enough, thank you, Mr. Jones."

"Then you did learn something of importance after all," I remarked as, seated once more in my car, we drove swiftly toward Broadway and headed uptown on our way to the Darwin home.

"Two things, one of which would have told me if I had not been positive before that Mrs. Darwin is innocent."

"Yes?" I prompted as he paused.

"There's entirely too much evidence against her. Why, man, it's overwhelming! One quarter of it would be sufficient to establish her guilt! Just go over it calmly. The quarrel, the change of will, the letter-any one of which would be ample motive. Her presence in the room when the shot was fired, your testimony that she held the weapon in her hand, the finger-prints on the pistol, the handkerchief, the closed room-It's much too much and thereby proclaims her innocence."

"And the second thing?" I asked.

He did not answer for he was employed in making what looked like a series of hieroglyphics on a page of his notebook. As I shifted closer to watch his occupation, between the traffic signals, he tore out the page and turning it over made four letters on it and handed it to me.

Keeping one hand on the wheel, I accepted the page with the other, and stole a quick glance at it. The letters he had made were capitals and were arranged in two sets. In the first group the L and the R were written with a flourish, so that the first stroke of the R resembled that of the L. In the second set the first stroke of the L was looped while that of the R was straight.

"Well?" I questioned, decidedly puzzled.

"I wish I knew whether Darwin made his capitals with a flourish," returned McKelvie. "The initial letter of the name on the scrap Jones so obligingly showed me had been burned away, leaving only the first stroke of the letter visible. If Darwin made his capitals like the first set on this sheet," tapping the paper I still held, "then the will might have been in favor of either the wife or the nephew and there is no way of proving which, except by taking Cunningham's statement as truth. If, on the other hand, Darwin made his capitals like the second set, then the will he destroyed was in favor of Lee Darwin, and Lawyer Cunningham was guilty of prevarication at the inquest. It makes a nice little problem to think about. I must find an answer to it as speedily as possible."

"Ruth would know Darwin's hand," I said eagerly.

"But the prison authorities aren't going to let us run in and out of the Tombs every time we happen to think of something we should like to know about," he replied dryly.

Piqued by the irony in his voice I remained silent, for I was not yet sufficiently accustomed to his manner to let his sarcasms pass unnoticed, and the remainder of the drive was accomplished in unbroken silence on both our parts.

CHAPTER XVII

THE LAMP

The moment we drew up before the house, McKelvie sprang out and disappeared from view. I switched off the motor and clambered out to find Jenkins waiting for me. He nodded in the direction of the grounds and as I had no mind to hunt for McKelvie I was on the point of ascending the steps when he appeared suddenly from behind a clump of bushes.

"Just taking stock of the general atmosphere, as it were," he said, waving his hand in the direction of the grounds, which made me take a second look at my surroundings.

My first visit had not been conducive to leisurely inspection and I now saw that the house was exceedingly unusual, a replica of the relic of a bygone age, although by no means so very old itself. It had been modeled after a type of dwelling that is now obsolete, but which was much in vogue when the English held sway over the Island of Manhattan, and was a massive affair with the servants' wing tacked on at the back like an after-thought (which it probably was, since it looked newer than the original domicile), and connected with the main building by a narrow enclosed passageway.

The entire structure, including the garage in the rear, stood directly in the center of the vast grounds, and was completely screened from the view of the curious by the forest of trees that surrounded it. It was an odd house, and it is a great pity it is no longer standing, but in a way I can hardly blame the heirs for having had it torn down and a modern home built on the site, since it must forever have remained coupled in their minds with associations which we who were in any way connected with the events which took place in that house, were all of us endeavoring to forget.

"Only two things to be learned here," said McKelvie. "First, that it would be easy for anyone to enter or leave the grounds unnoticed on a dark night."

"And it was dark that night, beastly dark," I interrupted.

"And secondly, that there is more space occupied by the left side of the house than by the right."

He pointed to the building and I saw what he meant. The left side jutted out almost beyond the steps. The right side was cut off level with the topmost gradient and in line with the front door.

"What a curious way to build a house," I remarked. "What's the interpretation, McKelvie?"

His answer was to spring up the steps and ring the bell. He waited a few minutes, then hearing no sound rang again.

"It's no good," said McKelvie, with a shrug, after our third attempt to rouse the inmates. "They've probably deserted the ship. It's a habit with servants when things go wrong in a house. Jenkins, go around back and see if you can unearth the butler. He can be depended upon to have remained behind. Tell him that Mr. Davies wishes to enter the house."

As Jenkins disappeared, McKelvie continued: "Strange that Orton hasn't the gumption to find out what's wanted."

"He left the house for good after the inquest," I returned. "I doubt if there is anyone living here now."

"What about young Darwin?"

"Lee? The last I heard of him he had gone South."

"Lee Darwin gone South?" he repeated. "How do you know?"

"I forgot to mention it last night, but when I first called on you I also went to the Yale Club. They told me Lee had left for the South the previous afternoon. At the time I thought it queer that he should go so soon after the murder, without waiting to attend his uncle's funeral."

"It was odd. I'll have to start somebody on his trail at once. Did you know that he was here the night of the murder?"

"Here in the house?" I gasped.

"No. Outside the study window," he returned.

"But McKelvie," I answered, thinking to trip him, "that footprint was made by Lee Darwin in leaving the study."

"What footprint?" He stared at me in evident surprise.

"I understood you to mean that you had deduced Lee's presence from the footprint that Jones discovered," I returned abashed.

He laughed heartily. "My dear man, where are your reasoning powers? Footprints don't last forever and we have had a shower since the murder. Besides I'm not clairvoyant enough to guess by a look at the imprint whose shoe made it. No, I base my deduction on this."

He held up a stick-pin of a peculiar dull brown hue, made in the shape of the head of a bulldog. On the gold setting around the base of the head had been engraved the name, L. Darwin.

"Where did you find it?" I asked eagerly, as he slipped it into his wallet.

"Beneath the first two windows of the study the ivy has grown very thickly. I found the pin close to the wall and directly beneath the second window, entangled in the vine. The head is exactly the color of the ivy stem and it had remained unnoticed. I saw it because I was hoping to find proof of his presence there."

"But I do not see how you could possibly know he had been there," I objected.

"I've learned to read between the lines and I spent the night in thoroughly acquainting myself with the inquest. Besides, Mr. Davies, you have a very retentive mind and you told me more than you guessed last night. One of the things you emphasized was the fact that Lee Darwin had seemed to know that his uncle was dead when he saw the coroner, and that he had turned deathly pale when suddenly accused of being outside the study that fatal night. You ended by saying that although that point was cleared up to everyone's satisfaction you were still persuaded that the young man knew more than he gave out, and I agree with you there."

"But if he witnessed events, why doesn't he clear Ruth then?" I protested.

"I didn't say he saw anything. I merely said he was there," he retorted, and refused to discuss the point further, which was just as well perhaps, for Jenkins was holding the door open and there was much to be done if McKelvie was to clear Ruth before her trial.

As we entered I noticed Mason hovering in the background, and I nodded to him. "Mason, this gentleman is a detective who has come to solve the mystery of your master's death. I should be obliged if you would let him in whenever he comes here."

"Yes, sir, indeed I will, sir. Master was my master and I'm not saying anything against the dead, sir, but I'd like to see someone else swing for it, indeed I would, sir," he said in a troubled whisper.

"Thank you, Mason. That is all. If we need you we shall call you."

He moved slowly toward the servants' entrance and I turned to look for McKelvie. He had been examining the lock of the front door, and now he was employed in measuring the respective distances of the stairs and the drawing-room door from that of the study. As Mason disappeared, however, McKelvie looked up at me with a smile.

"Ready?" he inquired, and when I nodded he opened the door of the study with an eager air and the light of battle in his eyes.

I had expected to see him whip out a lens and begin a minute examination of the room. Instead he adjusted the chair in the position in which it had stood on the fatal night, and seating himself in, closed his eyes.

This procedure did not at all impress me as the right way to go about solving the crime, when every moment was precious. I was on the point of remonstrating with him when Jenkins enjoined silence upon me.

"He's thinking, sir," he said low.

Thinking! I was thoroughly disgusted. With my intimate knowledge of the case thinking for five consecutive days had brought me nowhere, yet here was this man whom I had engaged to find clues and investigate the murder thoroughly, sitting back in a chair thinking-goodness knows about what, since all the thinking in the world would not produce the tangible material evidence of which we stood in such dire need!

"Jenkins!" McKelvie sat up with a suddenness that startled me. "Open that safe."

As Jenkins knelt before the huge contraption and manipulated the dial with deft fingers, McKelvie turned to me with a quizzical smile.

"Don't become annoyed, Mr. Davies," he said quietly. "Each man his own method, you know. I was just trying to decide a certain small point and now that I have satisfied myself as to my correctness in the matter, I'll be as energetic as anyone could possibly wish."

I felt the blood surge into my cheeks, as I said a little stiffly, "I didn't mean to criticize——"

"No harm done," he interrupted lightly, rising and laying a hand on my arm for a moment. Then he addressed my man. "You're mighty slow for an adept, Jenkins."

"An adept! Jenkins!" I could hardly articulate the words.

"A former adept in the art of safe-cracking," answered McKelvie with a flourish. "But I trust you won't count that against him since he reformed some years ago."

"No, of course not," I murmured hastily, as Jenkins looked up at me with pleading in his somber eyes. "He's a very good servant, whatever else he may have been."

With a beaming smile Jenkins rose and opened the door of the safe.

"Now," said McKelvie, "I'm going to show you several curious, but rather interesting facts."

He turned to the lamp upon the table and gazed at it thoughtfully for a moment, then he snapped it on and off. "Did you notice anything odd about it?" he asked.

In imitation of his manner, I too gazed steadily at the lamp. I had paid no great attention to it before, being too overwrought to notice details, but now I saw, or thought I saw, what he meant.

In keeping with the style of the room, the lamp though small was made in the shape of a bacchante who wore on her hair a crown of leaves and about her bare shoulders a wreath of the grapevine, so exceedingly heavy that she held it away from her graceful body with her hands, from which depended a rather large cluster of magnificent grapes.

"It is very beautiful," I responded, "but odd for a lamp, and that bunch of grapes seems almost out of all proportion to the rest of the figure."

"True, but that is not what I referred to," he returned. "Look here!"

Again he pulled the cord which cleverly imitated a stray tendril clinging to the wreath, and a pleasant glow suffused the table, but much as I looked I could detect nothing amiss.

McKelvie smiled involuntarily at my anxious endeavor to discover the flaw. "Don't you see that the light comes from the right side of that cluster and not from the center?" he remarked. "Which means a double socket of course. Why then doesn't the other bulb light also?"

"There may be no bulb in the left-hand socket," I suggested. "Or it may be broken."

He nodded. "We'll soon settle that." He unscrewed the bunch of grapes and revealed the double socket, each part of which was provided with a bulb. He exchanged the bulbs and when he pulled the cord the same condition obtained. Only the bulb on the right lighted.

"It isn't broken, you see. Therefore, it must be lighted from some other source. I divined as much when Mrs. Darwin declared she hadn't touched it, and that if it had been lighted from the table she would have seen the person who pulled the cord. The only thing remaining is to find the switch that operates it."

Without a moment's hesitation he made for the safe and I followed him hastily. Now that I was in front of it I saw that the safe was nothing but a closet containing three shelves, which were built into the side walls at such a height that by stooping slightly a man could pass under them with ease. I glanced along the lowest shelf, although I knew that it was empty since Jones' entrance at the inquest, but McKelvie paid no attention to the bareness of the cupboard. He was engrossed in fingering the wall beyond the door. Then with a grunt of satisfaction he caught my hand and placed it where his had been. Instantly my fingers came in contact with a small button. I pushed it, and lo! the left bulb of the lamp sprang suddenly into being.

"Well, I'll be hanged!" I ejaculated, looking at McKelvie. "Why does any sane person want to light his lamp from his safe?" I asked.

"Because, Mr. Davies, it's no more a safe than I am-well-Jenkins," he returned impressively.

"Not a safe?" I exclaimed.

"No."

"Then what—?"

"I'm going to show you." McKelvie again fingered lightly the wall, but this time it was the wall which formed the back of the safe.

Presently with that same peculiar grunt he took out a pocket-flash and a knife. Opening the knife he pried the point into what looked by the aid of the flash like a harmless knot-hole just beneath the lowest shelf. (He was kneeling on the floor of the safe and Jenkins and I were stooping to watch him.) The next moment the knot-hole had swung aside, revealing to our astonished gaze a tiny key-hole!

The back of the safe was in reality a door!

Silently we watched as McKelvie fished out his keys and tried them in the lock but without success. Then he spoke to Jenkins. "Tell Mason to give you all of Mr. Darwin's keys, but don't let him come in here."

"Very well, sir."

When Jenkins returned with the keys McKelvie tried them in the lock, one after the other, but the door remained as securely locked as before.

"Strange," he said, looking annoyed. "You are sure you brought me all the keys?" he added abruptly.

"Yes, sir, even the ones he had in his pocket when he was shot, sir," responded Jenkins.

"Odd. I hate to break it open. It might be useful later on."

Jenkins, who had been peering intently at the key-hole over McKelvie's shoulder, spoke suddenly. "No need to smash it, sir. I still have my old tool kit and if I'm not mistaken I have a master key that will fit this lock."

"Off with you, then. Break all traffic laws if necessary. Only be back as soon as possible," cried McKelvie gayly, and I never saw the solemn Jenkins move so fast before.

While we awaited the man's return McKelvie came out of the safe and resumed his indolent pose. Again I found myself growing exasperated with his attitude. Surely there were clues to be found in the room, and he wasn't thinking because those brilliant black eyes were wide-open and wore an expression of contented ease.

"Since you object to my inactivity," he remarked quietly, "let's talk. At least we shall be exercising our tongues, if nothing more," and he laughed oddly.

I ceased trying to understand him and welcomed the opening that he gave me. "Will you answer me three questions?" I inquired.

"Depends on what they are," he returned laconically.

"Nothing really startling," I answered, laughing. "I merely wished to know why if Lee Darwin was outside that study window he did not leave footprints for the police to discover, as they did the ones that he made in the morning."

"Because there is a flower-bed under all the windows except the first two. Beneath those two the cement walk reaches to the wall. He stood on this walk that night, but in the morning having just come in the door he rushed out of the window nearest to him and stepped into the flower-bed."

"I see. Now here's question two. How did you know so unerringly that the lamp was also lighted from the safe?"

"Childishly simple. I had already deduced a secret entrance."

"How?" I broke in.

"Sherlock Holmes says, 'Exclude the impossible, whatever remains improbable must be the truth.' Mrs. Darwin didn't kill her husband or I should not be here. The case is one of murder, not suicide, therefore someone else must have been in the room at midnight. He couldn't leave by the windows or the door and flesh and blood doesn't vanish into air, ergo he must have gone out by some other entrance, natural inference a secret one, since it wasn't discovered."

I nodded. So far it was absurdly simple and clear. I was a trifle mortified that I had not divined it myself, but then such things were not in my line and the affair stuck too close to home to leave me any capacity for ratiocination.

"The question that had to be settled then," he continued, "was the situation of this entrance. I called your attention to the peculiar architecture of the house. When I entered the study I noticed that the safe occupied the wall in question. Jenkins opened it for me and I saw that it was the size of an ordinary closet and not very deep. What was more reasonable than to deduce that the remaining space between the back of the safe and the outer wall of the house was occupied by a passage of some kind!"

Again I nodded. "Of course. It was just a question of accounting for the extra square footage of house. But you haven't answered my original query."

"About the light? Mrs. Darwin said she didn't touch it, the dead man presumably couldn't, therefore the murderer must have done so. If he had pulled the cord Mrs. Darwin would have seen him, hence he lighted the lamp from some other source. Where? Not at the main switch near the door, for he had to vanish at once, knowing the shot would rouse the household. Besides, Mrs. Darwin would have heard the click when he pushed the button. The only place left was somewhere near the entrance. It was more likely to be inside than out, since, as before, Mrs. Darwin heard no sound. So I looked for it in the most plausible spot and found it."

I smiled. "You have answered my third question, which related to the secret entrance, but I have thought of two more to take its place. If the murderer used Darwin's pistol, how is it that only Ruth's finger-prints are on it?"

"He'd be too clever not to use gloves," returned McKelvie shortly.

"To be sure. But here's a harder one. How did the criminal, if he was behind Ruth, shoot Philip Darwin with such accuracy in the dark?"

"Exactly, that's just the point," he replied enigmatically.

CHAPTER XVIII

THE SECRET ENTRANCE

When Jenkins arrived with the keys, McKelvie looked them over critically, selected a couple, and tried them on the door. The first was too large, but the second turned the trick. Cautioning us to stoop to avoid the shelves, McKelvie pushed open the back of the safe, which swung away from him into the darkness beyond. With the flash to guide him he stepped through the opening, then beckoned us to follow him. Though it was too dark to see, I knew I was in a room of some sort, for I felt the velvet softness of a carpet beneath my feet, and I also tripped over some article of furniture. By this time McKelvie had located the light and I saw that my room was really an alcove fitted up with a luxurious divan heaped high with pillows, beside which stood a small smoking-stand. But ornate and sumptuous as the alcove was I should not personally have cared for it, since the atmosphere was close and smoke-laden and there was no means of letting in the light of day.

McKelvie glanced hastily about and then striding to the divan he bent down and sniffed at it critically. Instantly I imitated him. To my amazement the same fragrance clung to the Persian cover of the couch that I had detected on the blood-stained handkerchief. I smelled it again to make sure and then as my memory still played me false I turned to ask McKelvie what it was. He was trying his key in the lock of a door at the rear of the room, and if he heard my question he failed to reply to it.

With less difficulty this time he unlocked this second door, which swung inwards and stood at the head of a flight of rather steep and dark stairs. As before, McKelvie preceded Jenkins and myself, but we kept as close as possible to him that his flash might guide us as well. At the bottom of the steps was another door of similar make, which also opened inwards, and to my astonishment it gave exit onto the garden at the side of the house between the first study window and the corner. So skillfully had it been cut in the masonry, however, that only one initiated into the secret of the entrance would have known it was there.

McKelvie examined the ground around the door and as at this point also the cement walk reached clear to the wall, I wondered what he hoped to discover. Whatever it was, his scrutiny satisfied him, for he stood up with a smile and applied his lens to the key-hole of the door. Then he nodded his head in a contented manner and remarked that we had better return to the study. I noticed that he locked all the doors scrupulously behind him, leaving the secret entrance exactly as he had found it, even to replacing the round disk which counterfeited the knot-hole.

Once in the room he knelt down and examined minutely the dial of the safe.

"Interesting and unique," he commented. "Look here, Mr. Davies!" He pointed to the inside of the door, and I noticed to my astonishment that the dial was duplicated within. "Do you get the significance?" he asked quickly.

"Why, that safe can be opened or closed by combination from the inside as well as the outside," I hazarded.

"Naturally, to be of any use as an entrance it would have to be capable of being opened from the inside," he said caustically. "No, what I meant was this. Supposing we want to lock the safe. Give me a combination."

"I gave him 'Darwin,' the first word that occurred to me, for it was one of those old style safes with the six-letter combination. He twirled the knob of the dial on the outside and pointed as he did so to the inside. Just as the inside handle of a door will revolve when the outer one is turned, so the inner knob of the dial duplicated the revolutions of the outer.

"Now, don't you see that in order to use this entrance it is necessary to know what combination was used to lock the safe from the study and vice versa?" he questioned.

71

"Yes, that's plain enough. To use the entrance the criminal had to know the combination. Well, what of it? A clever man would hardly be balked by so small a thing."

"You still don't get what I'm driving at," he returned. "I'll try to explain. You have arrived at the conclusion that I held a while ago; namely, that the criminal came in and went out by the secret entrance. Am I right?"

"Yes, that is my opinion."

"Now we come to my point," he said, rising and beginning to pace the room. "If the criminal entered by the safe, he must have been cognizant of three things: first, that there was such an entrance; secondly, that three of the doors were opened by a key of a certain size and make; thirdly, that the safe door was unlocked by a certain combination, that combination being the one which Philip Darwin himself had used. That the criminal should know of one, or perhaps of two of these facts, yes. But that he should be aware of all three of them seems incredible!"

"Why incredible?" I objected. "He may have known of the entrance. He could easily then take an impression of the outer lock and have a key made, and Philip Darwin himself may have revealed the combination to him."

"Very good, but not carried quite far enough," he said with his quizzical smile. "Before I show you where you are at fault, answer me a question. How do you suppose that entrance came to be there so very handy for the criminal's purpose?"

"I presume it was built with the house," I answered.

"Precisely. When?"

"Almost a hundred years ago—1830, to be exact."

"Exactly, and old Elias Darwin, the great-grandfather of Philip, who was a firm believer in the established order of affairs, modeled his home in the country (for this stretch of land was country then) on that which was built by his ancestors in pre-revolutionary days, secret entrance and all; for, of course, in those times secret entrances were indispensable for the concealment of friends, whether Tories or Whigs."

"Where did you learn all this?" I asked in amazement.

"I have a book home which details the histories of various mansions in New York," he replied.

"That accounts for the entrance. But what about the safe?" I continued.

"The safe is decidedly more recent. Doubtless the secret entrance had been blocked up, if it was ever cut through, and no one knew of its existence until Philip Darwin stumbled on the knowledge. I looked up the family history of the Darwins this morning while I was awaiting your arrival. Who's Who describes Mr. Frank Darwin, the father, as having been a strait-laced, Puritanical man, and you yourself know what the son was. Can't you imagine the clash between them?"

In view of Mr. Trenton's story concerning Dick's mother I could well believe that father and son had not agreed.

"In 1906 there is record that Frank Darwin went to Europe for a year. Of course, this is mere conjecture, but it is reasonable to suppose that Philip, who was then twenty-one, took the occasion to have the safe built, and the secret entrance unblocked."

"Mason should know," I said.

"I don't think so, or he would have mentioned it at the inquest. However, there is no harm in questioning him. Go and get him, Jenkins."

When Mason stood before us McKelvie said quietly, though his eyes sparkled: "You testified that you had been with the Darwin family thirty years. Did you remain in the house when Mr. Frank Darwin went to Europe in 1906?"

"Yes, sir. I remained as caretaker."

"Then you can tell us when that safe was built?"

"Yes, sir. It was that same year, sir. Mr. Phil complained he had no private safe and his father told him to have one built while he was gone. He chose that place, sir, because he liked the study. His father used the den upstairs."

"Why did he build such a large safe?"

"I don't know, sir. He sent me away to visit some of my folks, sir, while it was being built. He told his father it was to hold his fortune, sir."

McKelvie looked across at me with a triumphant expression which said as plainly as words, "Notice how accurately I deduced the truth," but his voice was subdued enough as he continued his questions.

"He did not get along with his father, I understand?"

"No, sir. They had different ideas on every subject, sir."

"Why didn't Philip Darwin live at his club then, when he came of age?" McKelvie inquired.

"Because his father told him, sir, that if he left the house it would be for good, and not one penny of his money would he get, sir. Mr. Phil knew that his father always carried out his threats, sir."

"That is all, Mason."

"Yes, sir."

The moment the door closed behind the old butler McKelvie said, with a smile, "Just as I thought. And what came in handy when his father was alive was doubly useful after his marriage. And thus we come back to the original discussion, whether the criminal would know the three necessary facts to enter by the safe."

"A member of the family might," I said.

"Yes, a member of the family. Lee, for instance, or even Orton might discover that there was such a passage and secure a key to it. Would either of them know the combination?"

"Orton was Darwin's private secretary."

"As far as his business down-town went, but not his secretary, as far as his personal affairs were concerned. Besides, recall Mason's testimony. He was surprised to find Orton in the study because Darwin always kept it religiously locked, to preserve his secret, of course. Then, too, Orton was Darwin's creature and, therefore, he would be doubly careful not to place himself in the fellow's power. He evidently considered he was running no risk, since he let Orton into the study that night. Besides, if you did not want anyone prying into your safe, what precaution would you take to prevent it?"

"I'd change the combination frequently."

"Exactly; and there you have an answer to my problem. Granted that the criminal knew the first two facts, was he going to depend on a combination that might be changed five minutes before he wished to use the entrance? No, no, we're dealing with a person too clever not to foresee that contingency. Besides, as far as I could detect, no one has recently taken an impression of the outer lock."

"Then we get back where we started and the entrance is of no value to us at all," I pointed out.

"You jump back too far. It merely shows that the criminal did not enter by the safe. That he left that way is proved by the fact that he vanished from the study without using door or windows, and that he very evidently took Darwin's key with him."

"But—the combination?"

"The safe was open, for Darwin had just removed the will from it. Even if it had been closed, a clever man could find an excuse for making his victim open the safe. Once inside any combination of six letters would close the door effectually against intruders."

"I suppose you are right, but how did he get in then?"

"Darwin let him in himself, either through the window or the door. Most probably through the window, since you would have otherwise heard steps in the hall. Recall Orton's testimony. He went to the garage to follow the maid. When he returned he heard voices in the study."

"And when he went in at eleven-thirty, Philip Darwin was alone," I remarked with a smile.

"Yes, to be sure, Philip Darwin was alone," he repeated, crestfallen.

CHAPTER XIX

THE LAWYER AGAIN

Before I could retort the front door-bell rang sharply. Turning quickly McKelvie walked to the safe and silently locked it. Then he spoke to Jenkins with his usual assured manner. "Tell Mason to answer the bell. And I sha'n't need you again to-day."

"Very well, sir."

As Jenkins opened the door and went out McKelvie dropped into a chair beside me.

"I wonder who that can be," he murmured, "but whoever it may be, not one sign, not one word of what we have learned."

I nodded comprehendingly, and in the pause that ensued I heard Mason shuffle to the door and fumble with the lock. Then a man's voice inquired for me. I heard an answering murmur and rose, turning toward the open study door just as Mr. Cunningham crossed the threshold.

"Mr. Davies," he said, with a smile, extending his hand. He had recovered his voice since the inquest and spoke in a rich baritone.

I gave him my hand, but not over-cordially as I said, suspiciously, "How did you know I was here?"

He laughed, not at all put out. "I called at your apartments to give you some information, and Mr. Trenton kindly told me where I could find you. He also explained your mission. A very laudable purpose. Mr. McKelvie, I presume?" turning toward my companion.

"I beg your pardon," I said stiffly, for I was ashamed of my unjust suspicion, which had its inception in the fact that he was the dead man's lawyer, and as such prejudiced against Ruth, and introduced the two men.

McKelvie, who had also risen at the lawyer's entrance, and who was standing with his hands behind his back, affected not to see Cunningham's extended hand and merely nodded. Annoyed at his incivility, and seeing that Cunningham frowned angrily, I hastened to make the peace.

"Mr. McKelvie put me out of his house when I first called on him," I remarked to Cunningham with a laugh. "You may consider yourself highly honored to have received a bow."

The frown melted from Cunningham's brow as he said, pleasantly enough, "I understand. The idiosyncrasies of the great must be indulgently overlooked," and he returned McKelvie's nod with a ceremonious bow.

"You have some information to impart?" broke in McKelvie briskly as we seated ourselves.

"Yes. I have discovered something that I thought might help toward freeing Mrs. Darwin. You remember," turning to me, "that I testified that Philip Darwin had removed his securities from my office. I learned yesterday that he had used them as I thought upon the market. There was a slump in the stock he was operating the afternoon of the seventh of this month and as far as I can make out he was completely ruined."

"Ruined!" I repeated, for I could recall no rumor to that effect on the Street that day. "You are sure?"

"Positive. He was completely, absolutely ruined," returned the lawyer. He looked at me thoughtfully a moment and then added, "You were wondering why, being a broker yourself, you had not heard of it? The explanation is simple. The world has believed Philip Darwin immensely wealthy for so many years that the truth concerning his financial affairs would have been a decided shock to his friends and associates. Naturally, though he lost heavily on the market on the seventh, no one suspected that he was wiped out, and so nothing was thought of the occurrence, for he had lost as heavily before without its making any appreciable difference to him."

"I understand. And, of course he knew that he was ruined?" I continued.

"He must have known it."

"Then why was he troubling himself to make a new will?" I said, perplexed.

Cunningham shook his head. "I never pretended to understand him. But I thought my information might help along this line. If he had no money Mrs. Darwin certainly didn't murder him to inherit his fortune."

"She may not have known that he was beggared," I retorted.

"Humph! If she swore she did know that fact, who could contradict her?" and he smiled blandly.

"Are you a criminal lawyer, Mr. Cunningham?" queried McKelvie suddenly. He had arisen again when Cunningham began to talk and had been pacing the room in apparent indifference to our conversation.

"No, I am not," answered the lawyer promptly, just a little surprised.

"What an infinite pity! You would make a great success in that line I am sure," responded McKelvie, and in his flexible voice I again detected traces of irony.

Cunningham looked at McKelvie undecided whether to take the remark as an insult or a compliment, and I saw McKelvie's lip curl just a trifle before he continued suavely, "I meant it, Mr. Cunningham. You would make a great criminal lawyer. I advise you to try your hand at that branch of the profession."

Cunningham laughed. "Thanks, but I'm too old a dog to learn new tricks. Besides, I am planning to take a little vacation presently. I expect to travel for the next few years, but I do not mean to intrude my own uninteresting affairs upon you. You have no time to waste in this case. Have you discovered anything of value so far?" he continued with friendly interest.

McKelvie shook his head and sighed. "I am afraid so far it is a losing game," he said with an air of great candor. "The trouble is, as I explained to Mr. Davies, that the scent is cold. The clues are in the hands of the police. Ah, if only I could have been here from the first!"

"It is a pity. They say you are a great detective. I should hate to see you defeated," answered the lawyer, giving McKelvie a Roland for his Oliver.

McKelvie laughed—a short, hard laugh.

"Don't fool yourself, Mr. Cunningham. I am not going to be defeated," he said tersely. "No, not even if the criminal is the cleverest fellow living."

"Pride goeth before destruction, Mr. McKelvie. By this time the criminal has doubtless betaken himself to other parts," returned the lawyer, sardonically.

"The world is small, and I am going to get him if it takes me the rest of my life." McKelvie's jaw snapped with grim determination.

The lawyer rose. "I must be going. Good-by, Mr. Davies. Farewell, Mr. McKelvie. Long life to you, sir."

"Damn his impudence," said McKelvie as the front door slammed, "but he's right. I have no time to waste. I'll call you up in the morning if I have news, and in the meantime say nothing to anyone of our discoveries."

"Not even Mr. Trenton?"

"Not even Mr. Trenton. I'm trusting no one but you and Jenkins. Also, I do not want that meddlesome old lawyer hanging around when I want to work. Good-by."

"Just a moment. How does what Cunningham told us affect the case as it now stands?"

"Not a hair's breadth. I told you before there was more than enough evidence against her. And I'm hanged if I don't believe he knew it, too!"

CHAPTER XX

DEDUCTIONS

Naturally, Mr. Trenton was eager to know what we had accomplished and bombarded me with questions the moment I stepped foot in my apartments, which was not until late, for I had stopped at the office to attend to some pressing business first. I put him off, however, by saying that McKelvie was just getting his bearings and we'd have definite news when I heard from him again. I expected that he would call me up next day, but I received no word from him, so that I had plenty of time to speculate on the little I knew.

Personally, I was not sorry that Philip Darwin had failed, because I did not relish the idea of Ruth's inheriting his money, but I could not understand why McKelvie had disparaged Cunningham's motive in giving us this information. Not that I wanted to side with the man. I felt the same unreasonable antagonism that McKelvie evidently experienced toward him, but I wanted to be fair, and as far as I could see he was desirous of helping us as much as he could.

At any rate, motives for the crime, as far as Ruth was concerned, were valueless, since we knew of the existence of the secret entrance. What troubled me most was this point. Why should any sane man (I presume that the criminal was sane, if criminality is not another form of insanity) I repeat, why should any sane man shoot another one in the dark in the presence of a third person with the chances ten to one against his hitting the one at whom he aimed, and ten to one in favor of his being discovered? It was absurd on the face of it, yet it was just what had happened in the study that night, and twist it as I would I could make neither rhyme nor reason out of it. McKelvie had said the criminal was a clever man and clever criminals don't usually leave anything to chance, for only chance could have directed his aim in a room so dark that he could not possibly see his prospective victim!

Though I thought about it continually, this point was still a puzzle when McKelvie phoned me, early the second day after our visit to Riverside Drive, and asked me to meet him there at ten o'clock, but to tell no one where I was going. As I was in the habit of leaving for the office about eight I said nothing of my ultimate destination to Mr. Trenton, but I ordered Jenkins to be at the office as near nine-thirty as possible. I did not know whether McKelvie wanted him or not, and it was simpler to dismiss him than to send for him.

When we entered Darwin's study at ten o'clock sharp McKelvie was standing at one of the windows whistling. He greeted us with a smile and the remark, "Well, I'm all ready to tell you how the murder was committed."

"You have discovered something new?" I asked quickly.

"One or two things, but nothing bearing on my statement. I knew before I entered this room day before yesterday how it was done. For another that might seem impossible, but for me, no. It was simplicity itself."

I couldn't help smiling at this piece of conceit and catching my look he laughed good-humoredly.

"All great detectives-and I am one, according to my friend, Cunningham-are egotistical," he said.

"Is that the reason that Sherlock Holmes is an egotist, sir?" asked Jenkins suddenly.

"Undoubtedly; and why not, since he is the greatest of his kind. You see great detectives seldom fail, and so naturally they become-well-self-opinionated," returned McKelvie.

But I had not come there to discuss the failings of detectives, great or small, so I proceeded to dismount him from his hobby.

"You said you knew how the murder was done. So does anyone who reads the papers. The coroner's inquest made that fact plain," I said to get him started. I had learned already that he disliked having his statements belittled.

"The coroner's inquest!" he scoffed. "Haven't you the wit to see that the inquest was in the hands of the police from the start? Jones questioned Orton in the morning and then calmly used Graves and his jury as a vehicle for tightening the net in which Mrs. Darwin had become entangled. What chance then had the truth for even so much as lifting its head? I suppose the police explained to your satisfaction how the murderer shot so accurately in the dark?" he ended, cynically.

I smiled inwardly as I realized that I had drawn the very fire I wanted. Now I would have the answer to my puzzle.

"Well, how did he do it?" I asked, unruffled.

"He didn't. He shot Darwin while the lamp was lighted, like any right-minded person," he answered triumphantly. "By the way, Jenkins, I don't believe I'll need you to-day."

"Very well, sir."

I waited until Jenkins had gone and then I replied to McKelvie's statement. "What you have just remarked is utterly impossible," I retorted. "Ruth heard the shot before she saw the lamp spring into being, and she was speaking the truth."

He laughed. "Certainly, I am not disputing that point. I am merely making the assertion that the murderer shot his victim while the lamp, and for all I know, all the lights were lighted."

"But——"

"On second thoughts I don't believe I'll tell you. You might be as skeptical of my information as you were triumphant just now at having roused my ire," he answered laconically, and I knew that I had not deceived him long with my pretense of blockheadedness.

"I promise to believe anything you may say and swallow it all, hook, line and sinker," I pleaded.

"Well, perhaps under those circumstances—" he appeared to reflect, then said abruptly, "Would you call Dr. Haskins a man who knew his business?"

"Yes, decidedly so," I replied, surprised at the turn in the conversation.

"He remarked, if you remember, that Philip Darwin lived twenty minutes after the bullet had penetrated his lung, and yet he also agreed with the coroner's physician that Philip Darwin died at midnight or shortly thereafter. You yourself can testify that the shot was fired at midnight. How then do you account for the discrepancies in these various facts, for facts they are?"

My mind reverted to the inquest, and I heard again the pompous coroner's physician explaining Dr. Haskins' mistake, and I also recalled the young doctor's face, which certainly belied his apparent acquiescence with the other's statement. And suddenly I saw what McKelvie was driving at. Yet, how could it possibly be?

"You mean that he had already been shot when Ruth entered this room?" I said slowly, hardly daring to believe that which I uttered. It was so incredible, so seemingly impossible!

"Yes, just that." The words came with quiet conviction.

"But I heard no other shot, and Philip Darwin was alive at eleven-thirty!"

"Of course you heard no shot. We're dealing with a clever man, I tell you, and he wasn't advertising his actions," returned McKelvie, with that note of impatience in his voice which crept into it whenever I failed immediately to grasp the point. "I'll show you how it was done, so that no one could possibly have heard that shot, even if there had been someone listening at door or windows, which, of course, there was not."

He walked to the safe, and unlocked the door. Then he inserted his key in the back wall and ushered me into the secret room.

"In here," he said, "no noise, however great, could be heard without these walls. They are sound-proof, for I have tested them myself. I fired a pistol by means of a mechanism, and then listened in the hall for its explosion. I heard nothing. When I returned to this room the pistol had gone off, as was intended. So you can see that shooting his victim in here with the doors closed there was no chance that the shot would be heard by anyone in the house at the time."

I stared at him in astonishment. "But, McKelvie, Jones proved beyond the shadow of a doubt that Philip Darwin had just risen in his chair at the table when he was shot," I protested.

77

"Jones proved it!" he jeered. "Ye gods! Jones proved it! Of course he proved it. What else would you expect of Jones? Why do you suppose the murderer took the trouble to make those marks in the carpet except to fool the police?" he raged. "Certainly Jones proved it when it was put there for that purpose!"

"Granted," I said pacifically. "He shot Darwin in this secret room. Then what?"

McKelvie calmed down and resumed his story. "Then he proceeded to manufacture evidence. He carried his victim through the safe," returning to the study as he spoke and relocking the entrance, "placed him in that chair and arranged everything to look as though Philip Darwin had been writing, as indeed he had been when Orton came in at eleven-thirty. Then, satisfied that all was as perfect as he could make it, he turned off the light and waited."

"What for?"

"Mrs. Darwin, naturally."

"How on earth did he know she would come into the room? How could he possibly divine that I would urge her to get me that letter when I only spoke on impulse myself?"

McKelvie sighed. "I'm not omniscient. If I could tell you how he knew it, or why, I could tell you who committed the crime. I am only reconstructing what actually happened, for he was in the room at midnight, wasn't he, since he fired that second shot and lighted the lamp? And is it reasonable to suppose that it took him twenty minutes to shoot his victim and place him in that chair?"

I acquiesced, but not because I could see through the affair. It was growing more intricate with every step we took. "But why, man, why?" I persisted.

"Because he needed a scapegoat. It may be, of course, and probably is, the fact that he was about to leave when he heard Mrs. Darwin try the door, and that the idea then came to him to incriminate her."

"Why-that's monstrous!" I cried.

McKelvie shrugged. "When you are dealing with a murderer, his little ideas are apt to be rather outside the pale of civilized folk," he returned ironically. "By providing the police with a suspect he escaped their vigilance. Mrs. Darwin had the most motive for killing her husband; therefore, she made the best possible victim. But he figured without me. It's like a game of chess. He makes a move. I block him. At present it's 'check,' with all the advantage on his side and every prospect of the jury finding Mrs. Darwin guilty of the murder."

He had forgotten my presence and was talking to himself, his eyes grown dreamy as he gazed into the distance. At my exclamation, he passed a hand across his eyes, saying in a different tone, "I beg your pardon. I forgot in my interest in matching my wits against his, that to you Mrs. Darwin is more than a pawn in the game."

"McKelvie, surely you can't be serious," I implored him.

"I'm sorry to say that I am," he returned. "The prosecution has a very strong case, and we have nothing we can offer that refutes a single point that they can make." He moved away from the window, where he had been sitting for some little time, and began to pace the room in long, even strides.

"If only I knew where that second bullet had lodged itself! The physician declares there was only one wound and only one bullet; therefore, it's not in Darwin's body. Also, I have searched every square inch of this room-walls, ceiling, floor, carpet and furniture. There's not a trace, nor even the faintest shadow of a trace of that bullet!"

He shook his head despairingly, but I had hardly listened to his harangue. My mind had leaped to a sudden joyful conclusion.

"McKelvie," I cried, "we have evidence to refute their arguments! Let's go before the district attorney and tell him what we have learned and insist on his releasing Ruth at once!"

"What evidence do you refer to?" he inquired a bit coldly. "Do you take me for a mere calculating machine without any human feelings and consideration for others? Don't you suppose that if I had any valuable evidence I should have used it to advantage long ere this?"

"Why," I stammered, all the wind taken out of my sails, "what about the-the secret entrance?"

"As to that, it may or may not have been used upon that fatal night. We conjecture because we are proving Mrs. Darwin innocent, but we do not positively know anything about it," he put in imperturbably. "Mr. Darwin may have lost or misplaced his key."

"How do you account then for the lighting of the lamp from the safe?" I persisted.

"Again, we do not know it was so lighted. Often, if a connection is loose, a jar or shock will light the lamp of itself."

"But the shot in the dark?"

"Ah, the police don't believe for a second that the room was ever in darkness at any time. They believe that you and Mrs. Darwin concocted that bit of evidence."

"When?" I spluttered.

"You gave the wrong impression about Mrs. Darwin the night of the crime. They would argue collusion before their arrival."

"But, McKelvie, what about the actual time when Philip Darwin was killed, twenty minutes before Ruth ever set foot in the study?" I continued, exasperated by his skillful refutation of my arguments.

"On what do I base that conclusion?" he asked quietly.

"On Dr. Haskins' testimony."

"Exactly. And do you believe for a moment that the district attorney will give credence to a fact which Coroner Graves practically ruled out of his court?" he demanded.

But I was still determined to have my way, for I wanted to free Ruth above everything else. "There's the second shot to prove it," I said stubbornly.

He looked at me a moment with a strange smile, then he tapped his head significantly. "Pardon me," he said quizzically, as I flushed angrily, "I had forgotten you are in love and that lovers are never logical. Don't be angry with me and I'll show you what would happen if I approached Grenville with your last statement as a proof of my previous deductions. You have no experience in such matters, but, unfortunately, I know Grenville so very well."

McKelvie drew his mouth down in imitation of the district attorney, whose picture I had seen more than once in the paper, and then continued his exposition, mimicking Grenville's soft voice, as I suppose, whenever the part demanded it.

"When I had been ushered into his office he would adjust his glasses and listen with an air of great politeness to all I had to say. Then, when I was through he would smile, still politely, very, if a trifle sarcastically, and remark in his purring voice (the purr of the tiger before he shows his claws):

"'Of course, since only one shot was fired from Mr. Darwin's pistol, you have brought with you the weapon that produced the second shot?'

"I would have to acknowledge that I not only had no such weapon, but not even the prospect of finding it.

"'No? Then, of course,' with a still deeper purr, 'you have brought me the bullet itself?'

"'Well, no,' I would answer sheepishly, 'I haven't even got that.'

"'What! No bullet either? Dear, dear, Mr. McKelvie, you really are a genius in your line. And you would actually have me credit the evidence of a chimera, a hypothetical revolver that fires a shot that leaves no trace——'"

Here McKelvie broke off abruptly and banged his fist against his forehead. "Stupid, stupid. Oh, that someone would write me down an ass!"

"What's the trouble, now?" I asked. "I thought you were doing very well."

"As regards Grenville? Well, I'm glad you realize that we couldn't prove anything with mere deduction unsubstantiated by facts, for any clever prosecutor could knock our evidence into a cocked hat. No, I was referring to something else," he returned, gazing somberly before him with a look akin to horror in his eyes.

"What is it?" I demanded.

He shook off whatever was troubling him and replied in a self-contemptuous tone, "Nothing, except that I must be getting old. I have actually allowed myself to ape that pompous idiot of a coroner's physician, and have thus been guilty of the worst crime in the decalogue of a detective. I have been fitting the facts to my theory instead of fitting my theory to the facts!"

"And that proves?"

"Just what I told you before, that we are face to face with a far cleverer, more cold-blooded man than even I had given him credit for being!"

CHAPTER XXI

THE STEWARD

I was taken by surprise when Mason knocked on the door to tell us that he had prepared some luncheon for us. We had talked for two hours and had virtually arrived-nowhere! The thing was beginning to get on my nerves and I said as much to McKelvie as we seated ourselves at the table.

"Yes," he returned. "It's getting on mine, too. I feel like-well, a person tied to a tree, who can go so far and no farther. But I'm going to break away."

"You mean you are going to try to locate the criminal since we can find no clues to help Ruth?" I asked.

"No, not directly, at present. I'm going to try to locate substantial evidence against him, for your clever criminal is not so easily caught. The trouble lies right here. Though I know the murderer is clever I have no idea as to his identity, because I do not absolutely know the true motive for the crime. Or, rather, I should say, no proof, for unfortunately there are any number of persons who might have been in the house at that time and who had sufficient motive for killing Darwin."

"Can't some of them produce alibis?"

"Alibis! I spent all day yesterday chasing alibis. Let's go over them. First, there's Mr. Trenton——"

"Heavens! You don't suspect him?" I gasped.

"Why not? Don't you suppose he realized as you did that he was primarily to blame for Mrs. Darwin's marriage? And didn't he, while living in this house, have an opportunity to witness and resent the treatment accorded to his daughter? And more than resent his own humiliation at the hands of Philip Darwin, a humiliation of which even young Darwin was cognizant, if he spoke the truth at the inquest?"

"You're right. I hadn't connected him with the affair at all. I suppose because he was away," I replied.

He smiled. "I think we can safely knock him off our list, for though he had motive he had not the opportunity. I motored to Tarrytown yesterday and had an interview with Mrs. Bailey. On the night of the seventh, Mr. Trenton was ill, too ill to leave his bed, and precisely at midnight she, herself, and her doctor were in attendance upon him."

"I'm glad of that," I said, drawing a long breath. "It's bad enough as it is without dragging Mr. Trenton into it, too."

"Though I made certain of his alibi because I am leaving no stones unturned in this case, still I never for one moment believed him guilty. It would be a monstrous father, indeed, who would let his daughter remain in jail if a word from him could clear her, particularly if he loved her and had bitterly repented of his former treatment of her."

"That's one off the list. Who else could have done it?" I prompted, as he remained absorbed in thought.

"Cunningham is clever, and though he may have had opportunity, he lacks motive. I saw the telephone girl in the apartment house where he has a suite of rooms. She says that he left town about the first of October and did not return until about ten o'clock the morning of the eighth. Of course he might have got in the night before, in which case he spent the night in the street or with a friend, for he is not registered at any of the hotels, although he could have registered under an assumed name, both of which presumptions are absurd, since he could have easily returned home and none the wiser. The girl said he looked as he usually did when he returned from out of town, but she had no idea where he went. It seems he has many out-of-town clients whom he visits occasionally, and it would certainly take quite a while to locate them and get the desired information, with the chances ten to one that he went somewhere else altogether, and had nothing to do with the murder after all. The only thing I have against him is that he is clever, and for that matter so I should judge was Richard Trenton."

"You think Dick might have done it?"

"I'm overlooking no one. I saw Jones and got from him all the data concerning Trenton's actions on that night. Also I telegraphed to the Chicago police to try to locate anyone who may have known him there and we should be hearing from that end in a day or two. There is one fact that stands out clearly, and can't be explained away. He left the hotel before eleven and did not return until one. Also there is no trace of where he went during that time since, though he taxied to the hotel, he was clever enough to take the Subway or the surface car to his destination. Then we have the letter he wrote his father, which certainly points to his intention to see Philip Darwin. Whether he did or not, we don't know, but it's quite probable that he did come here, and that the two men had a conference of some sort. Again I'm inclined to believe that he is innocent for the same reason that exonerated the father in my eyes. Yet there is his suicide to account for, and the still stranger fact that he left no word of any kind to explain his act."

He paused, then continued with a shake of the head, "There's not much use bothering with him at present, for he's beyond helping us in our predicament. There are others who may prove more useful."

"What about Lee?" I inquired, remembering the stick-pin and where it had been found.

"Lee Darwin is the most likely suspect that I have," he returned, then quietly busied himself with his dessert, for Mason had entered and was hovering around. "By the way," he added, as we left the dining-room, "I have an appointment with the steward of the Yale Club on this very matter. I went there yesterday but Carpe was away and I left word that I would call at one-thirty to see him. Supposing you drive me over."

"After this visit I'll be able to decide whether our young friend had the chance to commit murder," he continued when we were in the car headed for the Yale Club. "He had plenty of motive."

"Chance, too, McKelvie. Didn't you say yourself that he was there that night when you first showed me his stick-pin?"

"I said he was there and I still say it, but that means nothing at all. We have got to prove that he was there at the psychological moment."

I nodded. "But, even if he had been, I can't see where you find a motive. He quarreled with his uncle, I know, but there was nothing in that to cause him to shoot Darwin."

"Wasn't there?" answered McKelvie. "Surely you don't believe that he really quarreled with his uncle about Mrs. Darwin? It's absurd on the face of it, that he should suddenly object to treatment that he had accepted with utter indifference for five months or so. No, no, I have another theory altogether about that quarrel."

Our arrival at the Club put an end to our discussion. Carpe, the steward, whom I had interviewed the night I first sought McKelvie, came forward as we entered. He was a big, dependable fellow, this steward, and had been in the employ of the Club for years. Moreover, he could be trusted to give correct information about the doings of the various members of the Club, all of whom he knew well.

"Good afternoon," he said pleasantly. "If you will come into the office I shall be glad to accommodate you."

We followed him into a small room at the side of the hall and he invited us to be seated, as he dropped heavily into a chair at his desk, but McKelvie remained standing, and as he put his questions he paced back and forth with his hands clasped behind his back.

"I desire to ask you some questions about Mr. Lee Darwin, Mr. Carpe," he began. "You have heard nothing from him since he left?"

"No, sir, not a word," replied Carpe, slowly.

"Go back to October seventh, Mr. Carpe. Lee Darwin engaged rooms for that night, did he not?" continued McKelvie.

"Yes. He called me personally about noon and said he wanted a suite of rooms for an indefinite time. He came in some time during the afternoon but went out again at five o'clock."

"You are sure of the time?"

"Yes. There was to be a banquet of some kind to which he had been invited. It was just striking five as he came into my office here and told me he could not attend, asking me to make his excuses for him. He said he would not be back until late. It made an impression on me at the time because he was not in evening clothes and I had always known Mr. Lee Darwin for a very fastidious young man."

"Do you know what time he got back?" McKelvie inquired after a pause.

"He didn't come back that night," answered Carpe.

McKelvie and I exchanged glances. "You could swear to that?" asked McKelvie eagerly.

"I could. I sleep on the first floor at the back of the house. About five o'clock in the morning I heard someone knocking on my window and I got up to see who wanted me at such an hour. We don't keep open house at this Club. In the dim light I saw that the man was Mr. Lee Darwin, so I motioned him to the back and opened the door for him myself. It was quite a shock to me to see him, I can tell you. He was pale and wild-eyed and his clothes were rumpled and dusty. He stumbled in and I helped him to his room. He told me to keep quiet about him and naturally I promised. I thought he had been out on a spree of some kind. He acted as if he might have been drinking," explained Carpe ponderously.

"What did he do after you promised silence?" McKelvie took a turn around the room as he put the question.

"He went to bed, and at luncheon time I awakened him. He dressed hurriedly and rushed out without eating and did not return until three. There was a telegram waiting for him. He read it and then tore it up and his hands were trembling as he did so. Then he remarked that he was leaving for the South on business and asked me to leave his rooms undisturbed. He left in ten minutes and that is the last I have seen of him," replied Carpe.

"When he came back the morning of the eighth, were you really positive that he had been drinking, or did he give you another impression as well?" continued McKelvie.

"Well, to be candid, at the time he seemed to me to be scared, as if he had seen something that had terrified him plumb out of his wits. It was afterwards in thinking it over that I decided that he had been out on a lark," responded Carpe, after a moment's consideration.

"I should like to examine his rooms," said McKelvie abruptly.

"Certainly." Carpe rose and led the way up the stairs, along a hall and into a suite consisting of a dressing-room, bedroom, and bath.

The rooms were nicely furnished but were not unusual in any way and gave no indication of having been recently used. Everything was in immaculate order.

"Any of his belongings still around?" queried McKelvie.

"Yes, he left some things in the chiffonier."

McKelvie strode to the article of furniture in question and examined its contents with great care, as if hunting for some definite object. Then with a shrug he announced that he was through. I thought he had been disappointed in his search, but one look into his sparkling eyes told me a different tale. He had been successful, but what had he expected to find?

"Thank you, Mr. Carpe. I'm much obliged to you. Keep my visit a secret, particularly as your information may not be of value to me and might, if gossiped about, merely create an unpleasant situation for the young man," said McKelvie as we returned to the lower floor.

"Just as you say. Good afternoon, Mr. McKelvie," and the door closed behind us.

As we descended the steps I said curiously, "What did you find, McKelvie?"

For answer he pulled from his pocket a small yellow satin sachet bag with the initials L. D. embroidered on it in blue. He placed it in my hand and with the remark, "Take a good whiff. It's a heavenly scent."

I held the dainty bag to my nostrils and inhaled deeply. It was wonderfully, delicately fragrant. I had a distinct recollection of having been recently made conscious that there was in this world such a subtle, elusive perfume, but for the moment I could not place it. Like a melody that haunts by its familiarity even when its name eludes the mind, did this perfume waft across my senses the knowledge that I had breathed in its fragrance before and on two distinct occasions. Then memory awoke and I saw myself drawing back from a blood-stained handkerchief which had been suddenly thrust beneath my nose at Headquarters, and recalled wondering where I had come across that perfume before. Ah, I had it. It was Dick who first introduced me to it. He also had a tiny sachet of yellow satin embroidered in blue and when I noticed it with some astonishment among his things he laughed in an embarrassed way and said a girl he knew had made it for him. When I asked him what it was he named it for me with a shame-faced look.

The subtle perfume that now assailed my nostrils and delighted my senses was none other than the fragrance that scented Dick's belongings, that clung to the Persian silk cover in the secret room, and that had left its trace on that square of cambric that Philip Darwin had been holding, the fragrance of Rose Jacqueminot! And Rose Jacqueminot meant a woman and the only woman I could think of was-Cora Manning.

"What do you make of this, McKelvie?" I asked, returning the sachet.

He shrugged. "May be important and may not. I was more interested in hearing that he had been out all night."

"Which means of course that he had the opportunity," I interpreted.

"Yes, he had the opportunity, but he may not have used it. His stick-pin is no proof that he was there at midnight. There are all sorts of possibilities in a case like this one. However, he did have ample motive, for besides the quarrel there is the will. I examined specimens of Philip Darwin's handwriting. He does not make his capitals with a flourish. He makes his R's straight. So he was disinheriting his nephew and not his wife. Also the criminal knew that fact, or why his attempt to destroy the scraps by burning, which would account, you see, for his still being in the study when Mrs. Darwin entered."

"Somehow I can't believe Lee did it-unless it was on impulse," I said, recalling the young man's noble countenance. "Besides, McKelvie, surely he isn't so depraved as to implicate Ruth!"

"'Can there any good thing come out of Nazareth?'" he quoted. "He has the Darwin blood in his veins."

"So has Dick for that matter," I thought to myself.

"I don't mean to imply by that that he necessarily committed the murder," continued McKelvie. "I merely state that he had plenty of motive and chance. But so did several others, as we know. And even if he is the murderer we have no proof of that fact; nor does there seem to be at present any chance of questioning him. I have a man on his trail, but so far Wilkins has met with no success. He's evidently disguised, since no one recognizes his photograph, which, added to his use of Rose Jacqueminot sachet, looks very bad indeed."

"Why?" I put in.

"Ask me that again later and I may be able to give you a more definite answer," he retorted. "To return to the subject. It may take months to find Lee and we haven't months to waste on this case."

"What do you propose to do then?" I asked despairingly.

"I'm going to let you drive me over to Forty-second Street to see Claude Orton," he responded, entering my car.

CHAPTER XXII

ORTON'S ALIBI

As we drove toward Forty-second Street, I recalled my instinctive distrust of the secretary, his stealthy attitude, and very evident desire to see Ruth convicted. I had suspected him that very first night, and now I envisioned him sneaking through the secret entrance and returning to the house in time to follow me into the study.

"I know what you are thinking, but he couldn't possibly have done it," said McKelvie quietly. "He's the only one I don't suspect. He hasn't the nerve in the first place, and in the second place he hadn't the time. How long do you suppose it takes to lock all those doors-they were locked, remember-and return to the house and lock whatever entrance he used-not the front door, for you would have heard him-and enter the study a second after yourself?"

"He may never have gone out," I cried. "He could easily have stayed in the room all the time in a dark corner and have come forward when he turned on the lights. I swear I never heard him!"

"What about Mrs. Darwin's testimony that he was in the hall?" he asked.

"She may have been mistaken. He gave false evidence concerning her."

"That's what we are going to see him about. But, remember this, Mrs. Darwin would have no reason for saying she saw him if she did not."

To this last statement I had to agree, for Ruth I knew disliked Orton, and would hardly be likely to shield him. So I ceased discussing the point, knowing we would soon have the truth, for McKelvie could extract information from a stone.

In due course we drew up before a second-rate apartment hotel that was sadly in need of a coat of paint. We entered a dingy hall and inquired for Orton.

"Suite Four, third door to your left," droned the switchboard girl.

We walked down the hall, which would have been decidedly improved by an application of a mop and some soap and water, and knocked at Orton's apartment. As we waited we heard the sound of a door closing, and then the shuffle of feet and presently the door opened a crack and Orton's near-sighted eyes peered at us from the aperture.

"What do you want?" he asked impatiently.

"A moment's conversation," replied McKelvie, but at that minute Orton recognized me and, swiftly retreating, began to close the door.

McKelvie, however, was prepared for him and the closing door met an obstruction in the shape of the toe of McKelvie's boot.

"There is no use trying to keep me out," he continued sternly, "unless of course you would like to tell your story to the police."

At mention of the police Orton retreated still farther, and we followed him into the apartment, closing the door behind us. We found ourselves in a stuffy, gloomy little parlor filled with a lot of ugly, old-fashioned furniture. Orton, who was clad in dressing-gown and slippers, ungraciously asked us to be seated, but before we could state our errand a quavering voice from somewhere in the rear reached us.

"What is it, Claude? Who is in there with you?" it said.

"You have frightened my mother," said Orton, plucking at the cord of his wrapper, as if undecided whether to go or stay.

"Tell her it's all right and that you know who we are," commanded McKelvie. "And without leaving this room," as Orton started to move away. "I guess she can hear you from here."

Sullenly, Orton obeyed, and then seating himself on the sofa, demanded what we wanted.

"At the inquest you gave several bits of information which had no foundation in fact," began McKelvie, going straight to the point. "You lied and you know it. For that matter so do I. Now I want to know why?"

"Mr. Davies, of course I know," answered Orton with a sneer. "But what right have you to question me?"

"I am investigating the case for Mr. Davies on the quiet," answered McKelvie suavely.

"And that gives you the right to intrude on my privacy, I suppose?" continued Orton sarcastically (he had abandoned his rôle of "humble still," or rather he was Uriah Heep grown bold through triumph), "and to force yourself into my rooms?"

McKelvie shrugged. "Really if you would rather be put through the third degree at Police Headquarters it's a matter of indifference to me."

Orton's pallid face became livid. "Are you trying to frighten me by pretending that you believe that I killed Philip Darwin?" he cried, but his voice trembled in spite of himself.

"No, I'm not pretending any such thing. I know you didn't kill him. You're too much of a coward," returned McKelvie contemptuously, whereat Orton gave a gasping sigh of relief. "But I do say you know more of this murder than you gave out, and a hint to that effect in the ear of Jones will be quite sufficient to bring the police to this place. No doubt you have a telephone that I can use. I'll give you five minutes to decide."

But Orton didn't need five minutes, no, nor even ten seconds. McKelvie had hardly finished speaking when Orton flung himself forward with clasped hands, his prominent eyes fairly popping with terror.

"I'll tell you everything, anything, though I declare I know nothing. Only don't send the police here," he pleaded in a frightened voice.

I was amazed at his abject fear but McKelvie motioned him back, and said coldly: "Very well, but don't lie to me, for I know why you fear the police." He leaned closer and whispered a word that I did not catch, but which had the effect of making Orton wring his hands helplessly, and whine that he never intended to lie, and would tell us everything we wanted to know.

McKelvie silenced him with a gesture, as he said: "I want an account, a true one, of everything that you did and said and saw on the night of October the seventh between ten-thirty, when you summoned Mrs. Darwin to the study and midnight, when the shot rang out."

"I wanted to tell what Mr. Darwin had said and they wouldn't let me at the inquest," put in Orton, aggrieved.

"You're not dealing with the police now, and I want every word that has any bearing on the case, whatever its purport."

"Very well. At ten-thirty I told Mrs. Darwin that her husband wanted her and then I listened at the door. They were quarrelling about the love letter I had put together for him."

"When did you show him this letter?" interrupted McKelvie.

"In the morning after Lee left the study. Mr. Darwin told me to patch it together because he said it would come in handy some day. It did—that night," and he leered at me in a very unpleasant way.

"Go on," said McKelvie peremptorily.

"I couldn't hear what they said ——"

"Then how did you know that they were quarrelling about the letter?" I asked.

"I was going to say," Orton ignored me completely, "that I couldn't hear the words exchanged until I opened the door a crack. Then I heard very well, indeed. Mr. Darwin was threatening Mr. Davies, and Mrs. Darwin retorted that she would send for him and warn him, but he only laughed in a queer way and then I saw her coming, so I retreated. After that he called me in and told me to watch her. I crept upstairs and heard her orders to the maid, whom I followed to the garage. Then I came back and hung around the hall. Mr. Darwin had told me he was expecting a visitor, so when I came back I applied my ear to the door. I could hear voices, his and a strange one, but not what they said, though they spoke loudly as if in anger."

"Why didn't you open the door a crack?" I inquired sarcastically.

"Because I was too clever. Mr. Darwin had locked the door when I went out and I knew it was still locked. Besides at ten-thirty only the lamp was lighted and the region of the door was in comparative darkness, but at this particular time I could tell by applying my eye to the key-hole that the other lights had been turned on as well. So even if I could have opened the door I should still have been afraid of being seen."

"Never mind that. Go on with what's important," broke in McKelvie, impatiently.

"At eleven-twenty-five Mr. Davies arrived, and at eleven-thirty Mr. Darwin called me."

"How?"

"There's a bell connection between the study and my workroom. When I went in Mr. Darwin had resumed his seat at the table and looked pretty much as he did when we saw him later, except he was alive."

"A good deal of difference, I should judge," I thought to myself, "between a corpse and a well man. However, that's neither here nor there."

"He had just finished writing the name, Cora Manning, on his new will, for the ink was not yet dry when I reached the table. I told him all that had taken place. It was then he laughed and said: 'So we've a broker in the house, eh? He should know how to play fast and loose, eh? I'll make him useful, this broker lover of our stainless Ruth.'"

Orton mouthed the words with devilish delight and I had all I could do to keep my hands off of him. But McKelvie paid no heed to our feelings.

"Go on, man," he said with growing impatience. "Don't repeat what I know already."

"You said that you wanted to hear everything that was spoken," grumbled Orton.

"Yes, so I did. Only hustle along and get it out. Was that all he said?" demanded McKelvie.

"No. He said something else. I remarked that a broker ought to know how to play fast and loose, and he replied: 'Yes, and other things, too, eh? Mr. Davies doesn't know it yet, but he has done me the very greatest service by coming here to-night. See that the windows are properly locked and then go to bed.' As I locked the windows I could hear him laughing to himself, and he was still laughing when I closed the door behind me."

"What did you think he meant to convey by those words of his?" asked McKelvie.

"I thought he might be referring to the fact that now he had good grounds for divorce. I believe he was tired of Mrs. Darwin," replied Orton.

"You are sure that Mr. Darwin was alone at eleven-thirty?" continued McKelvie, after a slight pause.

"Yes, absolutely alone," responded Orton. "There was no place where anyone could hide. I examined the window hangings as I locked up."

"What about the safe?"

"It was partly open and I looked in as I passed. It was empty."

"Humph. Now I'd have sworn —" murmured McKelvie.

"What?" asked Orton inquisitively.

"Nothing. What's the rest of your story?" retorted McKelvie.

"I didn't go to bed. I wanted to see what would happen, for I was sure from the way he spoke that Mr. Darwin meant to call Mr. Davies into the study later on, so I continued to work in the little room until I grew weary and thirsty, and going out in the hall found that it was about ten minutes to twelve. Still nothing had happened, for I could hear the murmur of voices in the drawing-room."

He didn't have to tell us how he knew. We could guess. Ruth was right in saying that he was always spying upon her.

"I knew," he continued, "that Mr. Darwin kept a good brand of whisky, private stock of course, in a cabinet in the dining-room, and I determined to mix myself a drink. But just then I heard the key turned in the study door and thinking Mr. Darwin was coming out, I went back to my room and closed the door. I waited some time, maybe five minutes or more, and then looked out. No one was around and both drawing-room and study doors were closed. I decided I had missed the show, since there was no sound from either room, and I determined to have my drink before I went upstairs. I went in to the dining-room and had my hand on the cabinet key when the shot rang out. I hurried to the study and saw Mr. Davies in the doorway, Mrs. Darwin holding the pistol, and Mr. Darwin dead."

"You didn't see Mrs. Darwin go into the study?" questioned McKelvie.

"No, but I judged she had gone in when I heard the study door unlock. You see, I did not know what might happen, especially when Mr. Davies said I had no proof that I wasn't in the study also, so I decided to have an alibi for the police. That's why I said I was on the stairs because then they would not know where I had really been. I didn't know that Mrs. Darwin had seen me."

"A good thing for you that she did see you," returned McKelvie grimly, "or you might be occupying that cell in her place."

Orton blanched like the coward that he was. "But-but, I'm innocent," he said, indignantly.

"Well, you wouldn't be the first innocent person to grace a cell, I assure you," retorted McKelvie dryly. "You have told us everything?"

"Yes, everything."

"Very well, then you can answer several questions. You are positive you heard the key turned in the study door when you stood in the hall at ten minutes to twelve?" continued McKelvie. "Remember I want facts, and not impressions."

"I am as positive as that I am sitting here. But it was more toward five minutes to twelve because I paused to ascertain if Mrs. Darwin was still in the drawing-room and I listened for a minute or two before I started for the dining-room," replied Orton with conviction.

"A minute is a good long while, longer than you think, Orton," returned McKelvie. "But that point is, after all, immaterial. We will say that somewhere between ten and five minutes to twelve the study door was unlocked from the inside," and he looked at me significantly.

If he was right in his premise, then the person who unlocked that door could have been none other than the criminal, for at ten minutes before midnight Philip Darwin was past unlocking doors! Yet it seemed a foolhardy thing to do, for any one then could have entered and discovered him. But, no, after all, it was the sensible thing to do from his point of view, since otherwise the prospective suspect would have been unable to enter the room. Then I looked at McKelvie with dawning horror in my eyes. The unlocking of that door could have meant only one thing, that the criminal knew Ruth was across the hall, and deliberately, cold-bloodedly, planned to saddle her with the murder of her husband!

"Why, McKelvie," I began, horrified, but he tread on my toe as if by accident, and I recalled hastily that we were not alone.

"Even if I had not heard Mr. Darwin unlock the door," continued Orton ingratiatingly, "he must have unlocked it at some time, for I heard him turn the key in the lock when I left him at eleven-thirty and the door was open when Mrs. Darwin entered the room. But, I know I'm not mistaken in saying that I heard it unlocked."

"How do you know that it was Mr. Darwin who unlocked it?" I asked injudiciously.

McKelvie frowned, but Orton answered without apparent suspicion, "He was alone in a closed room. Who else could have opened it, Mr. Davies?"

"No one, of course," I lied cheerfully, and subsided into the background, not wishing to give Orton any further inkling of what we knew.

"When you came out into the hall the second time, you said that you heard no sound from either room. Did you open the study door even a crack that time by any chance?" resumed McKelvie.

"No. Again I feared to be seen. You see that all the lights in the room had been turned on," replied Orton.

CHAPTER XXIII

GRAMERCY PARK

Even McKelvie was taken aback by this statement, more so than I was, I could see, because he was firmly convinced that the criminal waited for Ruth in a darkened room. I stole a glance at Orton to see whether he was triumphing over us, but he was sitting in the same dejected attitude and did not act at all as though he had made a remarkable declaration. Yet if he spoke the truth, he sent our theories tumbling about our ears like a house of cards from which one of the foundation units had been suddenly removed. If the study was lighted at that time, then Ruth must have seen the criminal, yet she had said she was shielding no one and I believed her. What paradox was this, then? Even McKelvie was puzzled.

"I wish I were sure you are speaking the truth," he muttered, looking at Orton in a reflective way.

"It is the truth. Why should I make it up? I applied my eye to the key-hole to make doubly sure, even when I saw the light shining beneath the doorsill," said Orton, and there was no mistaking his sincerity and genuine surprise that McKelvie should doubt him.

"You did not chance to see anyone when you applied your eye to the key-hole?" went on McKelvie, putting aside his conjectures.

"No, I saw no one."

"You are acquainted with the details of Mr. Darwin's business, are you not?" McKelvie remarked, abruptly changing the subject.

"Yes, I'm conversant with a good deal of it," responded Orton.

"Is it true that he removed his securities from Cunningham's office and used them to speculate with?" continued McKelvie.

"I suppose so since the lawyer says it. I myself never even knew he had those securities. I attended strictly to his business in connection with the bank, answering letters, arranging committee meetings, taking notes of any agreements the directors came to, and so on. He speculated with his own private funds, and advised his brokers himself, so I know nothing beyond the fact that his transactions were large," answered Orton.

"You didn't hear any rumors that he was speculating in M. and R. stock, for instance?"

"Well, yes, he told me himself that he was going to take a chance on it," replied Orton after a slight hesitation.

"He didn't happen to mention that he was ruined, did he, on the afternoon of the seventh?" insisted McKelvie.

"Ruined!" Orton's eyes fairly popped with amazement. "No, I had no idea it was as bad as that."

"What do you mean?" asked McKelvie quickly.

"I was watching that stock go down, and when he came into the office that afternoon I asked him casually if he had invested. He said, 'Yes, heavily,' in a dull kind of voice, but I thought nothing more about it, because he was always pessimistic whenever he speculated and I also knew he was too cautious to put up more than he could afford. I can't believe he could have invested his whole fortune," and Orton shook his head with a shrewd glance at us.

"Rumors are apt to exaggerate," responded McKelvie lightly. "By the way, how much was his whole fortune?"

"I don't really know, but I believe he got quite a bit when he married Mrs. Darwin. At least I gathered as much from something she said to him one day when he had been particularly mean to her," explained Orton.

"Do you recall the exact words?" asked McKelvie, ignoring my frown.

"Not the exact words, but the sense of them," answered Orton with a smile. "She wanted to know if he hadn't humiliated her enough when he forced her to sign over to him her fortune,

89

thus leaving her dependent upon him, and he replied with a sneer, 'That's all I married you for, my dear.'"

At that moment I rejoiced in the murder, and should have thought no ill of her if Ruth herself had done it. It was not murder but the justifiable removal of a venomous snake. I was beginning to regret I had not done it myself six months before when it first occurred to me as the only solution to our trouble.

"I think that is all then. Say nothing about our having been here, and I'll do the same with regard to your affairs. By the way, at the trial you may use the alibi you gave the police. You might find it awkward explaining why you lied to them." McKelvie rose as he spoke, and walked toward the door.

"You're not joking? I can give the same evidence I gave before?" gasped Orton incredulously.

"Yes, only take care not to trip yourself up under cross-examination, though I doubt if there is much danger from Mr. Vaughn. Why on earth did you pick that old fossil to defend her?" he continued, as we re-entered my car. "The prosecution will put it all over him from the start."

"I went to him because he was the only one I could think of at the moment, but he will not defend her himself, McKelvie. He will employ other counsel. Though I can't see that it matters much what kind of counsel we have or if we have any at all, for the prosecution has the facts while we have-mere theories," I returned gloomily.

"You're right. We have only theories and for a moment mine got a mortal blow when Orton said the study was lighted, for as near as I can figure that must have been just before Mrs. Darwin went in. Lord, if Grenville knew that fact he'd laugh in your face when you testify, as I presume you will, that the study was in darkness. Yes, and how much store would the jury set by Mrs. Darwin's account then?"

"Is that the reason you told Orton to repeat his evidence?" I asked.

"Naturally. I'm not giving my opponents any more points in their favor. The game is unequal enough as it is," he replied, drawing his brows together in an effort to reconcile the various facts in the case.

"But, Orton may give us away," I said presently. "He may become frightened when he has to testify under oath."

"He's looking out for A No. 1 and he's an adept liar, to boot. Besides, he'd say nothing to make me reveal what I know about him," retorted McKelvie, coming out of his abstraction.

"What do you know about him?" I asked curiously.

"Only that he's mixed up in some boot-legging scheme. Not much of a hold, you think? Perhaps not, where a fearless man was concerned, but Claude Orton is the greatest coward I have met in many a day. The very word police is enough to scare him out of his wits, but he isn't worth a moment's thought. I wanted to frighten him badly enough to get at the truth and it netted us nothing in the end," he added, shifting impatiently in his seat.

I laughed sardonically. "You forget. It netted us a lighted room," I remarked.

McKelvie turned toward me with a look of deep concern in his eyes. "Tell me," he said, "do you believe it was cleverness or sheer bravado that made the criminal light the study with the door unlocked? Give me your opinion."

"How should I know?" I retorted glumly. "It's my opinion he was liable to do anything."

"He could hardly be cognizant of the fact that Orton was prowling around, and he could easily turn off the lights when he heard footsteps crossing the hall. That's doubtless just what he did, which would imply that he was somewhere near the door. What a pity Orton caught no glimpse of him! He would hardly leave Mrs. Darwin's entrance to chance. He'd want to know when she was coming, for he couldn't be certain of the time she would choose to enter, no, not if he were twice as clever." McKelvie was thinking aloud, his brows knit once more, but I did not hesitate to interrupt him. There was no Jenkins present to preserve the flow of his thoughts undisturbed.

"You seem to believe, or rather I should say, you seem absolutely convinced that the criminal knew that Ruth would come to the study. The same conviction, with all its attendant horror, flashed over me a while ago when you were questioning Orton. But, upon my honor, now I review the thing calmly, I can't figure on what you base your conclusion. Ruth had no more idea of going into that study than I had, until I suggested it to her on the spur of the moment. That's the truth. How are you going to get around it?" I said emphatically.

He pulled a briar pipe from his pocket and lighted it before he answered. "That's easy. The criminal was in the room when Orton came in at eleven-thirty. Probably he was hiding in the safe in the secret room——"

"I thought you deduced that the criminal knew nothing of the secret entrance until he forced the knowledge from Darwin just before he killed him," I pointed out.

"I said he did not enter that way, not that he had no knowledge of it. Orton said that Darwin and his visitor were quarreling. Darwin knew his secretary and divined that he'd be hanging around the door listening. So he called him in and got rid of him, in the meantime hiding his visitor in the safe, from which point of vantage he heard the conversation between Orton and Darwin. Am I correct so far?" he inquired.

"Sounds plausible enough," I replied.

"Knowing human nature (I make this deduction because throughout he has most certainly traded on his knowledge of human beings in general, and the police in particular), he put himself in your place. What would he do if he were in love with Mrs. Darwin and had learned of the existence of the letter. Why, naturally urge Mrs. Darwin to try to secure the incriminating evidence. So you see he was pretty sure she would come, but he did not know when. He couldn't possibly know when, could he?" he asked appealingly.

"No, I don't at this moment see how he could, unless he was a magician, which isn't likely. I think myself we are on the wrong tack altogether. We are trying to complicate a simple affair. The criminal, no doubt, came in at midnight and shot Darwin without knowing that Ruth was there. Then he went off again through the secret entrance, and Ruth was implicated by pure chance, for, after all, there is only one pistol, there was only one shot heard, and only one bullet found," was my contribution.

"All I can say to that, Mr. Davies, is that in that case the murderer must have been a magician after all, for surely you are not implying that Mrs. Darwin lied when she said the study was dark?" he remarked with a smile, blowing wreaths of smoke along Broadway, for we were driving slowly toward town.

I groaned. I had forgotten the problem of the shot in the dark. Assuredly it was a poser, for the feat was well-nigh impossible, unless we explained it by assuming a previous shot, which would have been all to the good if McKelvie could only have found the lost bullet.

"You have reverted to the theory that the crime was one of impulse," continued McKelvie. "Disabuse your mind of any such idea. That murder was premeditated. It was done in cold-blood, and planned down to the smallest detail, days before it occurred. And so very carefully was it planned that the criminal was able to work Mrs. Darwin into the scheme, without in the least disturbing his previous calculations. That is why we are stumped for the present, because I have not yet been able to put my finger on the weak spot in the link. There is bound to be a weak spot, there always is no matter how clever the criminal, but it may take longer than the time at our disposal before the trial. I shall have to pick up a new trail, since Orton had nothing of value to give us," McKelvie ended, knocking the ashes from his pipe. "Speed her up a little, Mr. Davies."

"What new trail?" I asked, obeying mechanically.

"The woman in the case," he said impressively.

"The woman in the case? You mean-Cora Manning?" I inquired.

"Yes. You know the old French saying, 'Cherchez la femme.' I have done my best to keep my promise to Mrs. Darwin to let Miss Manning out of it, but now it is a matter of necessity. I firmly believe she was in Darwin's study that night, somewhere between eleven-thirty and midnight," he answered.

"But, heavens, man, how did she get in?" I cried.

"She lodges, or did, at Gramercy Park. Drive me over there. She should be back by now and if she should prove to be the woman in the case, we'll make her talk. It ought not to take more than an hour at most, and if I am wrong, why we shall be no worse off than we are now."

I gave my car more gas and continued down Broadway, intending to cut across Twenty-first Street to Gramercy Park, remarking as I did so, "You haven't told me how she effected an entrance into that closed room."

"She must have entered by the secret entrance," he replied. "Eliminate the impossible, you know."

"That's all very fine, but it plays ducks and drakes with your previous reasoning, for how did she obtain a knowledge of those three all-important facts about the entrance that you said even the criminal could not divine?" I inquired.

"When we meet the fair Cora you can ask her to explain the facts for you, Mr. Davies. I confess that I cannot," he said a little wearily. "It isn't good to jump at conclusions and I make it a rule not to say anything which cannot be proved to have foundation in fact. Now I do not know how she got there, but I do believe she was present in the study. Until we make that a fact also, we will not discuss it."

Annoyed at his tone I remained silent, but my eyes betrayed me as I turned in his direction for a moment and he read curiosity in their depths. He smiled and clapped me on the shoulder. "I'm an old crank. You shouldn't mind my talk," he said. "I guess you have as good a right as anyone to all the knowledge that can be gleaned in this business. I owe my information to friend Jones. The blood-stained handkerchief is Cora Manning's, I'm pretty sure, though the police are positive it belongs to Mrs. Darwin. Perhaps you recall that I gave you an involuntary but generous whiff of it that day. Did you recognize the perfume?"

"Not at the time. I have since placed it as Rose Jacqueminot," I replied.

"That's right. It was very faint, but unmistakable. Now, I smelled the other handkerchief also. It was scented with violet. You see, I have made quite a study of perfumes and the different scents are as distinct from each other as different brands of cigars or cigarettes. A refined woman who has any taste at all chooses the perfume best suited to her personality, and sticks to it. She doesn't use one kind one week, a different kind the next. We will go over Cora Manning's room. If we find even the faintest trace of Rose Jacqueminot we will know without a doubt that the handkerchief is hers."

By this time we had reached Gramercy Park, and running up the steps of what was once a fashionable residence, we rang the bell. After an appreciable interval we heard a shuffle of feet in the hall, and a thin, emaciated-looking chap opened the door.

"Is Miss Manning in?" inquired McKelvie.

"I don't know," said the man, dubiously. "If you'll take a seat in the parlor I'll call Mrs. Harmon."

We did as he requested and entered a gloomy room in which all the shades had been lowered, and as McKelvie moved restlessly around I seated myself upon a very uncomfortable horsehair sofa.

"No wonder yonder fellow is pale and thin," I thought, then I rose hastily, more in astonishment than true courtesy, if the truth must be told, for coming through the narrow doorway was the very largest woman I had ever seen outside of a freak show, and when I say large, I don't mean that she was tall. She was hardly more than middle height, but so ample of girth that I expected to see her stick midway between the door-posts, and pictured McKelvie and myself frantically endeavoring to extricate her by hauling mightily upon her short, fat arms. But she was evidently accustomed to this particular doorway, for with a sidewise shift she entered composedly enough.

"I'm Mrs. Harmon," she said affably. "What can I do for you?"

"I wish to see Miss Manning," returned McKelvie.

"Miss Manning has been away since the seventh of October," she replied quietly.

A shade of disappointment crossed McKelvie's face. "You know where she has gone?"

"No, sir. I don't. I thought she had gone to see some relatives, perhaps."

"Please be seated, Mrs. Harmon. I should like to ask a few questions." She looked at him in evident astonishment, and he hastened to add, "I'm investigating the Darwin murder and any information you can give me will be appreciated."

"Land sakes, you don't mean to tell me, young man, that you think she did it?" she said indignantly.

"Oh, no, but her name was on the will and I wanted to trace the connection, that is all," he replied suavely.

"There was a young man here not so very many days ago who talked like that. I told him all I knew and he went and printed it in the paper. If that's the kind you are I shan't say one word," she retorted, her fat face flushing at the trick played upon her.

"We are not reporters, if that is what you mean," returned McKelvie soothingly.

Under the spell of his voice she heaved an enormous sigh of relief and lowered herself into a very wide arm-chair.

"You said that on the night of the seventh of October, Miss Manning went away from here?" McKelvie began.

"Yes, she left somewhere around eleven o'clock."

"On foot or in a taxi?"

"She went on foot and I watched her cross Gramercy Park and go toward the Subway," said Mrs. Harmon.

"Didn't you think it peculiar that she should leave suddenly at that time of night without leaving her address behind?" he continued.

The woman rocked back and forth several times before she answered. "Well, no. You see I didn't tell that other young man so, because he didn't ask me, and besides I didn't like his looks. But I guess you're all right. You have an honest face. I know pretty well why she wanted to go away. I would have gone, too, in her place, poor girl.

"It all comes of taking up with these idle rich young men who have more money than brains, say I," she went on with a self-righteous toss of her head. I smiled. I couldn't imagine any young man, rich or poor, taking a fancy to Mrs. Harmon. I wondered what kind of man Mr. Harmon had been, but then she may have been slimmer when he first met and married her. "I told Miss Manning she was doing a foolish thing, but she wouldn't listen and engaged herself to a young chap named Lee Darwin," the good lady continued. "I hadn't anything against the young man, he seemed a nice boy, but after a while another man took to coming around. He was older and wore a beard and eyeglasses. I didn't like him and told her there would be trouble, but she thought she knew best, and so there was trouble." Mrs. Harmon closed her lips on the words complacently.

"The morning of the seventh, Lee Darwin came here looking like a madman, and they had some kind of a quarrel in this very room. I don't know what it was about, but I heard him telling her that he was through with the likes of her, and then he bounced out again. Well, she acted kind of dazed for a while and then she made an appointment on the phone. When she came back from her lessons he just mooned around, and at ten-thirty that night she packed her bag and said she was going on a long journey, and if anyone inquired where she was, to say I didn't know. But she wouldn't tell me where she was going, and I figured she had decided to hide away till she got over her hurt."

"Yes, I guess you're right," said McKelvie. "And now one more request. I should like to see her room."

Mrs. Harmon eyed him suspiciously, but he gave her his best smile, which would have melted a harder heart than hers, and hoisting herself to her feet she led the way up the stairs to Cora Manning's room.

It was a small room but nicely furnished and very dainty, as befitted the bedroom of a refined young woman, but McKelvie hardly looked at it. He opened a handkerchief box on the dresser and when Mrs. Harmon had her back turned he slipped something into his pocket.

"Thank you, Mrs. Harmon, you have been most kind," he said, as we left the room.

"Not at all. I guess you can find your way out. It's kind of hard for me, climbing stairs so much. Give the door a bang and it'll lock itself," she returned, and we followed directions while she watched our departure from the head of the stairs.

"Well?" I said, as we descended the steps.

"It's hers. Look!" He removed from his pocket the article he had taken from Cora Manning's room and held it out on his palm. It was a tiny yellow satin sachet bag embroidered in blue!

"This is getting ridiculous," I said, as we took our places in the car. "How many more of these blooming things are we likely to run across anyway? That's the third one I've seen."

"Third? I have knowledge of only two, this one and Lee's, and it's not difficult to conjecture where he got his," McKelvie said, with raised brows, as he repocketed the bag.

I told him of my discovery that Dick possessed one of these sachets also, adding, "It's identical with this one. Do you suppose she gave it to him?"

"Richard Trenton," he mused, glancing at his watch. "We'll just have time before dinner. Take me up to Riverside Drive, if you will be so kind. I want another look at that secret room."

I turned my car, and drove as swiftly as I dared along Broadway, asking him, "Do you think that Cora Manning is in hiding because of that quarrel?"

He did not answer until we were skimming along the Drive. "No," he said quietly then, "I don't think so."

"Do you believe she killed Darwin?" I persisted.

"No, I don't. It was not a woman's job, but I do believe she can prove for us when he died," he answered. "And through her I hope to locate the criminal."

"If she is the woman in the case, she must be shielding the man or she would have come forward long ago to free Ruth," I pointed out.

"Or he may be holding her a prisoner because she knows too much for his peace of mind and body," he retorted. "That puts a different complexion on it."

"In that case he will murder her, too, before we can reach her," I said in a horrified voice.

"A man kills the woman he loves for only one reason, which does not exist in this case," he replied.

"Good heavens!" I said. "The criminal in love with Cora Manning! Then you mean that Lee killed his uncle?"

McKelvie shrugged. "That I can't presume to say. Perhaps it's Lee-perhaps it's another. Remember this. If Richard Trenton knew her, ten to one he was in love with her, too. I have seen her picture."

Which statement, since I was a man, only increased my eagerness to see the fair Cora.

CHAPTER XXIV

THE SIGNET RING

At McKelvie's request I parked my car a block from the house and we traversed that distance in silence, entering the grounds as though we had come on no good errand. When we reached the house McKelvie piloted me to the back and rang the servants' bell. It was late, after six, and growing dark so that Mason was hardly to be blamed if he failed to recognize us, especially as he did not expect to see us again so soon.

"It's Mr. Davies, Mason," said McKelvie. "Will you let us in to the main wing through the passageway, please?"

"Yes, sir," returned Mason. "This way, sir, if you please."

He led us through the passageway and opened the door into the main wing, going ahead of us to switch on the light in the hall.

"That is all. Leave the door open into the passageway. We shall probably depart the way we entered."

"Very good, sir."

McKelvie waited until the old man had shuffled away before he approached the study door. It was little more than six hours since we had been in that room, yet it seemed more like a week to me, so many things had cropped up in the interval, and I waited impatiently for McKelvie to turn the knob of the door.

"I thought I heard someone in there," he whispered, and flung open the door.

For one swift instant I had the impression of a glaring eye that winked and faded as I looked, then only darkness confronted us, darkness and a brooding stillness in which I could hear my very heart-beats.

McKelvie stepped into the room and found the switch, then as the study was flooded with light, he turned and sped toward the safe with me at his heels.

"The windows," he said tersely, as he spun the dial. "See if anyone is hiding behind those curtains."

I hurried to the windows and swept back the hangings. There was no one there, and I turned back to the safe just as McKelvie stood up and swung open the door.

"Come on," he said, thrusting his skeleton key into the inner door. "Don't forget to stoop and be careful to make no noise."

I followed him as he lighted his flash, and passed quickly through the secret room to the door at the head of the stairs. Unlocking this he motioned me to keep near him, and together we crept down the stone staircase and out into the night. We listened a moment, but the only thing we heard was the wind in the trees, which seemed to mock us shrilly as we peered into the dusk beyond.

"Come on back," said McKelvie quietly. "We have work to do yonder," and he nodded toward the entrance.

Wonderingly I obeyed him but asked no questions as he relocked the door and led the way back to the secret room. Here he paused to turn on the light and then lifting the divan aside with my help, he knelt and felt the wall against which it had been placed.

"What is it?" I whispered. His haste and mysterious actions made me feel somehow that to speak aloud would be to commit an unpardonable offense.

He raised his head as though listening to sounds from without, then he sprang to his feet.

"The divan, quick, and no noise," he whispered.

I stooped to help him and as we lifted the divan to its place the fringe of the cover caught in my cuff-link. I tried to untangle it, but McKelvie had no time for such niceties. He wrenched the fringe free, leaving a strand in my link, and as he did so something fell to the floor and rolled along the carpet. He pounced upon the object, then suddenly turned and switched off

95

the light. By the aid of his flash he crept to the rear door, and I distinctly heard the sound of steps on those stairs as McKelvie unlocked the door.

With a sudden movement he pulled the door open and flashed his light on the stairs. Again there was nothing but darkness and brooding stillness, and I could see that the door at the bottom was tightly closed.

"Well, I'll be hanged," muttered McKelvie. "I must be hearing things. Let's get back to the study."

We returned to the brightly lighted room and McKelvie locked up behind him with scrupulous care. Then he went over to the table and seated himself at its head in the chair in which Darwin had been found, and motioned me to take the place beside him.

"Funny thing," he said presently. "I could have sworn there was someone in this room when we first entered. I'm positive I saw this lamp go out."

"Was that it?" I answered. "It looked like an eye to me, a great glaring eye that faded as I gazed."

"You saw it too, then? I'm glad of that," he returned. "I was beginning to think I was the victim of hallucination. No, it was the lamp, which means someone was in that safe. However, he had the start of us, and there is not much use in trying to catch him at present."

"Who was it?" I asked eagerly. "Do you suspect?"

He made no answer but took from his pocket the object which had fallen from the divan. It was a heavy gold ring, evidently a man's. He looked at it critically and then held it out to me.

"Do you know whose it is?" he asked low.

Before I could take it from him he hastily slipped it back into his pocket and leaning closer, said in my ear, "Don't make a sound, but look at the safe door. Then turn back and listen to me as though nothing were amiss."

I was sitting around the corner from the head of the table with my chair turned slightly in McKelvie's direction so that my back was partly toward the safe. At his words I turned and looked at the safe door, expecting I know not what, and to my amazement I saw that the knob of the dial was turning silently and apparently of itself!

There was only one explanation. Someone was opening the door of the safe from the inside, somebody who knew the combination which McKelvie had used! And yet how could anyone have cognizance of the six letters McKelvie had picked out to close the safe. For this was no attempt such as Jenkins had made, no adept manipulation, since the dial was turning with precision, as though the hand that twirled it knew exactly how to spin it.

McKelvie's foot on mine recalled the remainder of his injunction, and turning back, I held out my hand for the ring. His lips formed the word, "No," and his eyes directed me to what he held in his hand. It was Lee Darwin's stick-pin.

"I thought there was someone in the room when we entered," he said in a clear voice, "but since you say you did not see the light, why I must have been mistaken. The case is getting on my nerves, and nerves are queer things when they begin to jump. I've been working too hard, and it's time I took a vacation."

He paused, and I had an uncomfortable feeling that whoever was in the safe had succeeded in opening it and was gazing at us from behind the shelter of the door. I shuddered as I realized the intensity of those unseen eyes which held me riveted to my chair. I longed to turn around and look and so break the spell, but McKelvie's glance on mine forbade it.

"I'm convinced that Lee killed his uncle," he continued. "The stick-pin proves his presence, and doubtless he had knowledge of the entrance. There is nothing more to be learned from this study. My work from now on must be conducted outside. As I said, I've got a man in the South and until he picks up Lee's trail there is nothing more to be done."

He stood up and put the pin away. "I'm dog tired. We've had a strenuous day. Take me home, Mr. Davies. I've earned a few days' rest."

Disappointedly I looked up at him. He spoke very convincingly and he did look tired, but somehow I had hoped that the ring had opened up a new line of inquiry for the morrow. Inaction was hateful to me while Ruth remained a prisoner. I wanted to be up and doing, even if it was only following a false scent.

"Come on, Mr. Davies. It's long past dinner time," he said impatiently.

"All right," I said reluctantly, rising and glancing casually at the safe as I did so. To my surprise the door was closed and had the appearance of never having been touched. Was I too beginning to have hallucinations?

A warning pressure as McKelvie took my arm made me mask whatever astonishment I felt, and also made me hasten with him from the room without a backward glance. When we were in the hall I opened my mouth to question him, but he shook his head and hurried me along to the door leading into the servants' wing.

"Wait here a moment," he said, indicating the passageway. "I'll be back in a second. Keep the door closed."

He disappeared down a side hall and I stepped into the passageway and closed the door, wondering what it was all about, and particularly who the man was who had evaded us to-night, if it was a man and not a freak of my imagination. Still, McKelvie had heard him, too, and it was hardly likely that both of us were dreaming.

"Come, we'll have to hurry," said McKelvie, returning suddenly.

In silence we let ourselves out the back door and crept through the grounds to the gate. In another minute we had gained the corner and my car.

As I drove toward town I remarked, "Was there really someone in that safe, McKelvie?"

"Certainly. I thought I was mistaken at first, but he came back again, as you observed. I thought you looked uneasy while I was talking," he said laughing.

I reddened. "It wasn't very pleasant to feel his eyes on me and be forbidden to see who it was. You were facing the safe. You saw him?" I questioned.

"No, I didn't see him. He was too clever to risk that. He knew we were there, and he came to find out how much progress we had made toward putting him behind the bars where he belongs," retorted McKelvie grimly.

"You don't mean to tell me that it was the criminal himself who had the nerve to come there to-night?" I said.

"It must have been, for who else has a key to those doors? Remember that he took Darwin's key, and mine is the only other one that will open those locks. Also he would be too clever to take anyone else into his confidence," he replied.

"How did he know the combination that you used?" I continued.

McKelvie laughed. "When I locked the safe the other day I used the word, Darwin, the one you suggested. He has since made himself acquainted with that combination. Just as he was too clever to change it so that I would believe the safe untampered with, so was I too clever to let him know that I suspected his visits."

I nodded. "Why didn't you go over to the safe and capture him then?" I asked. "You missed an opportunity."

"What happened when we chased him before? The moment he saw us making for the safe he would be gone. Besides, I was playing a little game. I had put him on his guard by hunting for him. I decided to trick him into thinking that I no longer had any interest in him."

"Then all that very convincing conversation———"

"Was mere bunk," he answered. "I'm glad it was convincing, though, for I was trying to fool a very clever devil."

He fished around in his pocket and drew out the ring. I could see it gleam in the light of the street lamps as we sped toward the park.

"Strange. I had an idea that there was a secret panel or something of the sort where he could hide such things as he needed, for I could figure no other reason for his coming to that house, and that is what I was hunting for when you so opportunely caught your cuff-link in that Persian cover. This ring must have been tangled in the fringe and when I yanked the cover I dislodged the ring. That was a stroke of pure luck, and it changes the whole course of the inquiry. Word from Chicago would have told me something, but not as much as this band of gold does. Take a good look at it and tell me whose it is."

He took out his flash and played it over the ring while I looked at it. Then I turned away, feeling sick at heart. The ring was a heavy gold signet with a deep-cut monogram, and it was a ring I knew only too well, since I had bought it myself at Ruth's request that she might give it to her brother on his birthday. That was three years ago, and what a very happy time it had been and how pleased Dick had seemed to receive the ring, for he always made a fuss over Ruth. I remember that he swore to wear it always as he slipped it on his finger, and now here it was cropping up to bring more misery to the girl I wanted most to shield from all harm and sorrow.

"Well?" McKelvie's voice broke the thread of my thought.

"It's Dick Trenton's," I said low. "And now shall I drive you home?"

"Home? I should say not!" he almost shouted. "We're going to get some dinner and then we're off to Water Street. The trail's too hot to turn aside now."

CHAPTER XXV

THE DECEPTION

I did drive McKelvie home after all, for he quite suddenly insisted that I partake of his hospitality, saying that we should find a better dinner at his house than at any restaurant in Greater New York. From there I phoned Jenkins to look after Mr. Trenton, and then followed McKelvie into a low-ceilinged old room lighted by a mellow glow which made the heavy mahogany furniture seem even more ancient than it really was.

I had not realized how tired I was mentally and physically (it's hard work racing around the city in a car) until I faced my host across the table, and saw how weary he looked. He smiled a little as I unconsciously relaxed after partaking of the soup which the old darky had served to us.

"Mr. Davies," he said, "I shouldn't drag you around with me. It's not fair to you. Go on home after dinner and I'll go to Water Street alone."

"You are tired, too," I returned.

"I'm paid to do this work. It's part of my business to chase after clues," he said. "You are my client, so to speak, and the client is not expected to aid the cause except in furnishing the means to carry it on."

But I shook my head. "I'm too keen on the result to stop now," I replied.

"Even if it should lead you into unforeseen channels?" he queried.

"Even so. Ruth is the first consideration," I responded firmly.

"Very well, and now the best thing we can do is to cease talking about it," and forthwith he launched into an account of a trip he had once taken through Africa.

He was a born narrator, and under the spell of his voice and the influence of that most excellent dinner, cooked as only Southern darkies know how to cook, I forgot the problem that was troubling me, forgot that there were such things as crimes and criminals; aye, even forgot that there was such a place on the globe as New York City, while I followed McKelvie on a lion hunt in the heart of northern Africa.

"And that's where I got that skin," he said, as we rose and sauntered into the living-room.

I gazed at the great rug spread out before the fireplace, and pictured to myself how it had looked the day McKelvie shot it when he spoke again.

"I'm afraid we'll have to smoke our cigars on the way. It's getting late."

With a sigh I returned to the business in hand, and as I drove through the poorer sections of New York on my way to Water Street my mind reverted to the first time I had visited that locality, which brought me around to Dick and the signet ring. So Dick had been in the Darwin home that night, and since his ring was in the secret room, then he must have been behind the safe at some time during the evening. McKelvie claimed that the criminal was hiding in the safe when Orton entered the room at eleven-thirty, but he also maintained that the criminal was the man we had heard when we ourselves had been in the study this very evening. If that were the truth then it could hardly have been Dick, since Dick was dead. Yet what did McKelvie hope to learn by visiting the scene of the suicide?

When we reached Water Street we pulled up before the lodging house where Dick had stayed and rang the bell. Mrs. Blake opened the door and eyed us suspiciously.

"No lodgings," she said uncompromisingly, beginning to close the door.

"Just a moment. We don't want lodgings," said McKelvie crisply, at the same time displaying a bill as he held his hand toward the lighted doorway. "We want you to answer a few questions."

Seeing that we were not of the class to which she was accustomed, and her suspicions allayed by the greenback, she wiped her hands on her apron and asked us in.

We went as far as the hallway, which was more ill-smelling than when I had first made its acquaintance, and paused near the shabby old staircase.

"On the tenth of October a lodger of yours committed suicide by drowning," said McKelvie abruptly. "Is this the man?"

He took a photograph from his pocket and handed it to her. As she grasped it I had a glimpse of the pictured face and was not surprised to note that it was Dick's.

"Well, I won't say for sure. It looks like the same man, only 'tother was more like the men I takes to lodge," said Mrs. Blake after gazing at the photograph.

"And this one looks like a gentleman, is that it?" supplemented McKelvie with a smile.

The woman nodded, and taking a piece of charcoal from his pocket McKelvie reclaimed the photograph and proceeded to blacken the lower part of the face, giving Dick an untidy appearance, as though he had not shaved for a week or more. Then he showed it to her again.

"Yes, sir. It looks more like him now," she added.

McKelvie pocketed the picture. "What's the name of the man who told you about the suicide?"

"Ben Kite."

"Thank you," and he placed the bill in her hands.

"Phew! It's good to get out into the fresh air. How do they stand it!" I exclaimed.

"So used to it they don't even notice it," McKelvie returned with a shrug. "Drive down to the wharves and we'll have a talk with Ben Kite, if we can find him."

"What do you expect to learn by all this questioning?" I inquired anxiously.

He did not answer except to draw my attention to a group of men lounging on the wharf. "Stay in the machine while I find out if Kite is among them."

He alighted and approached the group, but it was too dark for me to be able to distinguish more than a general blur of outlines.

"Can you tell me where I can find Ben Kite to-night?" I heard McKelvie ask.

"Who wants 'im?" growled a coarse voice in answer.

"I do," replied McKelvie.

"What you want, stranger?" remarked the same voice again.

"Are you Ben Kite?"

"That's the name me mither give me," the man returned, detaching himself from the group, which laughed immoderately at his words. "What you want?"

"A moment's conversation and I'll make it worth your while, but I don't care particularly for an audience. Do you see that car? Tell your friends to remain where they are. You'll find me waiting in the machine if you want a ten-spot."

McKelvie returned to my side and entered the machine. Hardly had he settled himself when the man was beside us. He was the same fellow I had questioned. I knew his ugly face in the light cast upon it by the lamp under which I had parked, but he failed to recognize me, since my face was in shadow.

"On October the tenth a man who lodged at Mrs. Blake's jumped into the East River and was drowned. Am I right?" asked McKelvie without preliminary.

"Sure. I told the bulls all I knowed at the time," responded Kite.

"I know. But I want the information first hand. He came to the wharf and jumped in. Was that the way it happened?"

"Sort of like that. When I seed him he was right on the edge. I hallooed and he flung up his arms high and duve in. I ran to the edge, but he never cum up. Current got 'im, I guess," answered Kite indifferently.

"And the body has not been recovered?" continued McKelvie.

The man grinned. "Well, they ain't had time. It's only four days. He might bob up yet."

I shuddered at the callous way in which he spoke of this boy of whom I had been fond.

"Is this the man?" McKelvie turned his flash on the picture.

"Sure, that's 'im, all right."

"Thank you. Here's your money. Drive quickly, Mr. Davies," McKelvie added in my ear as the man moved away. "If they think we have money they may try to get some of it for themselves."

I gave the car more gas and we were speeding round the corner before the man had more than joined his friends.

"Where did you get that picture of Dick? I do not recall having seen it before. It must be a recent one, for he looks older than I remember him."

"What picture of Dick?" he asked.

"The one you just showed Kite," I returned.

"Oh, that. I noticed it this morning when I examined the house, before your arrival, and that is what I went back to get after our adventure in the study to-night."

"Do you think the body will ever be recovered?" I asked as we turned into the Bowery from Catherine Street.

"No. It would be a very strange thing to recover a corpse that never existed," McKelvie responded grimly.

"A corpse that never existed," I repeated slowly and recalled my own doubts when Jones had first given me the news. "I understand. He was hardly likely to drown, since he could swim too well."

"Yes. Kite told us that plainly to-night. His words were: 'He flung his arms high and dove in,' which meant that he could dive; from which I deduced that he was probably a good swimmer. When a man who can swim, strikes the water his instinct is to swim, no matter how much he may want to drown. Besides, a suicide generally goes in feet first, not head first, for it takes a lot of skill to dive, even when you don't contemplate drowning," he replied, giving me his line of reasoning.

"Then he left his things at Mrs. Blake's to create the impression that he had committed suicide," I said heavily.

"Yes, so that the world would believe that Richard Trenton had drowned himself," returned McKelvie.

"But why? In God's name why? Not because he —" I broke off, unable to finish. Yes, I know I had dallied with the thought before, but then it had only been conjecture with the belief that such a thing was impossible to sustain me. Now, however, it was grim reality that stared me in the face. What other reason could Dick have for the deception which he had practised upon us all?

"We're not going to jump at conclusions, Mr. Davies." McKelvie laid a hand on my arm. "He may have had good reasons for his act."

"What reasons could he possibly have?" I said impatiently.

"When I hear from Chicago, which ought to be any day now, I can answer that question more definitely. Until then we will give him the benefit of the doubt, for, after all, he is not the only one who has vanished without a trace, nor, which is more important, is he the only one in love with Cora Manning," he added significantly.

"That's the second time you've mentioned that the criminal is in love with Cora Manning," I said, as we neared his house. "But there seems to me to be a flaw in that assumption."

"Why?"

"It stands to reason, does it not, that if the murderer loves Miss Manning he must know that she uses rose jacqueminot perfume?" I remarked.

"Yes, he knows it," agreed McKelvie. "In fact, it wouldn't surprise me if he owned one of those yellow satin sachet bags himself."

"Then he can't be as clever as you make out, or he would never have made the mistake of putting a handkerchief scented with rose jacqueminot in Mr. Darwin's hands, under the belief that it belonged to Ruth, particularly if he saw Cora Manning in the study."

McKelvie smiled. "Do you remember my saying that Lee's use of rose jacqueminot looked bad for him? It was because of that handkerchief that I made the assertion. The criminal, as

101

I said before, uses rose jacqueminot, and he has become so accustomed to the scent of it that his olfactory nerves have lost the power to respond to it except when it is present in a fairly detectable amount. There was only the merest trace on that handkerchief, indistinguishable to him, and, therefore, deeming it unscented, he decided it belonged to Mrs. Darwin. I have an idea that he found it somewhere near the door leading into the hall. He would have done better to carry away the handkerchief with him, but like all the rest of his kind, he could not resist the chance to strengthen the evidence against Mrs. Darwin and so put himself into our hands," he explained.

"But what applies to Lee, applies to Dick as well," I returned. "He also possesses a yellow satin sachet bag."

"Yes, that is true," he responded as he alighted before his door. "Therefore we have no right to condemn one more than the other until we have a few more facts at our disposal. I'll call you if there are any new developments. By the way, don't tell Mr. Trenton that his son did not commit suicide until we know definitely what happened in the study that night. *Au revoir*, Mr. Davies."

"I understand. Good-night, McKelvie," I replied.

CHAPTER XXVI

JAMES GILMORE

In the morning I returned to the office, for I could hardly expect my partner to carry on the business alone very much longer. He was extremely interested in the mystery because of my connection with it and also because he knew Ruth personally, and asked me what progress we had made so far. I told him all the various facts that McKelvie had dug up and he looked very grave when he learned the truth about Dick's pretended suicide. We were still discussing the matter when McKelvie called me on the phone to say that he had word from Chicago and would like me to hear what Dick's friend had to say.

"What is it, a new clue?" asked my partner curiously.

I repeated McKelvie's communication, saying that I was sorry to have to abandon him again, but that I would be back as soon as I could get away.

My partner clapped me on the shoulder. "That's all right, old man, you need not feel obliged to get back. I'll worry along somehow without you," he said kindly, adding with a laugh, "besides, you're worse than useless any way with this business uppermost in your mind. You'd be apt to make a bear out of a bull market," and his eyes twinkled.

So I drove to McKelvie's house and found him in his living-room talking to an old-young man of some thirty odd years, whose hair was quite gray and whose skin had a peculiar dead look, as though he had spent a part of his life shut away from the sunlight.

"Mr. Davies," said McKelvie when he had introduced me, "James Gilmore is a friend of Dick Trenton, and he has come from Chicago in answer to my request to relate to us what he knows of young Trenton's movements."

James Gilmore nodded. "If you have no objections I'm going to begin further back a bit so that you will understand how I came to be mixed up in this affair. Ten years ago I was a teller in the Darwin Bank. I was twenty-one, ambitious, and eager to make as much money as my pals. My salary was small, but the son of one of the directors, Philip Darwin, who was just a few years older than myself, took a fancy to me and told me that he could help me to make all the money that I wanted. I was young and foolish and I trusted him. I took money from the bank and gave it to him to speculate with, money that he feared to take himself, though I blame only myself for my folly. I did not have to steal, for, in a measure, I knew the risk I ran. But he was such a smooth fellow, and being the son of a director he declared that he could prevent any chance inspections, and I would have the money to replace long before an accounting was made. I believed him, and two days after I had given him the money we had an unexpected visit from the inspectors, and I was caught short. I went to Darwin for the money, but he shrugged his shoulders and said that the market had gone against him and that that was a risk that I had to stand. There was nothing to do but face the music, for, of course, his part in the affair never came to light at all."

James Gilmore broke off to add with bitter emphasis, "He was the son of a rich man, and I was poor, and so I paid for what he gained, for I have since learned that he made money on that deal and kept it all, damn him!

"Well, I got ten years, since it was my first offense," he continued presently in a quieter tone, "and when I got out last March I vowed vengeance upon him. I found out what he was doing and where he spent his evenings, and one night in the beginning of April I ran across a chap whom I had met in Sing Sing. He told me that he had been hired by a man to quarrel at cards with some boy whom this man was trying to ruin. The place was one of the resorts that Darwin attended and the scheme sounded like the sort of thing he would be capable of, so I asked this fellow, Coombs, if I could sit in at the game, and he answered, 'Yes, just drop in and I'll say you're a pal of mine.'

"That night I repaired to a private room in the rear of the gambling den and took a seat in a corner until Darwin and the boy had come in. They were disguised, but Coombs gave me the wink, and instinct, a feeling of antipathy, told me that the older man was Darwin, although I did not really see his face, for the light was bad. When I joined them, Darwin frowned, not because he recognized me (there was no danger of that-ten years in jail make a difference in a man), but because he wanted no one interfering with his plans. We began to play, and then Coombs, as per orders, cheated, cheated so openly it was a farce. But the boy had been drinking and he hadn't the wit to see that he was being made a fool of. He accused Coombs of double dealing, and Coombs jumped up and made for him with his chair, whereupon Darwin pulled out a gun and fired two shots in rapid succession. The first one bowled Coombs over, but I sensed what was coming and the second shot went over my head as I ducked. However, I dropped to the floor, deeming discretion the better part of valor. Then I saw Darwin press the pistol into the boy's hand, firing another shot as he did so and exclaiming, 'You've done for him, Dick, but don't worry, I'll get you away, never fear.'

"A terrific pounding ensued on the door at this moment and calls and yells came from the main room. Darwin sprang for the light and extinguished it, and seeing my chance I, too, sneaked away by the rear entrance just as the inner door gave way. I didn't want to be accused of having killed Coombs, and I knew that I could not implicate Darwin, since at no time had I seen his face. I was an ex-convict, and he a prominent and wealthy man. It was my word against his. What chance had I of using my knowledge to account?

"The murder of Coombs came out in the paper, and there was quite a to-do over it, and fearing that someone might recall that I had been there lately, and that I also knew Coombs, I lit out for the West. In September I drifted to Chicago, and having found a job, looked for a boarding-place. I found a very respectable home and there made the acquaintance of a handsome young fellow who called himself Richard Trenton. I wondered about him, since he seemed above his surroundings, but never was really intimate until I happened into his room to borrow a book that he had offered to lend me and found him at his desk writing the name Philip Darwin over and over on a sheet of paper.

"I was stunned for the moment, and then I found voice to say, 'You know him, too?'

"'Yes,' he said bitterly. 'Do you?'

"I nodded. 'Yes, I ought to know him. I served ten years in jail on his account,' I said.

"'Tell me about it,' he demanded.

"When I was through he sat for a while in silence and then he said, 'He has harmed me, too, but only in taking advantage of my own folly,' and then he told me the story that Philip Darwin had concocted for his benefit, a story which he, Dick Trenton, was too drunk to have been able to contradict. He had quarreled with a man and had pulled out a gun and killed the fellow and Darwin, like an angel of mercy, had got him away and saved him from the chair.

"When I heard that I let out a yell and told him the truth. He was mad then, mad enough to kill, and he swore he would go back to New York to have it out with Darwin. Then suddenly he seemed to recall something and just collapsed, and when I urged him to go and revenge himself, all he did was to shake his head.

"'He forced my sister to marry him to save my life,' he said hoarsely, clenching his hands. 'I must free her first and then-he shall pay.'

"Under those circumstances things were different, so we concocted a letter and sent it to Darwin, telling him we had proofs of his perfidy, and he must promise to let his wife divorce him at once or face the consequences. As soon as he got the letter there came a telegram from him, saying that his lawyer, who was in his confidence, was on his way to Chicago to confer with us. Well, we awaited the lawyer's arrival, and he came to the house and asked for Trenton. He was a red-whiskered, red-haired fellow called Cunningham, and he asked us for proofs of what we knew.

"Trenton did the talking, and he said that he could prove that it was Darwin who had fired the pistol, that he could produce several witnesses to that effect, that he had been investigating the thing for months. All this was pure bluff, of course, but the old chap came off his high horse and said that his client had deceived him and that under the circumstances he had nothing more to say. He would return to New York and advise that Mrs. Darwin be allowed her divorce and after that why he had no objections if we saw fit to punish Darwin.

"Seeing that we had won over the lawyer, we waited eagerly for news of the divorce proceedings, but in the beginning of October there came a long letter from Darwin. He explained that his lawyer had called on him and that in view of the fact that we had the proofs he was willing to grant Mrs. Darwin the chance to divorce him, but there was one difficulty in the way of that. Mrs. Darwin did not want a divorce, and he thought it was best for Dick to come to New York to see him personally before any actions were taken. Then Dick could talk to his sister and matters could be arranged to the satisfaction of all parties. If this was agreeable Dick would find him home at eleven-thirty on the night of October seventh.

"Well, we talked it over, and as Mrs. Darwin's letters had always been very cheerful and never held any complaint about her married life, why, we were in a quandary, for, of course, we couldn't expect Darwin to denounce himself to her. So the upshot was that Dick telegraphed that he would confer with Darwin. I told him to go armed, as I didn't trust Darwin around the corner, and Dick promised, though he said with a laugh that he knew where Darwin kept his pistol, and it would be easier to borrow that than to try to buy a new one.

"I saw him off, and then on the evening of the eighth I read about the murder in the papers. Right away I jumped to the conclusion that Dick had fired the shot, but when I read further I was amazed to see that the murder was the result of a quarrel between husband and wife and that Dick hadn't been there at all. I wondered why he didn't send me word, and then two days later I saw an account of his suicide in the papers. I couldn't quite figure it out, and finally decided that he had arrived too late to prevent the tragedy and drowned himself in a fit of grief."

James Gilmore shook his head in a perplexed way. "And now this gentleman tells me that Dick didn't commit suicide, and I understand it less than ever. There is one thing sure. He's not in Chicago. The police got your message, and after combing the city went to his boarding-place for information, and that's how I caught on that someone was looking for news of Dick. I said to myself, 'You're the boy to give it,' and here I am."

"And I am much obliged to you, I am sure," said McKelvie. "You have helped me immensely. And now that we may be absolutely sure that no mistake has been made, take a look at this picture and tell me whether you recognize it."

He handed Gilmore a photograph of Dick, an old one, not the one which he had blackened for Mrs. Blake, and Gilmore nodded quickly.

"Sure that's Dick Trenton, all right, except that he was wearing a very full beard when I met him. He told me he grew it as a disguise, but that he intended to shave it off the moment he reached New York. He said his sister would disown him if he looked like Daniel Boone."

McKelvie nodded, and I added, "He evidently kept his word, since he had only a stubble when he pretended suicide, poor boy."

"When you discover where he is, let me know," said Gilmore, rising. "Take my word for it, he is somewhere in this burg. Well, I must be going. There are some of my pals I want to look up before I go back to Chi. I'll keep my top eye open, and if I get a hint I'll let you know."

"I wish you would. Thank you again," said McKelvie, escorting Gilmore to the door.

When he returned his eyes were shining. "Well, that was worth-while news," he said smiling.

"It certainly was, providing he hasn't—" I said with a gesture.

"We won't spoil it by dwelling on that fact. Remember what I said last night. Stay for luncheon and then give me the benefit of your services as chauffeur. I know you will want to go with me, for I am going to ask Mr. Cunningham what advice he gave his client about this most interesting affair."

CHAPTER XXVII

THE STRONG BOX

After a luncheon, to which I did full justice, McKelvie flipped over the pages of the city directory and studied the section devoted to Cunninghams.

"That's rather peculiar," he said. "He has no office in the city. If he is a lawyer, where does he conduct his practice? Something wrong, somewhere. Come on. We'll get him at his apartments."

We drove to 84th Street and inquired for Cunningham.

"Mr. Cunningham? He's not at home," replied the switchboard operator in the hallway of the fashionable apartment house.

"Do you mean that he is out of town?" asked McKelvie anxiously.

"Oh, no. He'll be back at five, I guess. That's the time he usually comes in when he's in the city," said the girl, bestowing a fetching smile upon my companion.

McKelvie improved the acquaintance. He returned the smile. "Is he away very much?"

"Yes, quite a bit."

"Thank you, and you need not mention that I was asking about him. He might not like it," remarked McKelvie.

"You said it. He's closer than a clam about himself," she returned with a little toss of her head.

"Our friend Cunningham was once quite attentive in that quarter," explained McKelvie with a laugh as we drove away. "So much I learned when I first came here, and so I proceeded to make friends with Jane."

"Where to?" I inquired, laughing. "Home?"

"No, the Darwin Bank. I have a mind to see whether our lawyer friend, who has no office, possesses a sufficient capital to live on his income. Mr. Trenton is the best man to apply to I guess, since I have already learned that Cunningham keeps an account at his bank."

When we arrived at the bank I sent my card in, and we were admitted at once to Mr. Trenton's private office.

"What is it, Carlton?" he asked fearfully.

"Good news," I replied, "which I should like you to convey to Ruth" (I had ceased visiting her at her own request), and I told him Gilmore's story.

Mr. Trenton beamed on McKelvie when I had finished the tale. "My dear sir, this is all your doing. How can I ever thank you? You have lifted a great load from my mind, and I can think of him with great pity now instead of horror in my heart."

He bowed his head and I was glad he did not know that Dick was alive. It was far better that he think his son drowned than that he know that Dick was somewhere in New York, afraid to come home.

"Mr. Trenton," said McKelvie presently, "I came here primarily to obtain some information. Philip Darwin had an account here, did he not?"

"Raines can tell you," Mr. Trenton replied, ringing for the head cashier.

I nodded to the young man as he entered, for we were acquainted and Mr. Trenton introduced him to McKelvie, adding, "And Mr. Raines, you have my authority to tell Mr. McKelvie whatever he desires to know."

"I'm at your service, Mr. McKelvie," responded Raines, with a cordial smile.

"I wish to know whether Philip Darwin has a bank balance here and if so how much," said McKelvie, getting down to business at once.

"He closed out his account on the sixth of October," replied Raines. "I'm not likely to forget it, since it was the very next night that he was murdered."

"And the amount of his balance was —" repeated McKelvie.

"One hundred and fifty thousand dollars. I gave him the money myself."

"Did he take it in gold or notes?" asked McKelvie.

"In bills of large denominations, so that it did not make such a very large package to carry. He put it into a small bag and took it away himself."

McKelvie took a turn around the room and then asked abruptly, "Does a Mr. Herbert Cunningham, who lives on 84th Street, bank here?"

"Yes. He's a red-whiskered chap, is he not?"

McKelvie nodded. "Can you give me the amount of his balance?"

"I'll get it for you in just a moment." Raines left the room and McKelvie continued to pace the floor.

"What do you suppose Philip did with all that money?" asked Mr. Trenton.

"That's what I'm going to find out," returned McKelvie. "I have an idea I know where it is."

"According to Cunningham, Darwin lost it on Wall Street," I said.

"Yes, and according to Orton Darwin was a cautious speculator. I'll wager the secretary was the better judge of Darwin's character. Orton's shrewd for all that he's a wretched creature. No, that money did not go into Wall Street, and I'm going to locate it in just a moment. Well?" as Raines came in again.

"Cunningham's balance is ten thousand dollars," returned Raines.

"Any increase lately?" asked McKelvie.

"No, just a steady decrease," answered the cashier.

"Has he a strong box?"

"Yes, he has."

"May I examine its contents?" inquired McKelvie.

Raines looked at Mr. Trenton.

"It's all right. I'll come along, too," and Mr. Trenton rose.

"By the way, Mr. Raines," said McKelvie, "I should like this investigation conducted as inconspicuously as possible. I'm a rich eccentric who wants to hire a strong box, if anyone asks any questions."

"All right, sir. Whatever Mr. Trenton says goes. I'll meet you downstairs with the key," replied Raines.

Mr. Trenton conducted us through the bank corridor to the rear of the building and down a flight of stone steps to the entrance to the vault. The guard swung open the heavy door with a "good-afternoon, sir," to Mr. Trenton, and we entered the fireproof room where the safe deposit boxes were kept and paused before the one marked Cunningham.

When Raines came in he inserted the master key in the lock and opened the deposit box. Inside was a smaller tin cash box and when he lifted the lid, for it was unlocked, we saw that it was crammed with bills. Raines' eyes opened wide with amazement, and if McKelvie hadn't caught the box it would have fallen from his nerveless fingers.

"Mr. McKelvie," he said in a strange voice, pointing to the contents of the box, "those are the bills I gave to Philip Darwin!"

"I thought as much," said McKelvie seriously. "Lock up this box again. Until we can prove that Cunningham has no right to the money, we cannot confiscate it. Thank you very much, Mr. Trenton, for your kindness in allowing me this privilege, and I'd be much obliged if you will say nothing to anyone about our discovery. You'll excuse us if we hurry along?"

Mr. Trenton nodded and we hastened out, leaving the president and the cashier to lock up the one hundred and fifty thousand dollars in Cunningham's strong box.

"So Cunningham has the money," I remarked as we drove toward Stuyvesant Square. "Can it be he murdered Darwin, and then helped himself to the bills. The cash box in the safe was found empty," I added.

McKelvie smiled grimly. "Oh, no, he didn't steal the money. I don't believe it was ever in the house on Riverside Drive, but we will make our friend explain its presence in his strong box just the same. It should be an interesting account, to say the least," he ended sarcastically. "Call for me here at five and we'll hear what he has to say."

I pondered McKelvie's meaning as I returned to the office. The explanation should be interesting he had said. I agreed with him, yet after all it could have no direct connection with the murder, since Philip Darwin had never taken the money home. But how did McKelvie know this latter fact? Was he merely theorizing, or did he know more than he had told me? He had not appeared surprised when we discovered that the lawyer had the money, for he had even hinted that he knew where it was.

I determined to ask him what other information he had upon this point when I called for him at five o'clock, but at four-thirty, as I was making ready to leave, he phoned me to postpone our visit. His voice was so high-pitched with excitement that my questions vanished from my mind as if by magic, and all I could exclaim was, "What is it? What has happened?"

"Our friend Cunningham will have a pretty job on his hands explaining away all the facts I have gathered against him to-day," he exulted. "He's no more a lawyer than I am, Mr. Davies!"

"Not a lawyer!" I repeated.

"No. He's not registered, and he cannot practise law in New York City! I'm going to look up one or two more details before we call upon him. Be at the house at quarter to eight, please, providing, of course, that you desire to accompany me."

"McKelvie, if you dare to go to 84th Street without me, there's going to be trouble between us," I warned and he laughed gayly as he rang off.

CHAPTER XXVIII

GOLD AND BLUE

Though I was impatient to interview Cunningham, it was almost eight-thirty before we arrived at 84th Street, for on the way we had a blowout and the garage attendant was the slowest specimen of his type that I had ever had the misfortune to encounter.

Cunningham himself, debonair and genial as usual, admitted us into his apartment and invited us into what he designated as his smoking-room. It was a medium-sized room furnished in good taste, and as I sank into the depths of a luxurious arm-chair and accepted the cigar he offered me I felt assured that Cunningham could reasonably explain away the doubts which I had lately entertained toward him. Yes, the personality of the man and the soothing influence of that rare cigar had combined to make me as eager to hear him justify himself as before I had been anxious to prove him the murderer of his friend.

But McKelvie was not so easily won over. He accepted a chair and a cigar, it is true, yet I knew well that he was waiting as a person does at chess for the next move of his adversary.

"It is very pleasant to have you gentlemen call upon me," said Cunningham, breaking the silence. "Have you come in a friendly or an antagonistic spirit, Mr. McKelvie?"

"I have come with an open mind," responded McKelvie quietly.

"Explain yourself, please." Cunningham leaned back and puffed leisurely at his cigar.

"In an investigation of the sort that I am conducting one stumbles upon many queer things." McKelvie paused to draw a long puff and to blow a series of rings toward the ceiling. "As these smoke rings cross and recross each other and finally merge together, so do the trails in this case cross and recross each other until they all come together in the final solution. To distinguish the truth from the myriad bypaths of coincidence and false testimony is quite an art, I assure you, for I do not believe in doing any man an injustice. Therefore, I have come here to-night to give you a chance to explain certain curious facts which have come to my knowledge."

Cunningham bowed. "I thank you for the consideration, and I shall do my best to satisfy you."

McKelvie laid aside his cigar. "Are you a lawyer, Mr. Cunningham?" he asked bluntly.

If he thought to startle the man facing us so calmly McKelvie was mistaken in his estimate of the lawyer's character. Cunningham removed his cigar from his mouth, contemplated its lighted end for a moment, and then replied simply, "I am not registered in New York, if that is what you mean."

"Then may I ask by what right you constituted yourself Mr. Darwin's lawyer, and acted as Mrs. Darwin's counsel at the inquest?" continued McKelvie imperturbably.

Cunningham grinned sardonically. "I fancy that my estimate of the police coincides with yours, Mr. McKelvie," he said. "They got the idea, from Orton possibly, that I was Darwin's lawyer. They asked me to attend the inquest. I assumed the position they thrust upon me. What would you?" he shrugged whimsically. "It was no time to explain the complicated relation between us. As far as Mrs. Darwin is concerned, I did not advise her. In fact, I did not even see her until she entered the study."

He paused, and then leaned forward and said pointedly as he eyed McKelvie coolly, "You have asked me if I'm a lawyer. Yes, I am in this way. I have studied law and was ready for my bar examinations when the death of an uncle in a foreign country left me wealthy. I had to go abroad to secure my inheritance, and when I returned I had no desire to restudy for those examinations. So you see, I am a lawyer without a sheepskin, but, nevertheless, Philip Darwin had more confidence in my judgment than in that of the men who legalized his affairs. I have given him legal advice, yes, as between friend and friend, because I was his confident and he asked me for it, but I have never attempted to practise law in New York City or elsewhere. If you doubt my statement you are at liberty to verify it."

"I don't doubt you, Mr. Cunningham," responded McKelvie quietly. "I know you haven't practised law. I was merely trying to get the connection between you and Darwin, since you know so many of his affairs and represented him in a legal capacity when you went to Chicago to see Dick Trenton."

A slight tremor of Cunningham's eyelids was the only indication that the shot had told, but he replied as coolly as ever, "Not in a legal capacity. He sent me because I was acquainted with the details of the affair and understood merely that I was to find out how much real proof the boy had. What Darwin called me in his telegram I do not know, since I did not see it."

"How do you know he sent a telegram?" queried McKelvie.

"Is this the third degree, Mr. McKelvie?" asked Cunningham, frowning.

"No, Mr. Cunningham. I know it sounds very much like it," apologized McKelvie, "but it isn't meant to be. You have shown a disposition to aid us before, and you will help me immensely by making certain matters clear. Will you answer a few more questions?"

The frown cleared. "Certainly. Glad to assist you. Fire away," Cunningham returned indulgently. "And I don't mind saying that Darwin told me he had sent a telegram when he asked me to go out to Chicago for him."

"What advice did you give Darwin when you returned from Chicago?"

"I told him that the boy had a strong case and advised him to write and request Dick himself to see Mrs. Darwin and arrange for the divorce. Whether he followed my advice or not I don't know."

"For your information let me say that he did follow that advice, that Young Trenton came to New York and, without apparent cause, committed suicide. Whether there was an interview between them or not I cannot of course say positively," was McKelvie's astonishing reply. Why was he permitting Cunningham to remain in ignorance of our latest discovery concerning Richard Trenton?

"I'm very sorry to hear this," murmured Cunningham. "I should hate to think that my advice had brought him to such an end."

McKelvie changed the subject as abruptly as he had introduced it. "You said you had charge of Darwin's securities. What made you keep them?" his eyes on the other man's face.

"He was a very peculiar man and hated responsibility. I have cared for his securities and valuables for many years."

"Are you also caring for the one hundred and fifty thousand dollars that he drew from the bank and that is now reposing in your strong box?"

Cunningham looked annoyed, and then laughed cynically.

"Nothing escapes you, does it?" he sneered, then in a different tone, "No, that money is mine. A year ago I loaned Darwin enough to cover a slump in the market and thus saved him his fortune. I told him I was in no hurry for it, but as I've remarked more than once, he was peculiar. He came to me on the sixth and handed me the cash. I asked him what I should do with all that money in that shape and told him I'd prefer a check. He said that I'd given him cash and he felt better returning it in kind. And so he left it. I was going to add it to my bank account, but I'm going on a trip shortly and decided the cash would be useful to me. Therefore I put it in my strong-box for safe keeping."

"Thank you very much. Sorry to have disturbed you," said McKelvie, rising.

"Answers satisfactory?" asked Cunningham with a wry smile.

"Quite."

"And how much nearer to the solution have I carried you?" Cunningham continued with great politeness.

"Unfortunately I have remained static. Your answers though satisfactory as far as you yourself are concerned, have not helped me a particle toward solving my problem. I shall have to resort to desperate measures, I'm afraid," responded McKelvie, smiling rather oddly.

"Desperate measures, eh? That sounds like business. Before you undertake this work, honor me by drinking to your ultimate success," returned Cunningham. "My man is away, so if you will pardon me a moment I will get the whisky and soda."

The moment Cunningham left the room, McKelvie to my astonishment, sprang to the heavy portieres through which our host had passed and looked out. Then he drew back and walking swiftly to a door at the side of the room, he opened it and darted within.

Wondering what he was up to, I rose and followed him to this doorway and looked into the room beyond. To my surprise it was a bedroom, extravagantly but exquisitely furnished in gold and blue, a woman's boudoir, but I had no time to fix the details in my mind, for at this moment McKelvie came toward me hurriedly from his search of the dressing-table.

With a final comprehensive glance, and a whispered, "I thought I heard his step in the hall," McKelvie closed the door silently while I retreated to my chair and sank into its comfortable depths, none too soon. With a clink of glasses, Cunningham entered through the portieres. He glanced at us rather suspiciously, I thought, but McKelvie was contemplating the ceiling as he puffed his discarded cigar, and I was deep in the pages of a book, what book I have no idea.

Cunningham set the tray he carried on the table and poured out the whisky, allowing us to help ourselves to the soda. Then we raised our glasses and drank to the toast Cunningham had proposed, though I noticed that McKelvie merely touched his glass to his lips and set it down untasted.

"I never drink whisky," he said quietly, as Cunningham raised his brows in interrogation.

"Is there anything else I can offer you?"

"No, thank you. I appreciate your efforts in my behalf. Good night, Mr. Cunningham," and McKelvie bowed, a trifle too deeply to be really sincere.

"Good night, Mr. McKelvie," responded Cunningham, returning the bow. Then he offered his hand to me. "Good night," he said again as we left.

"What on earth were you doing in that bedroom?" I inquired as we parted at McKelvie's door. "By the way, it was rather an odd room—for a bachelor."

"Did you remark the gold and blue? Rather a familiar combination, eh? Here's the true significance of that very charming room."

Holding up his hand, he dangled before my eyes a tiny yellow satin sachet bag embroidered in blue, a satin sachet whose fragrance was the fragrance of Rose Jacqueminot!

CHAPTER XXIX

THE REWARD

Cunningham and the fragrance of Rose Jacqueminot! Cunningham and a yellow satin sachet embroidered in blue!

These words kept pounding in my brain and though I went over them in the light of the facts which we had gleaned, I could see no plausible reason for Cunningham's having committed that murder. He could have no possible motive for wanting to harm Ruth since he did not know her, nor could I believe, despite the gold and blue room, that he was in love with Cora Manning. He had evidently never called on her at Gramercy Park or her landlady would have described him to us, and it was not likely that being engaged to Lee, Cora Manning would have received the advances of other men, at least so I judged from the manner in which Ruth had spoken of her.

Cunningham's explanations, too, had been eminently satisfactory, and had cleared him even in McKelvie's eyes, as far as I could judge last night. Besides, it wasn't as though Cunningham were the sole possessor of one of those sachets.

McKelvie was in much the same position as that robber in "Ali Baba and the Forty Thieves," of which I used to be fond in my childhood days, that robber who led his chief to the cross-marked house only to discover that all the neighboring houses were also cross-marked. As a clue, then, the fragrance of Rose Jacqueminot and the yellow satin sachet were as useless as the robber's chalk-mark.

It might also be that Cunningham's use of that particular fragrance, and his acquaintance with a woman who also affected yellow satin sachets embroidered in blue, was one of those coincidences that often occur in life, where truth is in many cases stranger than fiction.

As McKelvie had truly remarked, the trails crossed and recrossed until the right one was lost to view in the labyrinth of paths. As I looked back over the facts we had learned I was amazed to find how little real progress we had made toward the solution. It was all conjecture and except for Dick's ring, we had no clues which could rightly be termed such. And when it came to suspects, Lee and Dick and Cunningham ran a close race, though the greatest amount of evidence pointed toward Dick, since McKelvie was inclined to hold Lee guiltless, and Cunningham had no adequate motive.

About two o'clock McKelvie called at the office and found me alone.

"Can you spare me a few minutes?" he inquired, as he glanced at the work on my desk.

"I should say so," I returned quickly, pushing aside my papers. "Anything new?"

"No, I've come to the end of my tether—"

"You don't mean that you're giving up the case?" I interrupted, dismayed.

He laughed. "Giving up the case when it's just becoming exciting? You don't know me, Mr. Davies," he cried, and his voice was exultant, his eyes fairly dancing. "I was going to say that I have reached the point where skirmishing in the dark is no longer satisfactory. I'm coming out in the open and I'm going to fight him with the plan of campaign spread out for him to read."

"You think that is wise?"

"Yes, decidedly so. I'm going to let him know I'm after him, and then we'll watch him struggle to escape my net," he declared.

"Then you know who the criminal is?" I asked.

"No. I suspect, but I have no proof," he replied. "Ah, he's a clever devil, that fellow, and we're just beginning to break below the surface in this affair. Here's my scheme."

He drew from his pocket a folded sheet, opened it, and handed it to me with the remark, "I've distributed copies of that around the city."

I looked at the sheet, which still smelled strongly of the printer's ink, and saw that it was a hand-bill offering a reward of one thousand dollars for any authentic information which might lead to the discovery of the present whereabouts of Lee Darwin, last seen about four o'clock at the corner of Twenty-fifth Street and Third Avenue, on the afternoon of October the eighth. There followed a description of the young man, accompanied by his photograph and the added announcement that the reward would be paid by Graydon McKelvie, at No. — Stuyvesant Square.

"Ought to bring results, eh? When some six million people become interested in finding him we ought to locate him in short order."

"What makes you think he is in New York?" I inquired.

"Wilkins returned yesterday morning and reported that Lee never went South at all. There is no trace of his having gone there. So I started Wilkins at this end again. Last night when I got back from Cunningham's, Wilkins was waiting for me. He had discovered that Lee had taken a taxi as far as Third Avenue and Twenty-fifth Street. After that he vanished completely. So the presumption is that he is still in the city."

"In the city and in hiding," I mused. "Yet you said the night we chased the criminal, that in accusing Lee you were putting the true culprit off his guard by making him think you had no interest in him. That would imply Lee's innocence, yet what other possible motive could he have for disappearing?"

"There are two reasons for his disappearance, as far as I can see. One is the assumption that he is the criminal. This reason, as you remarked, I have discarded. Lee did not kill his uncle. I'll tell you why I make this assertion." He rose abruptly and took a turn around the room, then halted in front of me again. "You saw and heard him at the inquest? How did he impress you, as regards his character, I mean?"

"He struck me as being a rather passionate, quick-tempered chap, one who also possessed the power of self-control. He has a frank face and clear eyes. Also I've heard Mr. Trenton say in discussing him that he is a fine, upright boy, and that he liked him very much indeed," I replied.

"Passionate and quick-tempered," repeated McKelvie. "Is he the type to commit murder in cold-blood?"

"No. In a moment of passionate anger, yes, but not in cold-blood," I returned with conviction.

"Just what I decided from the first, and as this murder was premeditated, that let's him out. Now for the second reason for his disappearance. He was engaged to Cora Manning, yet he denied knowing her. When the coroner showed him the handkerchief he was in mortal dread that he would recognize it as hers. Therefore he knew something of what took place in the study, in which Miss Manning was involved. Or, perhaps, he knew of her intended visit to the Darwin home. However that may be, he knew something of importance. He left the inquest before all the evidence was brought in, therefore he was in ignorance of the verdict when he returned to the Club. Nevertheless he was a menace to the criminal's plan to implicate Mrs. Darwin, for Lee would come forward and tell what he knew the moment he learned of Mrs. Darwin's predicament. What does the criminal do then? He decoys Lee from the Club with a telegram, and keeps him a prisoner somewhere in the city, to prevent him from giving evidence."

"What a fiend the man must be!" I exclaimed. "But how did he know so quickly that Lee was a menace to him. The papers were hardly out by that time," I added.

"Because he was at the inquest, and he deduced danger to himself from Lee's actions," replied McKelvie. "That is, of course, he must have been there to act so promptly since he has no confederate, I am sure. There were any number of extra persons in the room. He could easily form one of the curious, or disguise himself as a reporter, or any other character that happened to occur to him. He is daring enough to have impersonated the District Attorney himself."

I agreed. "But, in that event, when the man realizes you are after Lee because you need his evidence, for of course he will see your reward, won't he murder the boy to get rid of him? He seems to be capable of any outrage."

"Unfortunately that is a risk I shall have to run. Now that I am persuaded that the criminal is holding Lee a prisoner I've got to rescue him, since the murderer is not likely to hamper himself with the boy overlong-if he hasn't done away with him already. We have wasted much valuable time following a false lead. Well, it can't be helped now, and there is nothing to be gained by crying over spilt milk. Wilkins is combing the East Side and I hope to have news in a few hours. From now on it's a fight to the finish," he ended, exultantly. "I have shown the criminal my hand. I want Lee, and the man I'm ultimately going to get will do his best to balk me-if he can."

"Here's to our side," I said, catching his enthusiasm. "And remember that I want to be in on anything that happens."

"Right. I won't forget you."

But he did, for I heard nothing further from him during the remainder of the afternoon, which I spent in an endeavor to pin my mind to market quotations which I considered merely trivial beside the problem that was worrying me, and when I called his house that evening Dinah reported that he had gone out and she had no idea when he would return. Disappointedly I sought my favorite chair and my pipe, offering Mr. Trenton a cigar, which he declined. He had been to see Ruth that afternoon and as usual after such a visit he was very disheartened. I tried to cheer him, but with little success, since my feelings coincided so accurately with his own and I could ill bear the thought of Ruth in that dreadful place day after day, with no hope of release. I finally turned in, determined to forget my troubles in oblivion. But I could not sleep. Over and over I reviewed the case, particularly the latest phases of it, and wondered if Dick's ring in the secret room, where it certainly had no business to be, might not serve as a clue upon which to secure Ruth's release. Then my mind wandered to Lee and the girl of the perfume, to Cunningham and the gold-and-blue room, until gradually it seemed to me that a delicious fragrance pervaded the room, and I drifted into the land of dreams.

And in that sleep I dreamed a weird and awful dream. I thought I stood in the secret room behind the safe, which somehow resembled the gold-and-blue room in Cunningham's apartment, and as I stood there breathing the fragrance of Rose Jacqueminot a man dashed by me and entered the study. He had a pistol in his hand and as he fired at Darwin, whom I could see dimly in the distance, I heard a woman shriek. Then the man came back, dragging a girl by the arm, and as he went by me he dropped Dick's ring at my feet, and turned toward me such a face as I hope never to see even in my dreams again. It was the face of a demon distorted by passion, and it bore no resemblance to anyone I knew, or rather, it was a composite of those concerned in the case, for he had Dick's eyes, Lee's nose and chin, and Cunningham's red hair. A moment I looked into his mad eyes and then I saw him raise his arm and fire at the girl and I realized with horror that she was Ruth. With a cry I flung myself toward him-and woke with my arms around my pillow.

CHAPTER XXX

THE CURIO SHOP

I sat up and passed my hand dazedly across my brow and then suddenly I was broad awake and listening intently to the sound that had startled me, the sound of my door opening stealthily. I peered through the darkness but could discern nothing.

I waited a moment, but hearing no further sound reached under my pillow for my revolver, for I knew I wasn't dreaming now, noticing by my radium-faced watch that it was close to midnight. Then as I became conscious of another presence in the room, the light was switched on without warning, and I flung out my arm, covering the man who stood there before me.

He was a rough-looking customer in an ugly, worn blue suit, and his cap was pulled low over his brow. His face was unshaved, his lips were coarse, his nose was thick, his eyebrows bushy, and the eyes beneath were sunken and dull, a dead black in color.

"What are you doing here?" I demanded, holding the pistol in line with his heart.

But he did not reply except by a chuckle, and I flung down the pistol with the cry, "McKelvie!"

"I'm glad I pass muster," he said, chuckling again, but I could only stare at him in genuine amazement. Except for that chuckle I should never have known him!

"Here," he said, flinging a bundle on my bed, "get into those things as fast as you can, and meet me in your library. We have no time to waste, but I knew you would never forgive me if I left you out of this."

As soon as he was gone I attired myself in the battered old suit of brown which he had provided, and clapped a greasy cap upon my head. Then I surveyed myself in the mirror and turned away disappointedly. I was disreputable enough in all conscience, but no one would have taken me for anyone else but Carlton Davies, grown somewhat seedy in appearance. How did McKelvie do it?

In the library I found McKelvie talking to Jenkins, the latter clad in bathrobe and slippers, as though he had just been dragged from his room.

"Ready?" asked McKelvie, as I entered, and when I nodded he turned again to Jenkins. "Stay out in the hall beside the phone and don't go to sleep. If I do not phone you by one o'clock, call Headquarters and tell them to rush some men to Hi Ling's curio shop. You understand?"

"Yes, sir," answered Jenkins, blinking.

"Don't fall asleep, as it may mean our lives," repeated McKelvie impressively.

"No, sir. I'll stay awake. You can depend on me, sir," said Jenkins in a hurt tone.

"Yes, I know I can," returned McKelvie. "Come on, Mr. Davies."

McKelvie swung toward me and then began to laugh. "You're far too clean. They'd spot you for a fake in a moment."

He took what looked like a box of lampblack from his pocket and applied it to my face. As we hurried down the hall I glanced at my reflection in the mirror. My face was a dirty gray, sallow, unshaved. I smiled as I followed McKelvie into the outer hall.

"Ever read Gaboriau?" he asked as we crept stealthily down the stairs.

"Yes."

"Then you know the advice that Lecoq gave his men when they wanted to disguise themselves. 'Change the eye,' he said. 'The eye is the important factor in disguise.' He was right and I have spent some time practising the maxim. Try to look stupid and your eyes will deaden. Not that way," and he caught my arm as I made for the lobby. "The back entrance for ours unless we want to land in a cell at the police station."

We sneaked out into the back yard, around the building, and out into the street, where a motor car was waiting.

"All right, Wilkins. Full speed ahead," said McKelvie as we got in. With a jerk we were off toward the Park.

"Now," I demanded, "what's it all about?"

"You've got your pistol with you?" he asked, and when I answered in the affirmative, he went on, "Don't use it unless I give you leave. The less shooting the better for us, I expect."

"Is it Lee?" I inquired.

"Yes. My offer of reward hustled things up a bit." McKelvie leaned forward and called out, "Faster, Wilkins. We'll never make it at this rate."

"He's in danger, then," I said, as we tore around corners and down side streets to avoid the cops.

"Yes. But let me begin at the beginning. Wilkins got onto the track of a mysterious taxi that had been seen on Mott Street about four-fifteen the afternoon of October the eighth, and while he was hanging around one of those Chinese joints, he saw two toughs lounging down Pell Street, and evidently discussing the reward, since one of them was waving the hand-bill in the other's face. Wilkins followed them into an eating-house and by securing a table next to them, overheard their conversation. It seemed that they had identified Lee as the young man they had kidnapped and they were weighing the respective merits of giving their information to me or blackmailing the 'old man,' as they called whoever had hired them. The younger tough was for telling me, but the older one seemed to think they could make more from the 'old man.' Whereupon the younger one declared that the old fellow was stingier than hell and reminded his companion that Hi Ling had tipped them that the young man was to disappear that night, after the boss's visit at one o'clock. When the men separated Wilkins followed the younger one and by many judicious hints and the added compensation of some money and promised immunity from the police, he got the rest of the story.

"This fellow and his companion had been hired to kidnap a young chap and they had deposited him in Hi Ling's back shop in an upstairs room. There was something the young man knew that the 'old man' wanted to learn so much, he had gathered from the Chinaman who kept the shop. In other words, Lee knew something of the murder and the criminal wanted to find out just how much, or else he wanted to keep Lee from giving evidence. It doesn't matter which. The main fact remains, that he is holding the boy a prisoner.

"Well, when he realized that through my efforts I was bound to learn where Lee was, since he did not trust the toughs, he gave orders that when he had paid the boy his customary visit at one o'clock, they were to get rid of Lee for him. One more murder wouldn't disturb his conscience very much, I guess. Our only chance lies in getting there ahead of the criminal."

"How do you know it's not a trap?" I asked.

"I've provided for that by my orders to Jenkins. If it's a trap the police will have to rescue us, that's all. I feel conscience-stricken, lugging you into what may turn out to be a fight for life," he added.

"You needn't. I wouldn't have missed it for anything," I returned. "But why don't you surround the place with the police right away?"

"Do you know where we are going?" he asked curiously.

"To Chinatown, I should judge," I answered.

"Exactly. They keep scouts on the watch at those places, which are respectable without and hells within. The moment they saw the sight of a uniform Lee Darwin would disappear and no one would ever learn what had become of him. Days later an unrecognizable corpse would be dragged from the river."

I shuddered. What a horrible end for the boy if we should fail to reach him in time!

At this juncture the car stopped with a jerk at the corner of Mott and Hester streets, and we piled out.

"Wait here for us. If we do not come by one-thirty, you can go home," said McKelvie.

The man turned off his engine and settled himself to wait, and the next moment we were hurrying toward Pell Street. Then we turned another corner and modifying our pace, lounged carelessly toward the back entrance of Hi Ling's curio shop.

Remembering Lecoq's advice I tried to look dull and stupid as McKelvie opened the door. We stepped inside the shop and faced the Chinaman seated behind a counter at the rear of the room. He was a fat old Chinaman and he gazed at us stolidly as he smoked his pipe.

In a coarse voice McKelvie asked whether the "old man" had come, saying he had sent us to stay with the prisoner until his arrival.

The Chinaman looked at us unblinkingly for five steady minutes, then he waved his pipe toward a rear door. We shuffled toward it as fast as we dared, and I for one, expected that every minute he would call us back and question us more closely. But he did not move and we gained the doorway and saw before us, in the flickering light of a gas-jet from above, a staircase, steep, narrow, dirty. This we climbed and found ourselves in a small entry with a door at the back. Stealing to this door, McKelvie listened intently for a moment, then drew his revolver and tried the door softly. It was locked. Shifting the gun to his left hand he took out a long, narrow steel instrument, which he inserted in the lock. As the door yielded silently, he stole into the room and I followed him closely.

I did not hear but I knew he had closed the door behind us, and then his flash glowed and the disk of light darted here and there over the black interior of the room, or, rather, hole, in which we found ourselves. It was empty save for a narrow cot, on which lay an inert figure, apparently asleep. We moved closer to the cot and McKelvie let the disk of light rest upon the face of the man before us.

It was Lee Darwin, I could not be mistaken, but he looked as though he were in the last stages of some terrible disease. His form was quite wasted, his eyes were mere sunken hollows in his ghastly face, and his cheekbones stood out prominently where the flesh had fallen away. I contemplated him in horrified silence, until a touch on my arm recalled me to action.

"I'm afraid he's too far gone to walk," whispered McKelvie. "We'll have to carry him. The main thing is to get him out before the criminal arrives. I don't think the old Chink will give us much trouble."

Silently McKelvie bent over Lee and shook him into consciousness. The boy opened his haggard eyes, stared at the flash, then shuddered away from McKelvie's restraining hand.

"Go away," he said feebly. "I have nothing to tell you. Nothing, I say."

"Mr. Darwin," said McKelvie soothingly, "it's all right. We only want to help you get away."

Lee turned toward the sound of the voice, a dawning wonder in his eyes, then as the sense of McKelvie's words penetrated his dulled brain and the sound of McKelvie's rich voice fell like balm on his spirit, which had been harassed for days by harsh voices and coarse threats, he put out his hand and pushed aside the flash which McKelvie still kept focused on his face.

"Help me-get up," he said.

In the darkness we helped him to his feet and got him out into the corridor, where he collapsed again. So we lifted him by his head and feet and carried him down the stairs.

When we reached the bottom we looked across into the placid face of the old Chinaman contemplating us fixedly from the doorway!

CHAPTER XXXI

THE RESCUE

"Lord," McKelvie muttered low, as we set Lee down upon the lowest step. "He's evidently in the game, too. No wonder he was so obliging about letting us pass, since there probably is no outlet yonder," and he jerked his head toward the top of the stairs.

He pulled out his gun and leveled it at the Chinaman. "Now then, Hi, or whatever your name is, just raise your arms above your head and back into that room, or you'll get a taste of this," and he tapped his revolver menacingly, but the Chinaman only continued to regard us placidly, with no change of expression on his yellow countenance.

McKelvie spoke to me in an undertone. "He knows darn well I won't shoot, damn him, since it would bring the house about our ears. I have a better plan. I'll take Lee on my back and you can give yonder Chinaman a punch in the jaw. Then we'll make tracks for the door. Once we get outside we'll be fairly safe, for these Chinamen don't want a row with the police if they can avoid it."

He slipped his automatic back into his pocket, and while he slung Lee over his shoulder, I swaggered up to the Chinaman.

"Better let us pass, bo," I said roughly in character, to gain time. "You might get hurt, Chink."

Again that stolid indifference, as though to him we did not exist, which made my blood boil and gave my arm an added impetus. The next moment the Chinaman was sprawling on the ground and we had gained the other room. With my cap pulled well over my face I was making tracks for the door to get it open for us to pass, when I heard a yell from McKelvie.

"Duck!" he cried, and as I obeyed I heard something whizz over my head and a hatchet buried itself in the wall ahead of me. I turned sharply and grappled with a lithe, yellow-clad figure that had sprung at me from the side of the room.

In tense silence we struggled, each striving to reach the other's throat, and as we fought I caught a glimpse of some heavy metal object on a stand near one corner of the room. Warily, inch by inch, I forced my adversary back until he fell against the stand, losing his balance and almost carrying me with him. With an effort I kept my feet, freeing my arm with a sudden movement, and as he swayed clutching at me, I grasped the metal candlestick and brought it down upon his head. His fingers loosened from my arm and he went down with a sickening thud.

Then, panting, I turned to look for McKelvie. He was standing in the opposite corner, shielding Lee's unconscious form, with his gun covering the old Chinaman whom I had first knocked out and who had succeeded in joining the fray again, and now stood as stolidly as ever beside a third Chinaman, who lay prostrate on the floor.

I advanced to McKelvie's side and as I did so I glanced again at the prostrate Chinaman. To my horror he was not as insensible as I had at first supposed. One arm was drawn back and he was on the point of hurling a murderous looking hatchet at McKelvie's head.

"Look out," I yelled, but McKelvie had seen him too.

There was a spat from McKelvie's gun, the hatchet went flying backwards and the Chinaman rolled over, howling with pain and rage. The momentary diversion, however, had served the other Chinaman in good stead. Before I could reach him he had glided to a counter, lifted a clapper and struck upon a gong. The next moment the Chinks came pouring in about us like rats from their holes.

I managed somehow to reach McKelvie's side before the onslaught began, and together we kept our backs to the corner where Lee lay huddled. Then McKelvie raised his pistol and deliberately shot out the light. After that, confusion reigned. I could hear the scuffle of feet, an occasional flash from McKelvie's gun, and a scream of agony as the bullet tore its way through soft flesh, followed by a quick report from my automatic, which I had drawn even though he had given me no leave, then again the shuffle, shuffle of feet, while we warded off blows and tried to keep our unseen enemies at a distance.

And then into the midst of this turmoil a high pitched voice cut like a knife. It was not a Chinaman's voice. It was a refined, cultivated, but distinctly American voice, and it seemed to me that I had heard its intonation before at some time.

Querulously it demanded a light, and as someone lighted the gas the Chinamen fell away from before us. We were battered and bruised, McKelvie and I, but otherwise unhurt, and we still stood with our backs to Lee Darwin, protecting him from the assault of his foes.

In the flickering light of the one poor burner I could see that the room was filled with Chinamen, or perhaps I mistook shadows for the reality, since though they remained inactive they shuffled about in the background, passing and repassing each other continually. Then a man stepped forward into the limelight and I saw the owner of that cutting voice.

With arms folded and head thrust forward, he stood and glared malevolently at McKelvie, and I beheld with astonishment the bent old figure and the white hair and beard shining like silver in that light. Though he took no notice of me, still I could feel his antagonism and wished for a moment that he would cast aside the heavy blue glasses he wore and give me a chance to see his eyes.

"So," he said, in that high-pitched voice, sarcastically strident in its intonation, "you thought to get ahead of me, eh? You thought I was such a fool that I wouldn't prepare for your visit, eh? There are a few people still left who have more brains than you think, Mr. McKelvie."

McKelvie returned his empty gun to his pocket very coolly, and then laughed softly.

"Stand aside and let Hi Ling take that boy. Then I will settle with you, Mr. Detective," went on the old man, unfolding his arms and thrusting a hand into the pocket of the long coat he wore.

McKelvie laughed again. "Come and get him, you murderer," he said, quietly.

With a snarl of rage the man flung out his arm and fired. I saw McKelvie draw aside quickly and then bite his lips as his left arm fell limply at his side. With a curse I leaped forward, but McKelvie pulled me back just as there arose a banging on the outer door and a shrill whistle sounded clear and loud outside.

There was a cry of "Police, the Police" and with an oath the old man fired again, at Lee, and then he shot up tall and extinguished the light. Pandemonium was let loose. There was a scurry of feet, the banging of a door, yells and execrations, hoarse cries, men's voices shouting loudly, and then something struck me on the head. I fell heavily to the ground, and as I did so a flash was thrust into my face and I heard Jones' voice exclaim as from a great distance, "Mr. Davies, by all that's holy," and then blackness descended upon me.

I came to myself with the sensation that someone was pouring red-hot liquid down my throat. I sat up, gasping, to find Jones bending over me with a brandy flask in his hand.

"All right?" he asked.

Recollection swept over me. "Where's McKelvie?" I managed to reply.

"Yonder." Jones nodded his head toward the chair where McKelvie sat, grinning like a Cheshire cat.

His clothes were torn, his face was smeared with blood, and his left arm had been recently bandaged, but he wore the expression of a conqueror, as he commanded the doctor to cease fussing over him and to look after Lee, who was still unconscious.

Then I realized that we were no longer in the curio shop, but in McKelvie's living-room, and that Lee was lying upon a couch, as motionless and rigid as a corpse.

The doctor ordered that the boy be put to bed, and McKelvie told Jones to ring for Dinah. When she came in presently, wrapped in an old kimona and with her woolly wig more belligerent than ever, McKelvie asked her to get a room ready. Then the doctor and Jones carried Lee from the room.

"What happened after I went down?" I asked, feeling the lump on my head. "I remember hearing Jones, and that is all."

"I'm ashamed to acknowledge that when I knew that the police were actually in the room, I fainted," he replied with a grin. "When I came to myself, those Chinamen who could get away had vanished, and with them the old man. I'd have given ten years of my life to get a glimpse of his eyes behind those glasses. I have a feeling that once having seen them I should never forget them."

"So he got away," I said.

"Oh, yes, Jones of course knew nothing about him, and when I was in a condition to explain, the fellow was far away. The police searched for him, but without avail. So I told them not to bother and ordered Jones to bring us here." He sat back with a smile, but I could see that his arm was giving him pain. "It was a great fight and the best part was that we were able to rescue Lee."

"Yes," I replied. "I should very much like to hear his story. By the way, that vindictive old man didn't shoot him, did he?"

"No, I don't believe he more than grazed him, if he hit him at all. Naturally he was trying to prevent us from taking the boy away from there."

"He had no trouble recognizing you," I continued. "Has he seen you before?"

"Doubtless. A man of his caliber would acquaint himself with his adversaries for safety's sake. He saw me the night we chased him in the study, and what is more, I made no attempt to disguise myself to-night when he stood there looking at me. That's why he tried to kill me. I read his purpose though and waited until he had flung out his arm to fire, and then I moved aside, but not quite out of range, as you saw," and he glanced at his arm. "But here is Jones. What does the doctor say?"

"He'll pull him around. That black woman of yours is certainly a trump. She's making him some broth. The boy's starved," answered Jones, then he looked at us and grinned. "It's a good thing for you fellows that I happened to be at Headquarters to-night, when your man called us, Mr. Davies. I twigged what was up and had the dope in a second, so I was able to get to you in time."

"I'm eternally grateful to you, Jones, and so is Mr. Davies," returned McKelvie, holding out his hand, which Jones accepted with a sheepish smile. "But for you we might be occupying the river by now."

"Don't say any more," expostulated Jones, as I added my share of gratitude. "It's all part of the job. Well, doctor?"

"He's coming on fine. He's got a good nurse. I'll be around in the morning to have another look at him," said the doctor. "And now my advice to you, sir," turning to McKelvie, "is to get to bed and let that arm have a chance to recover. That was a nasty flesh wound you got. Come along, Jones."

"I'll be around again, too," said Jones, "to hear that young man's story. I don't know what all this has to do with the murder, but his tale should be interesting, to say the least."

We agreed and then went upstairs, where we got rid of our rags and had a good wash. Then McKelvie loaned me a pair of pajamas and a bed, which had never been more welcome to my throbbing head.

CHAPTER XXXII

LEE'S STORY

Despite his arm, which he had redressed himself and which was quite stiff, McKelvie was up ahead of me, and when I came down at noon attired in my own garments (McKelvie had phoned Jenkins to bring me my things) I felt quite like myself again.

"Has the doctor been here?" I asked as we had our luncheon.

"Yes, but he will be back later. Lee is still asleep. We shall hear his story this afternoon." Then he sighed. "I wish we had been able to catch that old chap. I am positive he is the murderer. I felt it in my bones when he looked at me and my bones are quite infallible, I assure you," and he smiled whimsically.

"It is a pity," I said, "for then this business would be over."

When we rose from the table and went back to the living-room, McKelvie moved about restlessly, and then said impatiently, "I wish the doctor would come. I want to get at the boy's story as soon as possible, for I think he may help us locate Cora Manning, and we shall have to work fast now if we expect to catch the criminal. He's too clever to hang around much longer, now that he knows the game is up as far as Mrs. Darwin is concerned."

I heartily indorsed McKelvie's words, for I was eager to hear what Lee had to say, but he did not waken until five o'clock and the doctor, who had come in some time previous, forbade our disturbing him. When we finally mounted to his room, Jones, McKelvie and I, we could hardly wait for the doctor's assurance that he thought it would not harm the young man to talk. As we gathered about the bed, Lee leaned back against his pillows, his hollow cheeks flushed and his black eyes glittering strangely as he looked at us. I heard Jones mutter something about "eyes like a madman's," which Lee evidently overheard, for he turned to the doctor with an appealing glance.

"Before I begin," he said, in a weak voice, "I want you, doctor, to answer me a question. Am I perfectly rational and sane?"

"Yes, perfectly sane," responded the doctor, quietly.

Lee breathed a sigh of relief. "Please remember that, gentlemen," he continued. "I may look mad but I'm not. No, nor ever have been, though at times I thought I was pretty near to it."

He paused to gather strength and then he told his tale almost without a break, for it gripped him too vitally to admit of his stopping, once he had begun.

"To explain my actions I must go back to the morning of the seventh. I testified at the inquest that I quarreled with my uncle about Ruth. I lied. We quarreled about Cora Manning."

At this name Jones leaned closer, a greater interest in his face.

"I met her a year ago when she came to New York to study for the stage. Three months ago we became engaged and I gave her, as is customary, a diamond ring. Later I introduced my uncle to her. Instantly he evinced a great interest in her, cloaking his infatuation (I know it was that now) under the guise of a desire to aid her in her career. He took her out a number of times and when I protested she accused me of being jealous of my uncle, which she said was unworthy of me if I loved her, since my uncle was an old married man.

"To make a long story short, on the morning of the seventh, as I was leaving the house, my uncle called me back into the study and there showed me the ring I had given Cora, swearing she had bestowed it upon him to return it to me, as she no longer cared for me and was coming to see him there in the study that night. He had the ring on the little finger of his left hand and he pulled it off with a laugh and held it toward me. I snatched it from him and flung it in his face, and would have leaped upon him to strangle him then and there, but he read my purpose in my face, and like the craven that he was, he called to Orton to come into the room. Then he ordered me to leave his house and I went out by the window, vowing vengeance upon him.

"I hurried to Cora's and accused her of treachery, declaring I'd kill my uncle before he should have her. I was mad, crazy, and refusing to listen to any explanations I rushed away and bought a pistol. That evening I hung around the house on Riverside Drive. I would wait her arrival and then go in and kill them both. I saw my uncle let himself into the house and about an hour later Mr. Davies arrived, but still no Cora. I began to think I had been a fool, but determined to wait a while longer just to make sure. About eleven forty-five, for I looked at my watch as I reached the gate, I saw her coming down the street with a suitcase in her hand. Mad with rage, I hid behind some bushes and followed her as she turned into the grounds. It was very dark and I lost her as she slipped around the house.

"I decided to enter by the front door and confront them, then I recalled that Mr. Davies had not yet gone, and determined to try the windows. I crept to the second window and by means of my flash saw that the shade did not come level with the bottom of the window. I knelt down and applied my eye to this space. By looking upward from the extreme corner of the window I discovered that I could see what my uncle was doing. The room was dark except for the lamp that threw its rays over the table and chair, and in the latter my uncle was reclining asleep. Then as I looked, suddenly Cora appeared beside the table and in her hand she carried a small pistol. She pointed it at my uncle, and just then the light went out. I judged that she had shot him, though I heard no sound, and so paralyzed with horror was I that I remained where I was gazing into the darkness of the room before me.

"How long I stayed there I don't know. Presently I thought I heard the sound of a step on the walk. I wrenched myself free from the entangling ivy and hastened to the gate. There was no one in sight. For a long time I stood there, debating whether to go back or not, and then I came to the conclusion that if she had really shot my uncle she needed every minute to get away. I fled the place and paced the streets in an agony of suspense. In the morning I returned to the Club, where I slept until noon. When the steward woke me my first thought was for Cora. I dashed around to Gramercy Park. She was gone, had been gone since the night before. Then I rushed up to my uncle's house, thinking she might have been caught. I found the coroner in possession. Persuaded that Cora had killed my uncle and not seeing her present, I determined to shield her by denying all knowledge of her. After my testimony I went upstairs to my rooms, gathered together a few necessary articles and went back to Gramercy Park. She was still missing. I thought of advertising for her and had gone as far as the *Herald* office when it occurred to me that by locating her I would only be putting her life in danger.

"Dejectedly I returned to the Club once more and there found a written message awaiting me. I read and destroyed it, but the words are burned into my brain:

> 'Lee, my darling: I killed him to save my honor. If you love me, help me to get away. I could not bear the notoriety of a trial. Meet me at the corner of Twenty-third Street and Third Avenue and I'll be waiting for you in a brown taxi. Cora.'

"I told the steward to hold my rooms as I was going South on business, and took a taxi to Twenty-fifth and Third Avenue, where I dismissed the man and walked rapidly to Twenty-third Street."

Lee paused and drew a gasping breath, whereupon the doctor hastened to administer a stimulant.

"The car was waiting?" prompted McKelvie.

"Yes, and when I appeared the door opened and a hand beckoned. I entered the car unsuspectingly, but I was no sooner seated and the door had been closed (it was dark as pitch inside, since all the shades were drawn) than I felt a hand on my face and smelled something that made me gasp. Some instinct warned me not to breathe and I thrust out my hand and my fingers closed on a man's rough coat. Then I realized I'd been trapped and flung myself toward my assailant. He grasped my throat and thrust a handkerchief over my face. The deadly fumes got into my lungs, for I felt myself suffocating, and drawing a deep involuntary breath I fell unconscious.

"When I came to I was lying in the room where you found me, and a couple of ruffians were guarding me. I do not recall much of this part of the affair, for I was kept in a semi-conscious state most of the time and left absolutely alone all day, with little or no food. I have an impression that once every night I was shaken into consciousness by someone who spoke in a harsh whisper and asked me a lot of questions about the murder. Fearing for Cora, I refused to answer. Every day I grew weaker and every day the harsh voice grew more insistent, until the man, whoever he was, started to torture me as well. The day before you rescued me I lost all consciousness of what was going on, for my mind had been partly drugged, I believe. I guess that's all except that I want to thank you fellows for getting me out of there."

Lee closed his eyes wearily, and Jones scratched his head in perplexity.

"If what he says is true," whispered Jones to me, "where does Mrs. Darwin come in? He must have dreamed all this. Darwin was shot at midnight."

"He didn't dream that he had been held a prisoner, at least," I returned. "As for the rest, I presume it's all true enough," and I turned toward McKelvie to get his opinion in the matter.

"Mr. Darwin," McKelvie said, as Lee opened his eyes again, "are you strong enough to answer some questions?"

"Yes," Lee answered.

"Describe the man who questioned you?"

"I never saw him. The room was always dark. I heard his voice, that is all. It was always a harsh whisper. But wait, once I put out my hand and felt a beard, long and silky."

McKelvie nodded quickly. "What questions did he ask you?"

"He asked me where I was the night of the murder, and he kept saying over and over, 'someone you love is in danger and when you tell me what you know about your uncle's murder, she will be freed.'

"I had a feeling this was another trap," Lee went on, "since if I told him that she had committed the murder they would send her to prison. I had no idea what his connection with the affair might be, but I determined not to be caught napping again."

"There is no connection between him and the murder," responded Jones authoritatively. "We've got the criminal locked up this minute."

"Oh, have you," returned McKelvie, sarcastically. "Just listen to what I have since discovered, Jones," and he sketched rapidly the main facts in the case.

They listened spellbound, as he told of the secret entrance and the second shot, declaring that Darwin was murdered at eleven-forty by the man we had seen in the curio shop, that this man was keeping Cora Manning a prisoner, and had deliberately set about implicating Ruth in the murder. Jones' eyes grew wide with astonishment as he listened, for it upset all his preconceived ideas.

"Then she didn't kill him, thank God, thank God," sobbed Lee, quite overcome by all he had been through.

"No, she didn't kill him," returned McKelvie kindly. "And now we are going to do our best to find her for you."

CHAPTER XXXIII

THE SECOND BULLET

When we were downstairs again and the doctor had gone, Jones turned to me. McKelvie was smoking his pipe and pacing the room, his brows knit in thought, and Jones did not like to disturb him.

"I say, Mr. Davies, can't you give a fellow a few more details?" he begged. "I seem to have got the dope all wrong in this case. Who is this mysterious man?"

I glanced at McKelvie, but he was paying no attention to our conversation. I decided that there was no harm in telling Jones all that we knew, since McKelvie himself had already disclosed the more vital points.

So I gave Jones a rapid account of our search for the criminal, how we had discovered the secret entrance, where the trail of the sachet bags had led us, how we had interviewed Orton, Mrs. Harmon, and Cunningham, and how the finding of Dick's ring led to the discovery that he was still alive.

"But as regards the mysterious man in the curio shop," I ended, "I can't tell you who he is since I don't know, but my impression is that he was disguised and that he is not old at all, for one moment he was feeble and bent, and the next, when he turned off the light, tall and strong."

Jones slapped his hand on his knee. "By George, you're right. What did he look like, anyway?"

"When I first saw him he was bent and his head was thrust forward, his hair and beard were silver-white, his eyes protected by blue glasses," I answered.

"Disguised all right," said Jones with conviction. "It's a remarkable thing now, Mr. Davies, but when a man runs to disguise he always chooses the appearance which is his very opposite, the idea being, I suppose, to look as unlike his former self as possible. He stooped and was old, therefore he really is young and tall. He wore whiskers and glasses, therefore he is smooth-shaven and has good eyesight. That's your man."

"And if you add the fact that he is dark, you have a pretty good description of the murderer," put in McKelvie suddenly.

"Good heavens!" I began, but McKelvie raised his hand.

"Keep your suspicions to yourself," he said, and returned to his meditation.

"Seems to me you've made pretty good progress so far," Jones continued, "but what you need is the police on his trail. We'd soon have him where he belongs."

"Well, I don't know that we have made so much progress after all," I went on, as McKelvie ignored Jones' insinuation. "We have reduced the number of suspects by finding Lee, but we really are no further than we were three days ago. We progress so slowly," I added, impatiently, "because we discover only unsubstantiated facts. We thought Lee might be able to help us but he cannot swear to having seen his uncle die, and without that proof Ruth must stay in jail."

"I'm sorry," returned Jones. "The only thing to do is to catch the criminal or learn his identity."

"How?" I demanded. Did Jones think he could win out where McKelvie had been unsuccessful? Then I recalled McKelvie's words before he took the case, when he had handed me his list of questions. "Find the answers to those questions and you will have the name of the man who committed the crime." We ought to be able to answer almost all of them by now.

I pulled out my wallet and opened it, drawing forth the sheets that I had placed there less than a week ago (it seemed more like years) and spread them out in front of Jones, explaining their purpose and how I came by them. He read them through, glanced at McKelvie's back (he was seeking inspiration from the falling night), and then he grinned.

"Say," he whispered loudly, "we ought to be able to dope it out, you and I. I'll read you the questions and you give me the answers." He took out his fountain pen, prepared to fill in my replies, and I humored him.

"Question one. Why was the pistol fired at midnight?" Jones asked.

"To implicate Ruth," I returned.

"Did the murderer also light the lamp?" Jones' pen scratched away as he spoke.

"Yes. He lighted it from the safe," I said, explaining how we had ascertained this fact.

"How did he enter and leave the room?"

"He entered by the window and he left by the secret entrance," I replied, remembering McKelvie's assertion.

"Wrong." McKelvie swung toward us for a moment. "He entered by the door."

"But I thought you said —" I began.

"I've changed my mind," he retorted, and turned his back on us again.

Jones' eyebrows went up a trifle, and then he asked, "What was the motive for the murder?"

"I don't know," I said frankly. "It seems to me that answer depends on who murdered him. Find the murderer and you have the motive, not learn the motive and you have your man, as in most cases," I added.

"We'll leave number four blank, then. Why did the doctors disagree, and which was in the right? I recall that fact now. They had quite a tiff over it and the young doctor was worsted." Jones laughed at the recollection.

My answer astonished him. "I'd say they disagreed because the coroner's physician was a pompous old ass," I returned vindictively. I could not forget that in very truth Ruth's accusal had been the result of this verdict. "Dr. Haskins was in the right, since Darwin was shot at eleven-forty."

"Why did Philip Darwin put that ring on his finger and then take it off again?"

"Cunningham explained that Darwin did it in a moment of sentimentality. It seemed an idiotic thing to do, after all, and I don't believe he was addicted to sentiment," I said.

"Well, no, he might have had it in his hand and slipped it on unthinkingly, and then had trouble taking it off," replied Jones, reflectively.

I shook my head. "No, I am inclined to believe that he hurt his finger with Cora's ring. Lee said his uncle was wearing it on his little finger and that he removed it hastily and handed it to him. It was probably tight for him, and so he bruised the finger," I said.

"Where's the diamond then?" asked Jones.

"It may have fallen out and the murderer may have found it," I returned. "Or better yet, Orton may have taken it. You know Lee flung the ring at his uncle."

"That's plausible, and I never liked the secretary's face, anyway. Whose was the blood-stained handkerchief?" continued Jones.

"Cora Manning's, because of the perfume which all her male friends seem to have adopted also," I remarked.

"Where did the second bullet go?"

"By the way, McKelvie, where did it go?" I inquired.

But he pretended not to hear me, so I said to Jones with a laugh, "Another blank. I have no idea where it went."

"Did McKelvie search the room?"

"With a magnifying glass. It's not there."

"That's queer. It's bound to be somewhere. I'll have to have a look myself. Why is there so much evidence against Mrs. Darwin?"

I permitted myself a smile at Jones' evident estimate of McKelvie's abilities as far as searching a room was concerned, then I replied to his question. "I suppose the criminal believed in being thorough while he was about it."

"Who and what is Cora Manning?"

"She is, or was, Lee's fiancée. As to what she is, I'll tell you better when I see her. According to McKelvie she's a beauty," and I smiled. "Also, if you can believe what he says, the criminal is in love with this girl, so she is not the one who fired the shot."

"So McKelvie says, but if the criminal loves her, how do we know she wasn't his tool. Even the boy upstairs thought she had killed his uncle," remarked Jones.

"Don't be an idiot, Jones," said McKelvie's voice. "She wasn't likely to shoot a man who was already dying when she entered the room. She got there at eleven-forty-five, or later."

"Oh, yes. I forgot that fact. But the boy's watch may have been fast at that," replied Jones, unabashed. "She pointed a pistol at him, you know."

"Yes, and I presume she kept the man she loves in duress all this time? But have it your own way," returned McKelvie, dryly. Then I heard him add to himself, "Where can she be? If I could only lay my finger on her hiding-place, I'd have him in my toils."

"What has become of Darwin's securities?" Jones returned to the paper before him.

"Cunningham says Darwin lost his fortune in Wall Street," I answered.

"What is Lee Darwin's connection with the affair?"

"Like Ruth he is a victim of circumstances and the criminal's machinations," I said.

"Why did Richard Trenton come to New York and then commit suicide?" Jones went on.

"He came to New York at Darwin's request to see him. This we know to be a fact," and I told Jones the gist of Gilmore's story. "Also we know that he did not commit suicide although he tried to give the world that impression."

"That looks very bad. What's Cunningham's relation to the murdered man?"

"Just his friend since Cunningham is not a lawyer."

"That looks bad, too," said Jones. "He acted as counsel at the inquest illegally then."

"He says not. That he did not see Mrs. Darwin and gave her no advice. You can prosecute him when the case is over. We have no time for that now," I added.

"Which one of those having sufficient motive for killing Darwin answers to the description: Clever, unprincipled, absolutely cold-blooded?"

"There's an immense amount of latitude in that question. There might be any number of men of that type, since we do not know how many may have had sufficient motive for killing him. I expect that we haven't met all the men who have grudges against him, not by a long shot. And now, Mr. Jones, having doped it out, as you expressed it, would you mind telling me who committed that murder?" I asked quizzically.

Jones grinned. "I'll be hanged if I know," he replied. "But then we have not answered all the questions, you know. There's the motive and that second bullet. Oh, I say, McKelvie, what about letting me get busy on the trail of the revolver that made that second shot? There's a good substantial clue for you, though I know your preference for deductions."

McKelvie turned away from the window laughing at Jones' irony, then said quietly, "I won't trouble you to locate it as it might inconvenience you sadly. You see, I know where it is."

"You do?" Jones looked incredulous. "You know where it is and you haven't produced it?"

"How could I when you have had it under lock and key at Headquarters right from the start," returned McKelvie, his eyes twinkling.

"I? Oh, no, you're wrong there. I have only Darwin's pistol," replied Jones.

"That's the one I refer to."

"But, man, there's only one shot fired from that, the shot that killed Darwin," expostulated Jones.

"Use your imagination, Jones. Did you never hear of a man's cleaning his pistol and recharging it?" inquired McKelvie sarcastically.

"By Jove," said Jones, then added quickly, "What about the second bullet, then? I don't happen to possess that, too, do I?"

"No, for there was no second bullet."

"No second bullet!" I exclaimed, remembering the stress he had laid on that fact.

"No," he returned coolly, "there was no second bullet because-he took the trouble to remove it before he fired the cartridge."

CHAPTER XXXIV

THE WOMAN IN THE CASE

My mind remained appalled before the contemplation of the devilish ingenuity of this man, who could plan the murder with such diabolical cunning. No wonder we were finding it a difficult matter to secure proof against him! Who was he? Was he someone I knew or a stranger who had hitherto remained unsuspected by us? Did McKelvie have any idea of the man's identity, or was he also groping in the dark? Persistently I discarded the thought of Dick, even though the ring was his, and Jones' description of the criminal fitted the boy, for I could not believe that he could have become such a fiend, unless indeed he had suddenly lost all sense of proportion and balance.

It was at this point in my meditations that Jones arose and declared that he must be going, but McKelvie refused to listen to him. He liked Jones, even though the two were so often on opposite sides of the case they were investigating.

"Stay for dinner," McKelvie urged. "I owe you that much anyhow. Also, I may need you. And now I wish you fellows would cease worrying about the criminal's identity and put your faculties to work on a more pressing subject. Where do you suppose he has hidden Cora Manning?"

Where, indeed, with the whole of New York to choose from.

We were enjoying our after-dinner cigars when McKelvie suddenly gave a shout. "Eureka!" he cried. "I've got it. She's at Riverside Drive. What an idiot I was not to think of it before."

"How do you make that out?" asked Jones.

"Lee thought he heard a step on the walk and assumed that it was the girl leaving the grounds. He hurried to the gate, but when he looked around there was no one in sight. If she had really left the place he would have been in time to see her as she walked down the block. There would be no place for her to disappear to unless she jumped in the river, which would hardly be likely."

"She may have hidden in the grounds and have waited for Lee to go away first," I objected.

"She did not know he was there and would have no reason then for hiding. No, no, she's at the Darwin house. It was the easiest place to hide her in, safe and secure, and it would not involve his having to take anyone into his confidence. The house, doubtless, has more than one secret room. We'll go out there now, and in an hour we'll have her free."

"Do you want a taxi?" asked Jones.

"No, we'll use the subway this time," replied McKelvie.

We walked to Union Square and took the Broadway Subway to Dyckman Street, walking from there to Riverside Drive. As we entered the Darwin grounds I paused to admire the brilliancy of the stars, and noticed how the reflection of the lights from the river craft twinkled in the waters of the Hudson as if in friendly rivalry.

But my companions did not wait to look at the scenery, and I had to hurry to catch up with them.

"We'll go in the back entrance again," said McKelvie. "I want to question Mason."

After a slight delay the old man admitted us and McKelvie asked him if he ever took occasion to go into the main wing of the house.

"Yes, sir. I have been in twice, sir, to open the windows and air the place against Mrs. Darwin's coming home," he replied.

"And while you were there did you hear any sounds, a person walking, for instance?" continued McKelvie.

Mason looked at him in great surprise. "Oh, no, sir. There is no one in the house now, sir."

"Is there an attic to the house?"

"Yes, sir; but I'm sure there's no one there. I went in yesterday morning to put away Mr. Darwin's things, sir."

"Have you any provisions in the house?" was the next question.

"Yes, sir, for myself."

"Prepare some broth for me, please. I'll send for it when I want it."

"Yes, sir."

"What's the idea? Do you think she's starving, too?" asked Jones, as we crossed the passageway and entered the main hall.

"Does he strike you as the kind that would be gentle with his prisoners? We'll ransack the whole house from attic to cellar, despite Mason's assertions."

We ascended the broad staircase to the second floor. McKelvie then apportioned the back rooms to Jones, the front ones to me, and reserved for himself the whole third floor, which was mostly the attic. My part comprised the sleeping apartments of Ruth as well as Darwin's suite.

I entered Ruth's rooms first, but did not remain in them long, since every article spoke to me of the girl I loved and who was at this moment enduring the hardness of a narrow cot in a barred and grated cell instead of enjoying the comforts to which she had been always accustomed, and all this because she had been accused of a crime that she was utterly incapable of committing.

Darwin's suite of dressing-room, bedroom, and bath were also unproductive of any clues to Cora Manning's whereabouts, although once I thought I detected a faint odor of rose jacqueminot and wondered idly whether Darwin, too, had caught the epidemic.

Out in the hall I encountered Jones.

"Nothing doing," he said. "Besides, she wouldn't be lying around loose, or that old butler would have come across her, unless he was lying. For my own part, I think this is a wild goose chase."

Before I could reply McKelvie descended from the attic. "Would you mind talking in a lower key," he remarked in a whisper. "I could hear you distinctly upstairs, Jones, and if the criminal should come here, we would frighten him off for good."

"You don't mean to tell me he'd have the nerve to come here!" exclaimed Jones.

"He's come here more than once, as Mr. Davies and I can prove," he returned, drawing us into a room and closing the door. "Don't you suppose he comes here to see the girl? It's my opinion he is trying to break her into going away with him, though I can't see what is to stop him from drugging her and carrying her away."

He walked to the window and looked out into the night. "She's not in the attic. There's no secret room up there; yet I'm positive she's in the house. He wouldn't come back for anything less important, though I did think once that he had a hiding-place in the room behind the safe. You remember that I was looking for it the night we found Dick's ring," he continued, more to himself than to us. Then he turned away from the window, his eyes shining, "Lord, I'm growing dull! Do you recall, Mr. Davies, that we heard steps on the stone staircase and that when I opened the door and turned my flash on the stairs they were empty and the door below locked?"

I nodded, and he went on quickly, "It never occurred to me before, but he must have vanished into a second secret room off those stairs. Come on, I'll bet that's where he's got her hidden."

At the door, however, he paused to issue final instructions. "Go softly and obey me implicitly. Also don't talk, and have your gun handy, Jones, in case of need."

We tiptoed down the stairs and crossed the hall to the study door, which McKelvie opened slowly and silently. The room was dark. With the aid of his flash we walked down the length of the room to the safe, our footfalls deadened by the thickness of the carpet. Then McKelvie manipulated the dial and opened the safe. It was Jones' first initiation into the mysteries of the entrance, and I pulled him down to a stooping position as we passed through to the secret room. Then we crossed to the door at the head of the stairs and McKelvie listened intently before he inserted his key in the lock. Then he turned to us.

"Stay here," he whispered. "When I locate the room I'll call to you. If anyone comes in that lower door, don't hesitate to shoot, Jones."

Jones and I obeyed and stood together in the darkness, watching the disk of light from McKelvie's flash dart here and there along the walls as McKelvie descended the stairs. Then the ray of light rested upon the wall into which the staircase had been built and which extended about three feet beyond the lowest step, that is, extended the length of the distance between the bottom of the staircase and the outer door, which, being but two feet in width, had plenty of margin with which to swing inwards. On this three feet of wall space the light danced up and down as McKelvie hunted for indications of a second secret room. Then we heard him calling to us softly.

We descended the stairs cautiously, and when we neared the bottom McKelvie pressed a depression which he pointed out to us. We saw a section of the wall disappear from view and the ray of light rested on the interior of a dark room. McKelvie stepped through first and called:

"Miss Manning, are you there?" he asked.

There was no answer, and telling us not to advance further, he disappeared into the darkness. We strained forward to look, and I distinctly smelled a musty, damp odor, as though the room or cell, or whatever it was, had been used as a vault, or maybe a tomb.

Then McKelvie came out again and swung the panel into place. He shivered slightly. "It's empty, but there are indications of a trap door in the ceiling. What is the room directly above this end of the study?"

"Darwin's dressing-room," I replied.

"Any windows on this side?"

"No."

"Just as I thought. There is a room above that vault. We'll try the second floor. I trust we are not too late," he added as we returned to the study. There we waited while McKelvie relocked the entrance, and when he was ready to lead the way upstairs again, Jones spoke in a troubled whisper.

"What's the idea of building a house with holes in the wall? It's a regular rat-trap," he said.

"I have a book at home that I'll have to lend you, Jones. The man who built this house was a nut on old-fashioned ideas. He copied an ancestral home, secret rooms and all. Not that he meant to use them, of course, but because it suited him to put them in. The one I just examined was used in ancient times, I think, to receive the bodies of those who fell through the trap door from the room above. A convenient way of getting rid of your enemy, that is all."

"This criminal of yours seems very familiar with this house," said Jones.

"Yes, he had been here many times before the murder, and he took pains to learn all he could about the place," returned McKelvie.

"I thought he only learned of the entrance on the night of the murder," I objected.

"Well, what of it. He is clever enough to have deduced what I did. He probably stumbled across the lower room in opening the outer door and then it was mere child's play to discover the room above."

Yes, that part was easy enough, but it was another matter to find the hidden spring that worked the panel. We turned on the light in the room, and divided the wall into three parts, each of us fingering a third carefully and painstakingly from top to bottom. It was Jones finally who stumbled on the spring. He had pressed the center of one of the mahogany flowers that formed the carved border of the dash-board and silently the panel slid back.

Never shall I forget the sight revealed to my eyes as the light from the dressing-room dispelled slightly the gloom of that interior.

In the center of the narrow room kneeled a young girl, with her dark hair streaming about her shoulders and her pale face raised to heaven as she pressed the barrel of an automatic to her heart. In that attitude of utter renunciation, she was very beautiful, so beautiful that she took away our breath and held us motionless.

That at least was her effect upon Jones and myself, but McKelvie was less susceptible, or perhaps his quick eyes noted a motion that we did not observe. At any rate, he sprang forward and knocked up the pistol. There was a sharp report, and the girl fell forward into his arms in a dead faint.

He carried her into Darwin's bedroom and laid her on the bed. While he worked over her, I descended to the kitchen where Mason was watching the broth McKelvie had ordered him to make.

When I returned she was sitting up, and as she sipped the broth I looked at her again and felt my pulses stirring as I looked into her face. I'm not much of a hand at describing beauty in a woman, and perhaps the greatest compliment I can pay her is to say that though she had suffered and her lustrous black eyes were dull and her face wan and pale, she was beautiful still, and her voice held all the haunting quality of the South in its depths as she told us her story, a story so unusual that it was almost unbelievable.

CHAPTER XXXV

A STRANGE ACCOUNT

"I come of a race whose blood is hot and easily provoked," she began in a low voice, "and who consider honor a thing to be cherished and guarded. A year ago I came to New York to study for the stage, which had always been my ambition, and before I left New Orleans my dear old teacher told me to beware of the pitfalls of that great metropolis, which I intended to make my home. In the beginning I followed his advice and was wary, receiving no visitors, although I made many acquaintances. But when one is alone one becomes lonely, and so I permitted two young men to call upon me, since I knew that both of them came from good families. I was playing with fire without realizing it, for the elder of the two, and he was hardly more than a boy, proposed to me when I had known him a month. I did not love him, and I told him so. In a burst of jealousy he accused me of being in love with his rival, and declared that since I would not marry him he cared not what became of him. He would go straight to the devil, he said. I tried to be kind and to reason with him, but he was spoiled and wanted only his own way, so I told him he must not try to see me again, and he never did, for six months ago he left the city for good."

As she paused in her recital, I realized with a shock that she was speaking of Dick Trenton. It was she who had given him the sachet then, and it was she who had been responsible, through the fault of that beauty with which nature had endowed her, for the attitude of devil-may-care, which had made the boy an easy prey to Darwin's fascinations. What a mixed up mess life really was!

"Three months ago I became engaged to Lee Darwin," she continued, "and in an evil hour for both of us, Lee introduced his uncle Philip to me. I knew Mr. Darwin was recently married, and so I deemed his interest in me what he said it was, a natural desire to aid me in my career. He took me to see the best actors and introduced me to one or two managers. Of course, Lee was jealous, but as I was never out with Mr. Darwin alone, and as Lee generally accompanied us, I felt I was doing no wrong, and that he was very inconsiderate to feel that way.

"The real trouble started on the sixth of October when I broke the setting of my engagement ring. I was afraid Lee would think I had been very careless, and I decided to have the ring mended and to say nothing about it. When Mr. Darwin came in unexpectedly that evening with plans for introducing me to an eminent playwright, he noticed that I wasn't wearing the ring, and asked why. I explained the circumstances and asked him to give me the name of a reliable jeweler, whereupon he offered to take it himself to Tiffany's.

"I had no suspicions of him," she said with an appealing glance for her indiscretion. "I gave him the ring."

She rested her voice as she sipped some more of the broth, which I brought up at McKelvie's request.

"The next morning about ten o'clock Lee came to Gramercy Park. His face was pale and his eyes gleaming wildly. He called me names and accused me of a liaison with his uncle, telling me that I might have saved myself the trouble of returning the ring, as he did not want it. Then vowing he would kill his uncle before the day was over, he dashed out, leaving me terrified, cowed.

"But not for long. When I realized Philip Darwin's perfidy I determined to avenge myself for the aspersions he had cast upon my honor. I recalled that Lee had declared that one of Mr. Darwin's assertions had been that I was going to the house on Riverside Drive that night. Very well. I would keep the appointment, and I would tell him I was coming, meeting guile with guile.

"I phoned his office and asked him whether my ring was ready for me. In a voice as false as his heart he apologized for not having taken it as yet to Tiffany's, but said he would return it to me, if I so desired, at dinner time, when he hoped to have the privilege of taking me to the Ritz. I pleaded a previous engagement, and asked him to let me come out to the house that afternoon to get the ring.

"He debated a while and then said that it was locked up in his study, and as he would not be home until late it would be impossible for me to come for it. I said that the lateness of the hour didn't matter, that I must have the ring, for if Lee should learn where it was he would break off the engagement. He inquired if I had seen Lee, and I said, 'Not to-day, but he was asking for it last night, and I put him off with an excuse.'

"Then he said all right, that I could come to the house at quarter to eleven. I wanted to know if there wasn't a window or some other way for me to enter, because I didn't want his wife and servants to know of my call. He laughed and said that I had only to use the secret entrance and no one would be the wiser. He explained how to find it and said he'd leave the doors unlocked for me.

"I had fully intended being at the Darwin house at ten-forty-five, but in thinking the matter over I became frightened. My anger had exhausted itself and I was horrified at my own thoughts. I decided not to go. When ten-thirty struck, however, the memory of all my wrongs swept over me again, coupled with the thought that Lee had threatened to kill his uncle, also. I must get there before my lover, since it was all my fault that he was planning murder. Yet even in my haste I took occasion to lay my plans with care. I would kill Darwin and myself since Lee no longer cared for me. I wrote a confession and put it in my pocket, that I might leave it in Darwin's study, so that no one else need suffer for the crime. It was eleven when I came downstairs, and meeting my landlady I informed her that I was going on a journey and should anyone inquire for me to say that she had no idea where I had gone.

"I took the Subway to Dyckman Street and walked from there to the Darwin home. I slipped into the grounds and around the house to the place where Mr. Darwin had told me there was a door in the masonry. I pushed against the wall, the door gave way, and I found myself at the bottom of a flight of stairs. I closed the door and then climbed the steps, feeling my way in the darkness until my hand came in contact with another door that yielded at my touch. I felt a carpet under my feet and knew I was in a room. I groped my way along until I reached an open space, and collided with what I thought was a bar. I remembered that he had told me to stoop when I passed through the safe. When I straightened up I saw that I was in his study and that the lamp on his table was lighted. At the head of the table sat Philip Darwin asleep. I advanced toward him, taking out my automatic as I walked. When I was close to him I pointed the pistol at him, then staggered back in horror, just as the lamp went out. There was a blood-stain on his shirt-front! Someone had reached him ahead of me!

"In the darkness I fled from him in a panic of fear, thrusting my pistol into the bosom of my dress. Then realizing that I had gone in the wrong direction, I ran back again-straight into the arms of a man! Before I could scream he had flung a cloth over my head and carried me to a couch. How long I remained thus I don't know, but just when I thought I must suffocate, someone removed the cloth, a glass was held to my lips, and Lee said, gently:

"'Drink this and you'll feel better, dear.'

"I thought he had rescued me. I drained the glass. Then I tried to ask where I was, but my head began to feel queer and heavy and my tongue refused its office. I closed my eyes and slipped into a dreamless sleep. When I awoke I could still feel the couch beneath me. I got up and groped my way around until I encountered the light switch. Then I saw that I was in a small carpeted room, which was furnished only with a divan and a smoking-stand. At either end of the room were doors. One of these was locked but the other had been left partly open and gave egress on the stairs that I had climbed.

"I thought of going down again, but felt too shaky to risk it, and returned again to the divan, deciding that I was in the room I had crossed to enter the study by the safe. There was a beautiful Persian cover on the couch and idly I examined it, lifting it clear of the floor. Then it was that I saw something bright shining where the fringe of the cover had swept the floor. I picked up the object and saw that it was a ring, Dick Trenton's ring.

"I knew it was his," she added, her pale cheeks flushing, "because when he proposed to me he wanted to take it off and put it on my finger.

"I gazed on the ring for a long time, trying to solve the mystery into which I had stumbled. Philip Darwin was dead, I was evidently a prisoner, and Dick's ring was in this room. If he had killed Mr. Darwin it was only right that he should pay the penalty. I would keep the ring and when the police found me, if someone else was in prison for the crime I would give them the ring and tell them what I knew.

"I still felt very drowsy, so I put out the light and as I lay down again the thought occurred to me that if Dick should come back while I slept and found the ring in my possession, he would take it away from me. Hastily I conceived a plan. I tied the ring to the fringe of the cover, where it would remain hidden until I could make use of it.

"I was dozing off when a step on the stairs aroused me. Someone came into the room.

"'Dick?' I asked, tentatively.

"He laughed oddly and replied, 'No, not Dick. Lee,' and I felt his arms around me and his kisses on my face.

"I was bewildered. Lee! Why had he drugged me then?

"'Lee,' I cried, 'why am I here?'

"'It's all right, dear. Uncle Phil was murdered and they think you did it.'

"'But I didn't kill him,' I protested, sitting up and pushing him away. 'He was dead when I entered the room!'

"'I know,' he answered. 'But just the same the police are hunting you. That's why I hid you away.'

"I heard him moving around the room, then he came back to me and said, 'You must be thirsty. Drink this.'

"But I was not going to be drugged a second time if I could help it, police or no police, so I said, 'I'm not thirsty, Lee.'

"'That doesn't matter. Drink, I tell you. I'm in a hurry.'

"His voice took on a sinister note as he held the glass forcibly to my lips. I gave his hand a shove, spilling the contents of the glass over him.

"'You she-devil,' he said, and crushed me to him.

"Then he flung the cloth over my head again and almost strangled me. I felt him lift me in his arms and carry me up a flight of steps. He placed me on the floor of a room and went away. I was in that room a long, long time before he came again. I was thirsty and hungry and heartsore to think that he would treat me so, for the room was narrow and bare and I hadn't even a bed to lie upon. My only comfort lay in the fact that my revolver still reposed where I had placed it. I took it out and held it in my hand, for I no longer trusted him.

"The second time he came to see me he opened the panel that formed the door to my cell and I could see his figure silhouetted against the dim light in the further room.

"'Lee!' I exclaimed. 'Why, oh why, have you done this! Is it because you killed your uncle and are afraid that I will tell what I know?'

"He did not answer and I went on: 'Why didn't you listen to my explanation that morning? You would have known then that your uncle only took the ring to have it mended. I do not know what he told you, but whatever it was, he lied.'

"'Did he lie about your coming to see him?' he replied then, in a hard voice. 'Did he? Answer me that, when I saw you enter his study!'

"'Yes, he lied,' I returned. 'I came to kill him and myself for his perfidy. Only you had already shot him. Oh, Lee, Lee, why didn't you listen to my explanation!'

"'I don't believe you. You came because he asked you to, but I got him first. And now your turn has come.'

"He made as if to step toward me and I put the pistol to my breast.

"'If you come any nearer, Lee, I'll kill myself,' I said steadily. 'Oh, to think that I could ever have loved you, you murderer!'

"He drew back. 'You'll pay for this. When you have starved for a couple of weeks you'll be more amenable, I guess,' and he went away laughing.

"I was horrified and I lay and wept for hours. Then as I moved about I discovered a jug of water. For a long time I was afraid to touch it, fearing it was a trap to catch me, but when my thirst got the better of my judgment I drank just enough to satisfy my worst craving. I waited to learn the results, and as I remained clear-headed, I decided the water was pure and hoarded it with care.

"I came to the conclusion that jealousy and its consequences had made Lee mad and that he was not responsible for his actions. Instead of horror, pity filled my heart for I loved him still.

"He did not come near me again until to-night, and then he was more fiendish than ever. He said he must leave the city, that he would come for me to-morrow night, and I could then make my choice between going with him and death. He pressed a button and showed me a yawning hole in the middle of the floor, telling me that he would throw me down into the pit below before he would let me go free to relate to the police what had happened to me. Oh, it was dreadful! I was glad when he was gone.

"I knew that nothing on earth could induce me to go with him, but the thought of falling through that black hole was more than I could bear. As long as I had to die I would choose a less harrowing way. I took out my pistol and was just going to kill myself when you flung up the barrel and rescued me."

She gave McKelvie a tremulous smile and burst into tears.

CHAPTER XXXVI

THE TRAP

For a space there was silence in the room while McKelvie paced the floor, a worried crease between his brows. As for Jones and myself, we looked from the girl to one another in undisguised perplexity.

How was it possible for Lee Darwin, whom we had rescued from the hands of the criminal at Hi Ling's shop, to be the same person who had kept Cora Manning a prisoner? Or had the boy been merely pretending to be unconscious, and the old man had been a confederate in the game which they were playing to trap McKelvie? Yet, the doctor had said that Lee was really ill, and the doctor could not possibly have any motive for lying, since he had been called in by Jones and was a stranger to us. Again, Cora had said that Lee had come to see her just previous to our rescue of her, and at that time I can swear to it that he was upstairs in one of the rooms in McKelvie's house.

Of course there was always the chance that the young man we had saved was not Lee Darwin at all (though who else he could be I had no idea), for I had only seen him once the day of the inquest, and the others had never laid eyes on him before. To counterbalance that hypothesis, however, was the straightforward story he had told, which tallied point for point with Cora's account. There was some deep mystery here which I for one could not fathom.

"My dear child," said McKelvie presently (from his tone one would have judged him old enough to be her father), "are you sure that you did not dream this tale?"

"Dream it? Oh, no, it was too horribly real for me to have dreamt it," she answered, astonished that he should doubt her.

"I was not referring to the treatment you had received, but to Lee Darwin's connection with your incarceration," he explained. "At the time of which you speak, Lee was himself a prisoner in Chinatown. And to-night he is at my home, ill in bed, too ill to have been able to come here at all."

"Lee—a prisoner? Lee-at your house ill? How can that be?" she asked in wondering tones.

"Miss Manning, did you see this man's face so that you could swear to it?" continued McKelvie earnestly.

"No. It was dark when he spoke to me in the little room, and up here the light behind him was always dim. But I heard his voice, Mr. McKelvie. I could swear it was Lee's," she insisted.

"Voices are easily imitated. He did not talk to you for any great length of time and he was careful that you should not see his face too closely. If he had been Lee he would not have cared how much you saw his features." McKelvie laid a hand on the girl's arm, as he added: "I want you to believe that Lee had nothing to do with this affair. On the contrary, he has done his best to protect you, almost giving his life for your sake. Let me tell you his story briefly. He can fill in the details for you later," and he told her of our trip to Hi Ling's shop.

"I'm so glad," she said, raising tear-filled eyes to his face as he ended. "You see I love him still, even though I thought him-all that was bad. May I see him soon?"

"Yes, but I'm going to ask you to remain in this house to-night. You are not strong enough yet to take a journey in the Subway and I have no desire to use the phone to call a taxi. The criminal may have a means of tapping the wire, for all we know. Now, Miss Manning, are you sure he is coming back to-morrow?"

"Yes, he told me he would return to-morrow night. He said he had to get money enough for our trip in case I should go with him, and that a woman always needed plenty of spare cash. Besides, he'd be sure to come, if only to give me my choice. He would not leave me here alive for someone to discover. He made that very plain to me," she returned, with a shudder.

"Very well, then, we will meet him in your place. I'm going to guard you to-night myself, in case he should change his mind and come again unexpectedly. In the meantime, I wish that

136

you, Mr. Davies, would spend the night at my house to protect Lee. And if you will come around to Stuyvesant Square at ten o'clock to-morrow morning, Jones, I'll give you the other details necessary to catch the murderer in his own little trap."

"Do you want a taxi for to-morrow, then?" asked Jones, as we were leaving.

"Yes, send one around about nine o'clock. Tell him to wait at the corner of Dyckman and Broadway. Or, better yet, send one of your own men with the car, in order that there may be no hitch in our plans."

Jones promised and we returned to town via the Subway, and parted company at Union Square. When I reached McKelvie's house I stopped at Lee's room and found that he was awake. He called to me to know whether I had any news, so I told him the latest developments, watching his face while I talked. He listened eagerly to what I had to say, was unaffectedly glad of the girl's release and thankful to learn that she was safe. His face darkened when I spoke of the impersonation, and he was just as much at a loss as myself to account for it.

When I turned in I had come to one conclusion at least, and that was that Lee had had no hand in the murder, either as principal or as confederate.

At ten o'clock the next morning Jones put in an appearance, but McKelvie had not yet returned, so we occupied ourselves with a discussion of the events of the previous night. Finally we came to the conclusion that Cora Manning in her dazed state had, perhaps, mistaken Dick for Lee, since both were more or less of a height. But in that event, Dick purposely misled her. Why? What reason could he have for such an action, unless indeed, his love for her, coupled with the crime committed in a moment of passionate anger against the man who had injured him, had turned his brain.

When McKelvie arrived he brought Cora Manning with him and asked me to conduct her to Lee. I helped her up the stairs and to the room where Lee was sitting, and as he rose and held out his arms to her I turned away and went back downstairs, where McKelvie was issuing his orders to Jones.

"I want you to bring three men to the house with you, Jones. Be out there at five o'clock and get Mason to let you in the back way. Wait in the passageway for me. Get Grenville to accompany you. Tell him it's important."

"You think you'll be able to catch him?" inquired Jones, as he picked up his hat.

"He has no suspicion of our visit last night. Our rescue of Lee, although in a measure it proves that Mrs. Darwin had nothing to do with the crime, does not in his opinion help us to locate Cora. He only kept Lee at Hi Ling's to prevent him from giving evidence in Mrs. Darwin's behalf. He will come to the house to-night without the least suspicion that there will be anyone there to greet him as he deserves," and McKelvie laughed.

"Then you know who he is?" I inquired, as Jones left the house.

"I still suspect. I shall not know positively until to-night. And now I'm going to get some sleep. Then we will go over to the Darwin bank. I have a mind to see whether that one hundred and fifty thousand dollars is still there."

Taking advantage of the respite, I went back to my own apartments for luncheon, and returned to Stuyvesant Square in my car. Evidently in McKelvie's mind Cunningham was still under suspicion, yet I could hardly credit that it was Cunningham who had kept the girl a prisoner. He did not resemble Lee.

When we arrived at the bank Mr. Trenton turned us over to Raines, who conducted us to the safe-deposit vault.

"Do you know whether Cunningham was in to-day?" asked McKelvie.

"No, I don't. One of the tellers might be able to tell you," responded Raines.

"Never mind. The strong box will tell me all I want to know," McKelvie answered.

We approached Cunningham's box and Raines inserted his key in the lock. As he pulled it open I leaned closer to look at the interior. Then I gave an exclamation of astonishment. The box was empty! The one hundred and fifty thousand dollars in bills was gone!

It was two days ago that we had interviewed Cunningham and he did not then contemplate removing the money from the bank. What had occasioned this sudden need for so much cash? I could think of only one reason. His must be the master mind that had conceived the crime and struck the blow against Darwin, even though he had since hired confederates to aid him in his scheme of holding Cora, as he had done in the case of Lee.

I spoke my thought to McKelvie as we drove back to his home, but he shook his head.

"The criminal had no confederates to aid him against the girl. He has played a lone hand all through with one exception, that is, in the case of Lee."

"Then why did he remove that money from the bank?" I asked.

"Perhaps he is going on that trip he was telling us about the other night," responded McKelvie cynically, and I knew by his tone that he himself did not believe any such thing.

"A trip which will end before it has begun, since it's very apparent his only reason for flight must be that he killed Philip Darwin," I said with a laugh.

"Oh, no," responded McKelvie, coolly, "he is clever and unprincipled, and all kinds of a blackguard, and I wouldn't be at all surprised if he had a couple of murders to his name, but this I do know. He did not murder Philip Darwin."

CHAPTER XXXVII

M'KELVIE'S TRIUMPH

When we drove into the grounds of the Darwin home at five o'clock that night, McKelvie ordered me to hide my car behind the garage and then to join him in the passageway. As I obeyed I saw him helping Lee, with Cora's aid, to mount the steps to the back door, for he wanted the two of them for purposes of identification, since both had been victims of the unprincipled man we had come there to-night to try to trap.

I parked my car where it could not be seen by anyone approaching the house and then returned to the servants' wing and entered the passageway, where McKelvie was disposing of his forces. The three burly policemen that Jones had brought with him McKelvie ordered to remain where they were until it grew dark, when they were to hide themselves in the grounds, toward the side of the house. When they saw a light in the study they were then to group themselves around the door to the secret entrance, which he had already pointed out to one of their number while I was parking my car. If anyone came out through this door they were to arrest that person, and under no circumstances to let him get away, even if they had to shoot him. The men saluted and I could see by the determination written on their faces that the criminal would have small chance of escaping their vigilance.

Then McKelvie opened the door into the main wing and asked Cora and Lee to remain in Orton's workroom until they were needed.

"And under no circumstances show a light of any kind," he added. They did not need to promise, for they preferred a darkened room in which to tell each other the sweet nothings that lovers are fond of murmuring, and I envied them their happiness as I thought of Ruth shut away where even my loving care could not reach her.

In the fading daylight the study was dim, but we managed to make out the outlines of the furniture, and so were able to move about without turning on the lamp. McKelvie grouped some chairs around the table and told us to seat ourselves, since at that distance we could not be seen by the criminal as he stepped from the safe. Then McKelvie arranged the shades, drawing them so that they did not quite reach the bottom of the windows, thus allowing the light to gleam through later, as a signal to the waiting policemen.

When everything was ready McKelvie spoke to us in an undertone. "I do not know how long we shall have to wait for him. He will come when it is dark, perhaps, and again he may not turn up until midnight. In any event, whether our vigil be long or short, I want to impress upon you the necessity for absolute silence. A false move and we may lose every advantage and the criminal as well."

We declared ourselves ready to obey his instructions, however long we might have to wait, and he crossed the room and took up his position beside the safe door with the metal handcuffs in his hand, prepared to snap them on the wrists of the man who should come forth from the entrance.

I glanced at Jones and Grenville and saw to my amusement that the police detective was sound asleep. He reminded me of a watchdog that though he might doze would yet be instantly on the alert at the least hint of danger. The District Attorney caught my look and smiled, then he leaned back in his chair and set himself to wait with what patience he might possess.

I turned to my thoughts, thankful that McKelvie had spared Mr. Trenton this ordeal, for now that Cunningham was exonerated, the burden of the crime must fall upon Dick, who, after all, was the only one well enough acquainted with circumstances to have attempted the schemes which McKelvie had foiled. Yet it seemed such a mad thing to do, to put his head in the noose a second time when he had just been cleared of his first crime, unless James Gilmore's story was all of a piece with the other deceptions Dick had practised upon us. Who was Gilmore any way? Had we any proof that his story was true? He may have been paid to put us off the scent by making us believe that Dick could not commit another crime since he was innocent of the first one. But, again, there was McKelvie's statement that with the exception of the Chinamen and those two ruffians, the criminal had steered clear of confederates. I could not divine Dick's motive for the deed, since the murder was not and never had been, one of impulse.

I wished heartily that the whole thing was over and this suspense ended, yet when the lamp suddenly lighted on the table and I knew that the hour was at hand, since it must have been the criminal's hand that had pressed the switch in the safe, I closed my eyes. I did not want to see the door swing open and Dick step out of that safe.

I heard a metallic click as McKelvie snapped on the handcuffs, and I opened my eyes with a start as I realized by the snarl of rage that had come from the murderer's lips that we had caught the man as neatly as one traps a wild and dangerous animal.

McKelvie laughed as he slammed the door of the safe, and the three of us rose precipitately (Jones had wakened when the lamp went on), for we could make out the criminal's figure as he came rapidly toward us. When he stood within the circle of light, confronting the muzzle of Jones' gun, I looked into his face, then I gasped audibly.

The man before me was not Dick, but the lawyer-Cunningham!

"This is an outrage!" he exclaimed furiously. "What do you mean by putting such an indignity upon me?" and he glared at McKelvie.

McKelvie smiled in an exasperating manner. "I was expecting the criminal to come through that entrance, since he alone possesses a key to it. I saw a man appear and clapped on the bracelets. It happened to be you. How do you explain the circumstance?" he inquired politely.

"Very easily," retorted Cunningham coolly, recovering his poise, "I was going over a lot of old papers and came across a sealed envelope addressed to me in Darwin's hand. Wondering what it could portend I opened it. Inside I found a small key and the explanation of the secret of the entrance. Darwin also went on to say that he was taking me into his confidence in case anything should ever happen to him. Having a fondness for amateur detective work, like yourself, Mr. McKelvie," here he bowed ironically to McKelvie, "I decided to use the opportunity which fate had bestowed upon me to do a little investigating on my own account."

"Very ingenious, but it won't do," returned McKelvie, adding with a sarcastic inflection, "I suppose he also told you the six-letter combination that I used to lock the safe-after he was dead?"

Cunningham flushed and bit his lip, but before he could think of an appropriate retort, McKelvie had turned to Jones.

"You won't need to use that gun, Jones," he said with a twinkle. "Our prisoner is too valuable to shoot-as yet. Call in the others, please, and light the room as you pass the switch."

Jones pocketed his gun, and departed on his errand, lighting the study, as we had agreed to do, for the guidance of the men outside. In a second he was back again with Lee and Cora. As Cunningham's eyes rested on the girl, who had her arm around Lee and was helping him tenderly to a chair, the man's face darkened and his eyes blazed upon her.

"Miss Manning, have you ever seen this man before?" asked McKelvie when Lee was seated and Cora had turned toward us.

The girl looked Cunningham up and down, from the sole of his patent leather shoes to the crown of his gray-streaked red hair, then she shook her head and answered simply, "No, Mr. McKelvie, I have never seen him before."

"Now I trust that you are satisfied?" demanded Cunningham, insolently, a gleam of triumph in his eyes. "You will oblige me by removing these things."

Though he held out his manacled hands to McKelvie, his eyes remained on Cora's face with a look impossible to mistake. The man was in love with her, though how that was possible when she did not know him, I was at a loss to decide. McKelvie took a step forward and I thought he was going to comply with Cunningham's request, but he made no move to release his prisoner.

"Sorry to have to refuse a gentleman of your standing, but you are far safer to me with the bracelets on," returned McKelvie imperturbably. "You are undoubtedly clever or you could not have evaded me so long, but the trouble with you, as it is with all clever criminals, is that you are egotistical. You commit a crime and get away with it and then you immediately think yourself a genius, so much more wonderful than your fellows who have paid the penalty for their deeds, so infinitely superior to the police and the detectives that you have no fear of being caught. But like all your class, there is a weak joint in your armor. There is no such thing as an infallible criminal and a perfect crime. You may get away once, or perhaps a score of times, but in the end your weakness trips you and you fall into the hands of the authorities. In your case the thing that tripped you and delivered you to us was—love for a woman. A dangerous game to play, the woman game, Mr. Cunningham, but love knows no reason. You were so desperately infatuated with Cora Manning that the thought of going away and leaving her to a more successful rival was agony to you, and so you remained to persuade her to go with you. That is why you are here now, facing arrest under an accusation of murder."

In wondering silence we listened to McKelvie's words and Cora said quickly, "In love with me? But I never saw him before."

Cunningham only smiled coolly. "You have no proof, my dear sir, no proof at all."

"Haven't I? I am not as amateurish as I look," said McKelvie, dryly. Then he faced the man before him squarely and addressed him in a tone of grim earnestness from which all hint of banter had fled. "You demand proofs. I will give them to you. I know why the murder was committed, why Mrs. Darwin was implicated, because I know exactly what took place in this room on the night of October seventh, from the moment when Richard Trenton stepped through that French window to the moment when the murderer left the room by the secret entrance. In other words, the game is up—Mr. Philip Darwin!" and McKelvie's hand shot out toward his prisoner's face.

I heard Lee's wondering, "Uncle Phil?" and unable to believe my ears I took a second look. Then, "Good God!" I cried, for the red hair and beard were gone and the man standing where Cunningham had been was indeed Ruth's husband, for whose murder she was even now enduring the horrors of prison life, Philip Darwin, but Philip Darwin without his eyeglasses and without his beard!

Who, then, was the man we had found dead in this room, the man we had buried under Darwin's name? A sudden conviction borne of McKelvie's last words flashed across my mind.

"Was it—?" I began.

"Yes," replied McKelvie, "the man who was so foully murdered in this room that night was—Richard Trenton!"

Cora cried cut, "Dick, oh, not Dick!" and I put my hand to my head, for my brain was in a whirl. Yet I was conscious of a feeling of thankfulness that he was the victim rather than the perpetrator of the crime.

With a snarl of rage Darwin broke from McKelvie's hand and fled toward the safe. Jones started to follow, but McKelvie checked him with a laugh.

"Let him go, Jones. Have you forgotten that there are three men guarding the outer door?" he said.

Darwin paused abruptly and turned a hate-distorted face toward us, then he recovered his cool manner and walked back calmly to where we stood.

"You win," he said to McKelvie with a shrug. "What do you want of me?"

"If you will kindly be seated I should like to explain, with your corroboration, just exactly what did take place in this room that night," answered McKelvie.

"No," returned Darwin, "let me tell the story, for you would bungle the tale. I'll accept your word that you know what happened, since otherwise you could not have unmasked me. Kindly take off those bracelets, they annoy me, and give me a cigar. I swear to you that I shall make no attempt to leave this room."

For a long minute the two men looked into one another's eyes, then McKelvie stepped forward and removed the handcuffs. He bestowed them in his pocket, took out a cigar, and offered it to Darwin.

The man accepted the cigar with a bow, lighted it, and then drawing a chair into the center of the circle which we had formed, he leaned back nonchalantly and began his tale.

CHAPTER XXXVIII

THE MOTIVE

"You must know, then," said Philip Darwin, "that I was the child of a second marriage contracted between my father and a young woman who had just begun to earn a name for herself upon the stage. She endured two years of walking the straight and narrow path as his wife, and then she eloped with an actor friend. My father hushed the scandal and withdrew from social life, becoming morose and bitter and narrower than ever, watching over me with a zealous eye as I grew older, and endeavoring to eradicate the talents which I had inherited from her, looking with particular disfavor on my ability to act and mimic the speech of those about me.

"Knowing my inherited love of pleasures of all kinds he strove to curb me by refusing to let me go out in the evenings with my young companions. This I considered an indignity since I was then old enough to be my own master, and so I took matters into my own hand, retiring early and then sneaking away from my rooms to join my friends. This practice I continued until by an unforeseen chance I was among those arrested in a raid upon a gambling-house. I would have given a false name but unfortunately the Sergeant knew me, and of course the affair came to the ears of my father.

"He was exceedingly wroth and threatened to disinherit me if I ever disobeyed him again. I did not want to lose my chance to secure his fortune, which would come to me intact since Robert, my older brother, was dead, and my sister, Leila, had run away from home, so I remained at home on my best behavior. It was just at this time that I came across an old book in the study that gave the history of the house from which ours had been copied. I investigated and found the door in the masonry, took an impression of the lock, had a key made, and so discovered the secret room. That room gave me an idea. I knew that it was next the study although it had never been cut through, but this fact did not trouble me. My father had planned to take me to Europe with him, but I told him that I preferred to remain at home and look after the business, into which I had been taken as junior partner on my twenty-first birthday. Thinking that I had reformed he gave his permission for me to have a safe built in the study, since I had pointed out to him that now that I was a man of affairs I needed such a contrivance for my personal papers. But though he left for Europe without me he did not altogether trust me, for I discovered that his lawyer had orders to telegraph my father if at any time he learned that I had deviated from the rule of conduct laid down for me to follow.

"I determined to outwit him. I sent Mason away, hired some workmen, had a door cut between the study and the secret room and had a safe built into the wall as a blind. Then I spent the rest of the year in evolving the character of Cunningham. He should be a young law student, red-haired, red-bearded, fastidious. Also as Darwin, I adopted glasses to make myself and Cunningham as opposite as possible in appearance.

"When my father returned he heard no scandal of me for Cunningham had taken young Darwin's place in the beaumonde. Thereafter I had no difficulty in getting away, retiring early and then leaving the house by the secret entrance, after changing to Cunningham in the little room.

"After my father's death Cunningham was of no further value to me, but I was too clever to utterly destroy him, since I had no idea when I might need him again. So he told his friends that a relative had died abroad, leaving him a fortune, and that he was going on a trip around the world. Then Darwin came back and took his place in the social world.

"I pass over the next few years, in which I played the fool and speculated beyond my means. Eight months ago I was in desperate need of money, although none knew of it, and I saw that my only course lay in marrying some wealthy woman.

"I looked around me and decided that Arthur Trenton's daughter would serve my purpose. I made friends with her brother and discovered to my annoyance that the young lady in question had just engaged herself to a young broker by the name of Carlton Davies and that the wedding was scheduled to take place in a very short time. This was something of a set-back, since I knew that Miss Trenton was not likely to jilt her lover for a man she was barely acquainted with. But once I make up my mind to obtain a thing I never give up until that thing is mine. I cast about for a way to make her marry me, and having cultivated her brother, Dick, for a month, I laid my plans accordingly.

"I enticed the boy, who was inclined to be wild, to a gambling-den, after I had taken the trouble to get him fairly intoxicated. I had hired a jail-bird to quarrel with Dick and when the man pretended to go for the boy, I shot and killed him, telling Dick that he had done it. He became frightened and I took him to his home, where his father was told my version of the tale, and Dick was dispatched to Chicago. Then I forced Ruth to marry me to save her brother from going to the chair for something he had never done!"

Darwin paused in his narrative to puff his cigar and to let us sufficiently admire the cleverness that had conceived such a plan. Admire! I could only shudder at the thought that there could be in existence a man who could carry out such diabolical schemes in cold-blood, and actually pride himself on his accomplishment.

"After the marriage I made Ruth sign away her dower rights as well as her dowry, all to save her brother. Then I took up my old way of living again. But now there was a fly in my ointment. People began to talk, and I had enough of my father in me to make gossip distasteful to me. Yet marriage was a bore, I discovered, and so I resurrected the lawyer, Cunningham. If as Darwin I must endure life with Ruth, as Cunningham I would be as gay as I chose. I hired an apartment and began my double life.

"When Darwin was bored to distraction by prosaic affairs, he would take a business trip and Cunningham would have his fling. When pleasures cloyed, Cunningham would be off to see his out-of-town clients and Darwin would return to the city. The excitement and the danger of detection that this sort of existence afforded fascinated me and I should have kept it up indefinitely if fate in the person of a former teller of the Darwin Bank had not intervened.

"This man, James Gilmore, who had been my dupe ten years before, and had since been in jail, was at the gambling-den the night I shot Coombs, and he realized the trick I had played upon Dick. I thought at the time when Gilmore fell that I had killed him also (I did not know him at the time. I merely shot at him on the principle that dead men tell no awkward tales), but by some freak of chance he escaped unhurt and became acquainted with Richard Trenton.

"The first intimation I had that my plans had gone awry was in a letter from Dick explaining the circumstances. I thought the matter over and finally made up my mind to go to Chicago as Cunningham, to kill Dick, and then return as Darwin, abolishing forever the character of the lawyer.

"When I reached Chicago, however, and saw Dick, a new plan, more daring, more subtle, more pleasing in every way leapt fully matured into my mind, since by means of it Darwin would disappear and Cunningham would remain, free to live his life unhampered by the marriage tie.

"Dick had grown a beard. Trim it as mine was trimmed, give him a pair of gold eyeglasses, and he could pass superficially for myself. I marveled at the likeness then. Now I know it was only natural, since it seems he was my nephew as well as my brother-in-law.

"I pretended as the lawyer to be on his side, returned to New York, and wrote him a letter in which I declared that as Ruth refused to divorce me, which was one of the terms of reparation Dick insisted upon, he had better call upon me and talk things over. He walked into the trap I had laid for him, and telegraphed that he would come to see me."

Again Darwin paused and eyed us in that strange exultant manner.

"You will think, perhaps, that it was a daring thing to do, this that I had in mind, but its very audacity would serve to carry it through, I knew. Have you ever studied psychology? I commend it to you, for my knowledge of that subject was the foundation stone upon which I built.

"When a man is found shot in his own study, remaking his own will, looking like himself to all outward appearance, the conclusion is naturally that the dead man is the one whom the world believes him to be, that is, the master of the house. Also I had no fear that the deception would be remarked. Orton was near-sighted, Mr. Davies (for as I shall show you presently, I intended to bring him into this affair also), knew me only slightly, had not seen Dick for six months, and never with a beard, besides being under the belief that the boy was in Chicago, and Ruth would be too overwrought to notice anything amiss. The only one I really feared was Lee, as he knew me thoroughly. I determined to get rid of him. The question was, how? and the answer was supplied by the girl, Cora Manning.

"I had been intrigued by her beauty, but had no thought, despite my nephew's assertions, beyond being allowed to gaze upon her occasionally, but the night of the sixth as she told me of her broken ring I knew I loved her and wanted her for my own. I saw a way ahead of me and seized the opportunity presented to me.

"I inveigled her into giving me the ring and the next morning I gave Lee to understand that the girl had been false to him. He believed me and I knew him well enough to guess that he would break off the engagement, leaving the way free for me later. I also ordered him to leave my house for his insolence to me, thus getting him out of the way for that night.

"It was at this point in the game that a new element was introduced. I had meant merely to leave Ruth a supposed widow, but when Orton showed me the letter she had written to her former lover, I determined to make her pay for my crime. I told him to piece the letter together and bring it to me, and then I left for the office.

"And now I was guilty of my first error. I permitted my infatuation for Cora to get the better of my discretion, and told her to come to the house at ten-forty-five, knowing I would have time to see her in the secret entrance and get rid of her before Dick was scheduled to arrive. I should have known better, for it was too dangerous a game to play.

"At ten-thirty that night I called Ruth to the study and upbraided her, threatening Mr. Davies in such terms that she took fright and declared she would send for him to warn him. I only laughed and thoroughly roused she left me to call her lover to her, as I hoped she would.

"Then I locked the study door, opened the secret entrance as I had promised, and waited for Cora. She did not come, and when eleven struck I gave her up and was on the point of leaving the study to relock the entrance when Dick suddenly stepped in through the window, one half-hour before he was due. We talked for twenty-five minutes, while I waited for Mr. Davies' arrival. Dick insisted upon seeing Ruth at once. I told him she had gone out with friends and would not return until eleven-thirty.

"At eleven-twenty-five I heard a motor drive up, and guessing it must be Mr. Davies who had come, I set to work to carry out my plan. I told Dick Ruth had come, and he sprang up and went to the door. I followed him and as I did so I soaked a handkerchief with chloroform from a bottle I had in my pocket, and as he fumbled with the key I came up behind him and pressed the handkerchief over his face. As he sagged into my arms I switched off the light and carried him to the secret room, depositing him on the couch.

"Then I returned to the study, unlocked the door, and called in Orton that he might take away with him a mental image of myself seated in my chair, as I later intended that Dick should sit. When Orton was gone I relocked the door, and returned to Dick. I exchanged clothing with him, and it was no easy task, for he lay an inert mass. Then I trimmed his beard and placed my eyeglasses on his nose. Finally, I took out my revolver and shot him through the heart as I supposed, but he had come out from under the influence of the anesthetic and as I fired he moved so that the bullet only penetrated his lung. I knew that he was done for in any case and as I bent down to pick him up I noticed the ring on his finger. I never wore rings, and that one was too familiar to Ruth to risk leaving it. I was removing it with care when I heard a step on the stairs of the entrance. I remembered Cora and dared not let her guess the truth. Hastily I snatched off the ring, slipped it in my pocket and carried Dick into the study, setting him down in my chair. Then I hid behind the curtains of the window, which was nearest the safe. I saw her enter, and as she advanced toward the table where only the lamp was lighted, I slipped into the safe and switched it off.

"I took off my coat and as she fell against me in the dark I flung it over her head, and carried her to the divan in the secret room. Then I went about my other business, for I had much to do. I cleaned my gun, and recharged it, removing the bullet from the cartridge I intended to fire later. I returned to the study, pushed back the chair so that it would look as though Darwin had been shot when he rose to meet someone, arranged the matter of the wills, and left a word half finished upon the testament I was supposed to have been making, burning the old one which I had torn up when I recalled it was in Lee's favor and not Ruth's.

"When I saw that I had bruised Dick's finger I flung Cora's ring, from which the stone had dropped that morning, on the top shelf of the safe in order to explain the abrasion with some degree of plausibility, since I knew that Lee had seen the ring on my finger in the morning. Then when everything was as perfect as human ingenuity could make it, I went to the door and unlocked it, that Ruth might find no obstacle to her entrance. I switched on the lights for a moment for a last survey and saw a handkerchief lying near the door. When I picked it up I saw that it was Ruth's, but caution prevailed and I smelled it to make sure, knowing well that Cora used Rose Jacqueminot, since I had adopted it myself after becoming acquainted with her. The handkerchief was unscented and I decided to add it to the evidence against Ruth. I put out the light, stained the handkerchief with blood, arranged it in Dick's hand, turned out the lamp, and waited for Ruth.

"How did I know she would come to the study? Because I had decoyed Mr. Davies to the house to bring about that very result. He was a man and he loved her and he feared what I might do to her if I remained in possession of that letter. I had purposely told her I was going out and had let her see me throw the letter in the table-drawer. Mr. Davies, I knew, would urge her to get the letter.

"When she came in and I heard her fumbling with the contents of the drawer I fired my revolver. I knew it would startle her, and that she would move away from the table, so I slung the gun along the carpet, trusting that it would carry as far as her feet. Then I hastened to the safe and turned on the lamp, closing the door to behind me, but remaining where I could hear what occurred in the study.

"I heard Mr. Davies' order to Orton, and locking the safe I hastened through the entrance to the front door, letting myself in just as they disappeared into Ruth's apartments. I went into the dining-room and opened a bottle of wine, into which I mixed a sleeping potion. While I was there I heard the doctor arrive and go upstairs, then I returned the way I had come, poured out a glass of the wine and gave it to Cora. Then I locked the entrance doors and left her there to sleep while I returned to the Corinth as Dick, so that there would be no undue search made for him. The next morning I went back to my apartments as Cunningham, and from there to the inquest.

"When Ruth had been adjudged guilty, I determined to get rid of Lee, since his actions told me plainly he knew something of Cora's visit. I decoyed him from the club with a fake message and had him kidnapped, but could get nothing from him. I decided to keep him a prisoner until after Ruth had paid the penalty for the crime.

"My thought now reverted to Cora, but I dared not return to the house that night, as the police were still in charge. I waited until they had left about nine o'clock the next morning, and went to the secret room, where I found Cora awake. It was too risky a matter to take her to my other apartments, besides she knew too much to suit me, so I impersonated Lee to kill her love for him. Then as Cunningham I would rescue her and through her gratitude I could earn her love. I did not guess she had a revolver or things might have taken a different turn.

"The afternoon of the ninth I carried out the plans for the suicide of Richard Trenton. It was necessary to account for his disappearance, since two men were gone and there was only one body which could be produced. It was I who jumped in the river. It was an unpleasant duty, but I had to make some sacrifice to attain my ends. I swam down the shore and made my way to Chinatown to my refuge at Hi Ling's.

"From then on I faced the world as Cunningham, and in the end I should have triumphed but for one thing. Mr. Davies' refusal to believe Ruth guilty brought a new element into the case, a man with brains as keen as my own, who was not to be duped as I had fooled the police. He was suspicious of Cunningham from the first, but I did not think that even he could uncover the truth, so in the end I lost."

Darwin ceased speaking and there was silence in the room for a moment, then unexpectedly he rose and turned to McKelvie. "You are clever, but you haven't got me yet. You think to try me. The man doesn't live who can put me in a cell."

Even as he spoke, before we could grasp the meaning of his rapidly uttered words, he sprang down the room toward the door, wrenching it open as Jones fired. We saw Darwin make for the stairs and we were after him in a second. On the floor above he rushed into his dressing-room, and as we entered we saw him disappear into the secret closet. There was a whirring sound and a cry of dismay, then silence, horror-filled.

CHAPTER XXXIX

CONCLUSION

Leaving Jones in charge of the house and its gruesome burden, McKelvie, Grenville and I drove to Center Street to secure Ruth's release. On the way Grenville asked McKelvie whether he would mind explaining how he first divined the truth. McKelvie obligingly complied.

"I owe my success to Miss Manning's quick-wittedness in leaving us that clue in the secret room. But for that the case might still be hanging fire. Until we discovered the ring I had no suspicions of the real truth of the matter. I merely mistrusted Cunningham, because he was the only clever unprincipled person connected with the case, but I could conceive of no plausible motive which would cause him to commit the crime.

"I had never swallowed that neat account of how Darwin's finger came to be bruised. The reason was deeper than mere sentiment, I felt. When we stumbled on the ring, the truth flashed across my mind. The ring had to be removed because the dead man was Dick, not Darwin. If that were so, then Dick could not have committed suicide. I determined to test my theory.

"I took with me to Water Street a photograph of Darwin taken when he was Dick's age (I had seen it in an old album in the den upstairs when I first examined the house on Riverside Drive). Both Mrs. Bates and Ben Kite recognized it as the picture of the man who had jumped into the river. So far, so good. Dick had been murdered and Darwin was alive. What was the motive? James Gilmore supplied the answer and the case was simplified. With Darwin as the murderer every fact fell into place with the ease of a carefully pieced puzzle.

"Darwin wanted to rid himself of his wife, Darwin knew she had written a love-letter, Darwin knew that Mr. Davies was in the house and would urge Mrs. Darwin to secure the epistle. Also the quarrel with Lee took on a new phase, a scheme for ridding himself of a pair of keen eyes.

"The only question to be solved was the one, Where was Darwin? Was he still in the city or had he left the country? I could not rid myself of the idea that Cunningham had some share in the affair. He was too keenly interested to be a mere on-looker. Could it be that Cunningham was Darwin, I asked myself. I investigated and discovered that the two men were never in the city at the same time, that they had never been seen together, although they were more than lawyer and client. The finding of the one hundred and fifty thousand dollars in Cunningham's strong box clinched the matter for me. I knew that Darwin was not likely to give another man the money which he would need himself with which to get away."

McKelvie paused and turned to me. "Do you remember the night he told us that pleasant fiction about the one hundred and fifty thousand dollars? I was positive then that he was Darwin, but I had no way of proving it and I had no desire to put him on his guard. That is why I advertised for Lee. I wanted to frighten him into thinking I was on to him and so catch him with the goods, which we were able to do, thanks to his own folly."

"And thanks to you, Mrs. Darwin's life has been saved," I said, as he ceased speaking. "I can never repay you for what you have done," and I held out my hand.

He grasped it with an embarrassed laugh. "Don't thank me. I enjoyed running him to earth. I'm glad he got his deserts."

"Did he really mean to kill himself?" I asked presently.

"No. I examined that closet. It had a double purpose. There was a trapdoor in the ceiling as well, and when you pressed a button in the wall a ladder was let down and you could escape over the roof. That was Darwin's plan, but in his haste he touched the wrong spring, for they were near together and it was dark, and so he fell to his death. Thus is evil punished in the end."

"How did Cunningham happen to have a sachet bag embroidered with his initials when Cora did not know him as Cunningham?" I inquired.

"He had foolishly preserved the one she had given him as Darwin. The initials on it were P. D."

"You told me that when I learned the answers to those questions that I should know who committed the crime. Why was it then that Jones and I did not guess the truth the night we heard Lee's story?"

"Because you had no idea of the motive for the crime. Also you answered some of the questions wrong," he replied with a smile.

"Wasn't it odd that Ruth failed to recognize Cunningham as her husband when he spoke to her at the inquest?" I asked.

"No. He kept his voice disguised. Didn't he say he had a bad cold or something of the sort? When I was positive that Cunningham was Darwin I had a second interview with Mrs. Darwin. She told me then that when Cunningham spoke to her she had an impression that she was hearing the voice of her husband, but as she was persuaded that Darwin was dead she thought it must be her own foolish fancy, and so said nothing about it."

I nodded, recalling the puzzled look on Ruth's face when she glanced at Cunningham at the inquest, for which I had at the time been unable to account, and while I waited McKelvie's return in the reception room of the Tombs, I pondered upon the kindness of Fate in having disposed of the man who had stood so long between me and the one desire of my heart. I wondered how I would tell Ruth the actual facts in the case, and was debating the wisdom of enlightening her when McKelvie returned with a beaming smile.

"She'll be here in just a minute," he said, adding quizzically, "You won't need my help in solving this problem, I'll wager," and he waved his hand toward the door.

The next moment Ruth was in my arms.

Printed in the USA
CPSIA information can be obtained
at www.ICGtesting.com
CBHW072210031224
18410CB00007B/392